BOOK 2

BATTLE
DRAGONS
CITY OF SPEED

BOOK 2

BATTLE DRAGONS

CITY OF SPEED

ALEX LONDON

SCHOLASTIC INC.

Copyright © 2021 by Alex London

This book was originally published in hardcover by Scholastic Press in 2022.

All rights reserved. Published by Scholastic Inc., *Publishers since 1920.* SCHOLASTIC and associated logos are trademarks and/or registered trademarks of Scholastic Inc.

The publisher does not have any control over and does not assume any responsibility for author or third-party websites or their content.

No part of this publication may be reproduced, stored in a retrieval system, or transmitted in any form or by any means, electronic, mechanical, photocopying, recording, or otherwise, without written permission of the publisher. For information regarding permission, write to Scholastic Inc., Attention: Permissions Department, 557 Broadway, New York, NY 10012.

This book is a work of fiction. Names, characters, places, and incidents are either the product of the author's imagination or are used fictitiously, and any resemblance to actual persons, living or dead, business establishments, events, or locales is entirely coincidental.

ISBN 978-1-338-71658-0

10 9 8 7 6 5 4 3 2 1   22 23 24 25 26

Printed in the U.S.A. 40

This edition first printing 2022

Book design by Maeve Norton

TO THE READER WHO IS READING THIS
RIGHT NOW. I'D BE NOWHERE
WITHOUT YOU. ISN'T IT COOL
YOU HAVE A BOOK
DEDICATED TO YOU?
YES, I MEAN YOU!

PART ONE

"WHO NAMES THESE DRAGONS?"

THE FIRST RACE OF THE season brought the whole city of Drakopolis out, or so it seemed to Abel. The bleachers were packed uncomfortably close around his parents and his two best friends beneath the heat of a blazing blue sky.

The raceway held over a hundred thousand people, and it was full past any measure of safety. At the top of the arena perched the luxury boxes of the wealthy owners and sponsors, set where the dragons would race right past their windows. At the bottom was the flat oval infield, where a motley mixture of crooks, gamblers, and goons stood shoulder to shoulder, their necks craned straight up, as far from the aerial raceway as you could get while still being inside the arena.

In between the luxury boxes and the gritty infield were the bleachers, where a ticket bought you a reclining seat to look up at the race above and a discount on one extra-large Firebreather Soda. You could enter a code in the app on your phone to place bets, order food to your seat, or even look up the statistics of your favorite racing dragons.

"This technology is better than anything we have at school," Abel's best friend, Roa, lamented. "Why does a sport have more advanced stuff than our educational system?"

"Because racing is fun and cool and school is boring," their friend Topher said, popping sour gummy serpents into his mouth. "Anyway, school is for tomorrow. We have one more day of summer. Live in the now."

Roa nodded. This was the last day of summer break for all three of them—Abel, Roa, and Topher—but Abel was actually excited for the new school year. They'd been out since an emergency closing in the spring. During that time, Abel had learned how to ride a dragon, learned that his sister was a dragon thief and his brother was an undercover Dragon's Eye agent, and flown in a dragon battle, a match between all the criminal kins that controlled the underworld of Drakopolis. He'd ridden a powerful Sunrise Reaper named Karak. Together, he and Karak and his friends on his ground crew had won. Then he let Karak go free into the wilds beyond Drakopolis. Word got around. For the first time in all their lives, Abel and his friends were considered . . . cool.

He couldn't wait for school to start.

Abel was also excited because he liked the beginnings of things, when everything felt like potential and nothing had yet gone horribly wrong.

"Summer's over," he told his friends. "This trip to the races feels a little desperate, right? Like trying to lick the icing off the box a cupcake came in."

"That's the best icing," Roa replied. Topher agreed.

The racing dragons were still in their starting pens behind a fiery gate at the far end of the arena. The air around the gate shimmered with heat, and the holographic display above it showed the racing positions of the dragons waiting to start. People in the stands all around the arena cheered and clapped and placed their bets, gossiping about how *this* dragon flew faster on windy days or *that* dragon hurt its claw last week, so might be hesitant in close flying. Abel's parents didn't gamble, and no one under sixteen was allowed to place a bet, so they didn't have much to do before the race except wait and eat snacks.

As far as Abel was concerned, the best part of any sporting event was the food.

Still, he realized as soon as his order arrived that a dragon pepper ice cream sundae had been a bad idea. He stared at the hot-pink mound of spicy ice cream and felt his stomach churn.

Topher grinned. "Eat up!" his friend said. "A dare's a dare."

To thirteen-year-olds, an accepted dare was as unbreakable as a dragon's scales. He couldn't back out now. What had possessed him to agree to eat this?

"You don't have to eat that if it's going to make you sick," Abel's father told him. "Dragon peppers are the spiciest found in nature."

"Actually, they were developed in a lab," said Roa, who loved science. "Geneticists fused regular peppers with dragon blood."

"Why would they *do* that?" Abel wondered.

"Scientists do stupid things all the time," Topher mumbled between licks of his simple chocolate–peanut butter swirl cone. "Just admit defeat."

There was glee in Topher's eyes, and it wasn't just from his ice cream. He'd issued the dare, and if Abel didn't eat the spicy sundae, Topher could claim victory for . . . well . . . how long did the shame of a ditched dare last? Eternity? Eternity plus forever?

"Technically, you'd have to actually *try* it to be defeated by it," Roa added unhelpfully. "This would just be giving up. There *is* shame in just giving up."

Abel looked to his father.

"That's true," his father said, licking his salted caramel scoop.

Abel had thought he could at least count on Roa to have his back. They had gotten a mango bubble tea and sipped it loudly and happily.

"You're are *all* incorrigible," Abel's mother said, glaring at her husband and then looking gently at Abel. "If you don't want the ice cream, don't eat it." She paused, and Abel saw a glint of mischief in her eyes. "Of course, it *was* expensive, and you know we've spent a lot on your school supplies for this year . . ."

"Flaming skies, Mom!" Abel cried out. "*You're* guilt-tripping me? Is no one on my side here?"

His mom smiled. "A dare's a dare, honey."

"I can't believe you brought us to the races today, on the last day of our summer, just to torture me!" Abel exclaimed. "Your youngest child!"

That made his mom and dad lean their heads together and grin.

"Aw, he's right, sweetheart," said his dad. "He's just a wittle-bitty baby."

"Maybe he needs his binky," cooed his mom. "Does witty-bitty Abey Baby need his binky boo?"

"Maaaaa-uuum!" Abel blushed.

Topher and Roa looked smug about his ordeal. What were friends for, if not to dare you to eat things you shouldn't? He'd have felt the same in their position.

The people around them in the stands at the Drakopolis Raceway weren't paying attention to Abel's spicy sundae situation. They were more interested in the racing dragons about to compete.

"It's a sure thing!" the man next to Abel shouted into his phone. "Furious Drifter pulled a wing muscle last month, and the treatment gave her extra thrust! I'm telling you, I heard it from the trainer's cousin's best friend's manicurist's ex-boyfriend's landlord!"

Abel turned back to his friends and family. They were all staring at him and the bright pink blob of dragon pepper ice cream in the plastic dragon claw dish.

"Now or never," said Topher.

"The race is gonna start soon," Roa reminded him. "Do it if you're doing it."

"You remember where the bathrooms are?" his mother asked.

He rolled his eyes at her, at *all* of them. Then he took a breath and slammed those rolling eyes shut as he shoved a spoonful of hot-pink dragon pepper ice cream into his mouth.

"Hmmm . . . s'good," he mumbled through the frozen deliciousness. It tasted something like cocoa strawberry swirl, with just a hint of a minty flavor, which he normally didn't like but totally worked here. The mint flavor blossomed a bit and brought out the taste of chocolate, and a surprising burst of sweetness. He smiled at the eager faces of his friends and family. *Ha! He was showing them!* "Not bad at all!"

He shoved two more spoonfuls into his mouth, letting that chocolatey-berry-mint flavor spread so it coated his tongue and slipped down his throat in a cool, creamy river.

"Careful," his dad warned. "Dragon pepper takes a few seconds to—"

"BAAAAAAHHH!" Abel yelled as the cool minty flavor turned into a hot chili burn. Then, like the sun rising over the great glass desert beyond Drakopolis, it turned into jagged, sizzling pain that tore through his teeth, his tongue and throat, filling his face and his head and then his entire body with a heat that no human word could describe. It was *agony*!

"OW, OW, OW!" Abel added to his previous cry. And then, because he couldn't help it, he started jumping up and down, while alternating between "OW" and "BAAAAAAHH!"

"Drink this." His mother shoved her jumbo Ice-a-coolada at him, which he immediately chugged. The whipped cream and iced coffee cooled the inferno on his tongue. Now it just hurt with a normal amount of unbearable pain. His skin tingled and he had tears in his eyes. He panted like Percy, his pet pangolin.

"Not to be *that guy*," Topher said, clearly enjoying being exactly *that guy*, "but the dare was to eat the *whole* sundae."

Abel looked down at his cup of frozen pink pain, and the thought made him want to scream, want to run away, want to throw himself on the ground and weep.

He also didn't want to lose the dare. Abel did not like to lose.

"Mom," he said, his voice scratchy. "I'm gonna need my own Ice-a-coolada."

With that, he dove back in and ate the entire dragon pepper sundae so fast he nearly passed out.

"Done!" he declared, dropping the cup at his feet. His hands shook. His forehead sweat and his skin tingled and he had the intense urge to jump up and down screaming, but he was triumphant.

"Wow," Topher said. Roa just whistled.

"That's all?" Abel shouted. "I just ate more dragon pepper ice cream than anyone in the history of ever and all you can say is *'wow'*?!"

"I mean, people eat that much all the time," Roa told him. "Otherwise they wouldn't sell it. They don't stay in business just because of kids daring each other to do dumb things."

"Dumb things!" Abel threw his hands in the air, looked around for support or a high five or, like, a medal. Surely he deserved one. But all eyes had drifted back to the gate. The race was about to start.

"Sit down and look up, honey," his mother said.

The horn blared, and the fiery gate burst open to unleash the racing dragons. The whole crowd roared as one, but at that moment, Abel's stomach made a sound that no human stomach was supposed to make.

The shadows of sixteen dragons passed over him, but he couldn't stay to watch.

"I think I need to go to the bathroom," he announced. "Right. Now."

He ran straight for the restrooms under the bleachers as the dragons flew their first lap of the arena sky. The crowd hooted and cheered. He didn't even look back.

When he got to the restrooms, he'd expected a long line and was relieved to find no one else there. Everyone was watching the start of the race; he had the place to himself. It was a nice surprise.

What was not a nice surprise was what he saw on the way out of the bathroom after he was done. His older sister, Lina, ran past, sprinting up the stairs toward the bleachers.

He frowned.

Lina wasn't supposed to be at the raceway.

Lina was supposed to be in hiding.

Lina was a fugitive from the law.

If the Dragon's Eye secret police caught her, she'd go to Windlee Prison for the rest of her life. And if one of her enemies in the kins caught her, she'd *wish* she'd gone to Windlee Prison for the rest of her life.

Abel ran after her, because whenever Lina made a surprise appearance, disaster followed.

This time would be no exception.

HE LOST LINA IN THE glare of sunlight. The dragons raced with furious wingbeats and thunderous roars. Their riders squeezed them as close to the edge of the hovering lane markers as they could, and the crowd cheered when the dragons made the first turn toward the straightaway. Fans jumped to their feet and waved their phones around—either because they'd just won a bet or just lost one.

At the races, you could bet on anything, not just the winners. The position of every dragon on every lap, or who changed lanes the fastest, or which dragon got disqualified first, or even the day's attendance were all fair game. (A digital sign near the starting gate said there were 107,498 racing fans there today, and that didn't count the workers or the security guards or undercover secret police from the Dragon's Eye or any of the countless people who'd snuck in without tickets, of whom his sister was surely one.)

Abel scanned the throngs of racing fans for her. Everyone else was looking straight up, heads swiveling on their necks as they watched the lightning-quick dragons. A red short-wing Pincer named Mama's Thunderheart was in the lead, flapping like fury just a snout's length ahead of a pale blue Steelwing named Electric Clawface. Just above both of them was a black Heartrender Reaper named Two's-a-Crowd.

Who names these dragons? Abel wondered. His own dragon, the

Sunrise Reaper he'd trained to battle and then set free, was named Karak. "Karak" was a proper dragon name. He wondered what Karak was doing now. Was his old partner happy, out hunting prey over the Glass Flats or guarding a hoard in some distant cave? Did he ever think about Abel or was the world of people just a hazy memory? Did dragons even have emotions like that?

There was a lot Abel didn't know.

Suddenly, speeding from the back of the flight was a small green Moss dragon named Star Believer.

Karak was a Reaper whose scales looked covered in stars. This one looked like fresh green pond scum.

What does "Star Believer" even mean? Abel thought. *And why am I thinking about Karak so much today?*

The Moss dragon roared and used its muscled shoulders and barbed wings to knock other dragons out of the way. It might've looked like pond scum, but it raced like a river.

It flapped right behind Two's-a-Crowd and tried to dart past but caught a nasty swipe of the other dragon's black tail across its snout. The blow sent the Moss dragon crashing out of its lane, tangling with a Yellow Stinger who'd flown too close, hoping to use the Moss dragon's body to block the wind. Both of them fell from the race, shrieking and snarling.

Abel went back to looking for Lina.

The raceway was a huge arena high atop one of the tallest buildings in the city, shaped like a big open bowl. The seats all faced in and up, where the dragons flew between lanes of hovering drones. There were five lanes across and five lanes stacked on top of each other, creating a grid of flashing lights.

Unlike illegal dragon battles, which went in all directions and every way at once, the dragons had to stay in the lanes that matched their assigned colors. What kept it exciting was that the lanes kept changing colors, so the dragon riders had to change lanes quickly or be given a default. Three defaults meant a forfeit. Changing lanes could slow you down or make you bump into the other dragons as they changed lanes too, which could spark a fight, which would slow everyone down. It was important for the riders to figure out the patterns to the sudden lane changes so they could predict when the next one was going to happen and be ready to move first. During a lane change, anything could happen; a clever rider could go from last to first place in one move.

It was exciting every time it happened. When the lights flashed and changed colors, everyone got to their feet.

In a jumble of wing and claw, roar and rumble, the air turned into a tumultuous tangle for dragon dominance. Mama's Thunderheart dropped two lanes down and three to the right, falling back into third place. Electric Clawface and Two's-a-Crowd ended up in a tussle, fighting and snapping, wings beating on one another while their riders tried to break them apart. This gave six other dragons from behind the chance to race ahead. The melee—which was a word for a brief and bloody battle that Abel had learned from his favorite comic series about a dragon veterinarian—left the whole race rearranged. Gamblers in the stands let out a whole new spate of cursing and cheering and checking their phones. Some just cried into their extra-large sodas.

The tumult was when Lina made her move. Abel was the only person among the hundred thousand plus who was watching her, so he was the only one who saw the teenager slip a phone from the pocket of an unsuspecting older man who was watching the race with his grandchildren. She typed something on his screen before sliding it back into his pocket.

Then Lina gestured toward another section of the crowd. Abel followed her gaze to a dark-haired kid in a purple-and-gray jumpsuit, who picked someone else's pocket, typed on their phone, and put it back undetected.

Abel watched his sister and her accomplices do it again and again, moving through the crowd. The picked at least eight other pockets and signaled to at least three other accomplices. That was a lot of phones they were messing with. What were they up to? Installing a computer virus? Robbing people's bank accounts?

He wanted to get closer. He crept sideways across the section, keeping the crowd between him and Lina but losing sight of her in the process.

"Flaming frogs!" Abel cursed. He searched for her accomplices in the other sections. One of them, a young man dressed like he was a Wing Scout, was currently typing something into the phone of a Wing Scout leader who hadn't noticed he had one extra kid.

Just like when you see someone scratching an itch and you find yourself suddenly itching, Abel worried for his own phone. He searched his pocket to make sure it was still there. It wasn't.

He froze.

"The races are full of pickpockets," Lina said from directly behind him. He whirled around, and she was holding his phone out to him. "You need to more careful. Also, you are *not* good at following people. I spotted you right away."

Abel took his phone back and gawked at his sister. Her hair was short and streaked with red, orange, and blue—the colors of the Sky Knights kin—and she wore a jeweled nose ring and three lip rings and more earrings in her ears than actual ear. She also had a face tattoo of a pink cupcake. The last time Abel saw her, she'd had zero tattoos.

"What did you do to your—"

"Relax," she said. "They're fake. It's just to trick the face-recognition software." She winked up toward one of the security drones.

"Still . . ." Abel gaped at her. "You shouldn't be here!"

"Why not?" she said.

Abel threw his hands in the air. "You're on the run from the law!"

His sister shrugged. "Half this city is on the run from the law. Every kin has people here today. Jazinda Balk from the Red Talons even has her own box."

Lina pointed up toward the luxury boxes. The Red Talons were the biggest and fiercest kin in the city, and Jazinda Balk was the kin boss. She sat in her luxury sky box wearing a bright red leather outfit with her long dark hair tied up in an intricate crown, sparkling with jewels. Abel'd had unfortunate run-ins with the Red Talons before. He'd earned Jazinda Balk's respect by defeating her kin in a battle, but he'd also earned her deep dislike.

Jazinda's only child sat next to her, dressed in a Dragon Rider Academy uniform, looking surly and bored. The kid was Abel's age but was as much like Abel and his friends as a racing dragon was to a school bus. He was rich, powerful, and indifferent to broke municipal-school boys like Abel.

"One day we'll tear open those sky boxes and toss the selfish rich into a dragon's gullet," Lina snarled. The Sky Knights kin— her kin—were just as ferocious a gang of criminals as the Red Talons but not quite as powerful. Abel had *also* had unfortunate run-ins with them. They considered themselves revolutionaries, not criminals, but they stole and cheated and battled dragons just like any other gangsters. Their leader, Drey, didn't like Abel either.

"You're not a kin boss, Lina," Abel reminded her. "The Dragon's Eye could arrest and disappear you, and no one but me and Mom and Dad and Silas would even know."

"Silas would probably *be* the one disappearing me," Lina grunted.

Silas was their older brother. He pretended to be a cadet at the Dragon Rider Academy, but he was actually an officer in the Dragon's Eye, the secret police of Drakopolis. Needless to say, Abel's dragon thief sister and secret police brother did not get along with each other. Both expected Abel to keep their secrets . . . especially from the other sibling.

"No one will catch me here," Lina said. "Not the Red Talons or the Dragon's Eye. Or even Mom and Dad."

"What *are* you doing here?" Abel asked. "Why are you picking people's pockets?"

"Redistributing wealth," Lina said. As if he didn't know what that meant. "The Sky Knights aren't just a kin of thieves and crooks. We're revolutionaries."

"Ugh, I know." Abel rolled his eyes. "I think you're another bunch of thieves and goons, just like every other kin."

"'Flame and claw may cut me raw, but words can't break my armor,'" she recited at him like they were little kids. "Anyway, not that you deserve to know, but we're placing bets *for* other people. Including you."

Abel frowned and looked at his phone. Somehow, his sister had bypassed the app's security and the racetrack's age restrictions, and placed a bet on his behalf on a bright orange Reaper named Carrot Soup Supreme.

"That's a ridiculous name for a dragon," he grumbled. Then he clicked through and saw that the odds on Carrot Soup Supreme winning were twenty-two to one. He wasn't great at math, but he knew enough to know that those were not good odds. It meant no one thought Carrot Soup Supreme could win, so if the orange dragon did win, for every dollar a person bet, they'd get twenty-two dollars back. More likely, though, they'd just lose their money when that dragon lost.

Unless his sister and the Sky Knights knew something that the oddsmakers didn't.

Abel looked up at the sky and found the Reaper that matched the picture on his phone, a bright orange medium-wing dragon who was currently in last place. Reapers were the best fighters among dragons but not the fastest fliers. No way this one could come from behind and win, unless . . .

They were cheating.

"Wait for it . . ." his sister whispered.

Suddenly, the lane lights in the air changed: blue to red and green to yellow and purple to orange and so on. It was a sudden shifting rainbow, and Carrot Soup Supreme reacted just a split second faster than the others, crashing through three dragons above it, then turning in a corkscrew and spinning straight through toward the front of the flock.

Dragons screeched, and their riders screamed. Midair melees erupted. Through it all, the orange dragon charged, reaching its newly assigned lane before any other. Only the pale blue Steelwing called Electric Clawface was in front, flapping as hard as it could to stay in first place.

The crowd went wild; phones pinged, and Carrot Soup Supreme

accelerated even faster, catching up to Electric Clawface on the turn for the final straightaway.

With one deft snatch of its foot, Carrot Soup Supreme grabbed the lead dragon's tail and tugged. The blue dragon roared and turned back, shooting a blast of lightning, but the orange Reaper dodged without slowing down. Carrot Soup Supreme didn't seem to have a breath weapon, but it had a fury in its eyes that could've melted steel. It thrashed so hard, the blue dragon's tail cracked the air like a whip. The rider fell from the saddle and was left dangling upside down by their safety harness. Another thrash and Electric Clawface cried out in such pain that it seemed the whole crowd winced as one. Spectators on the oval infield directly below ducked and covered their heads, as if the dragon or the rider or both were about to fall from the sky.

In which case, covering their heads wouldn't do them much good. A Steelwing dragon weighed about ten tons. A medium-wing Reaper even more.

But Carrot Soup Supreme finally released the Steelwing and bolted into the lead. It jutted its neck out as it crossed the finish line in first place, leaving carnage in its wake.

Abel's phone dinged. Phones all over the stadium dinged. He looked down and saw that he'd won the bet his sister had placed. He now had $550 in his account that hadn't been there before. Judging by the whoops and cheers from surprised people all over the stadium, some people had won a lot more.

"How did you—" he turned to ask Lina, but she was gone.

He looked back up at the orange dragon taking its traditional victory lap. Fireworks erupted, and big holographic images of Carrot Soup Supreme and its rider fluttered in the air all over the stadium. The triumphal anthem of Drakopolis blared over the loud-speakers. In her luxury box, Jazinda Balk looked disgusted. Her son looked like he was crying.

Sore losers, thought Abel as he made his way back to his friends and his parents.

"Did you see that?" Topher asked excitedly.

"It was impossible," Roa said quizzically.

"How's your tum-tum?" his father asked embarrassingly.

Abel wanted to tell them about Lina—about the secret bets and the Sky Knights somehow knowing the dragon that would win and using that to give people money—but the winning dragon wasn't done with its victory lap yet.

"Something's not right," said Roa.

Abel saw on the live hologram that the orange dragon's rider was tugging the reins and shouting but couldn't get control.

That was when three things happened at nearly the same time:

- Dragon Safety Officers in full riot gear rushed into the stands, sealing the stadium exits.
- An announcement interrupted the Drakopolis anthem to say: *"This is a security alert. Do not move."*
- Carrot Soup Supreme tossed its rider and dove toward the crowd, jaws open to attack.

"**THIS IS A SECURITY ALERT.** *Do not move.*"

The blasted warning repeated again and again over the speakers. All around the arena, holograms turned into red exclamation points above the symbol of the Dragon's Eye. Every phone buzzed and lit up with the same emblem, a dragon with an eye for a head wielding a huge curved sword.

Dragon Safety Officers rushed the crowd. Abel saw them grab the old man with his grandchildren and pull him away. He saw the Wing Scout leader yanked from his troop. He quickly scanned the crowd for anyone else whose phone Lina and her crew had taken. Sure enough, they were all getting hauled away by the police.

That meant the four officers with their mirrored helmets and riot shields charging down the aisle were headed straight for Abel.

"*What did you do in the bathroom?!*" Roa cried, bracing themselves for the charging riot police.

"What's going on here?" his father called to the officers in his best dad voice, which was neither terribly loud nor very convincing against tactical body armor.

What *did* give the riot police pause, however, was Carrot Soup Supreme, the mad-eyed orange Reaper diving low over the stands.

Abel's mother yanked him and his father down to the ground; Roa dove on top of Topher, and they all lay in a heap as the dragon plowed through the riot police, slashing its huge claws and tossing spectators, stadium employees, and armored riot police aside like they were rag dolls.

Did people ever actually make dolls out of rags? Abel wondered, his brain doing that annoying thing where he dealt with panic by getting completely distracted with irrelevant thoughts.

Nothing focused the mind, however, like hot dragon's breath, which he now felt warming the air above him.

He bent around to see Carrot Soup Supreme surrounded by three Sawtooth Reapers in full military combat armor, ridden by Dragon's Eye pilots with weapon system modifications, like flash cannons and electric stun missiles. Above the Reapers, blocking the orange dragon's escape, was a Golden Wyvern, its mouth open to show a ball of poison breath building. The attack Reapers had balls of fire in their throats and their wing-mounted missiles ready to fire.

Carrot Soup Supreme, however, was insensate with rage.

"Insensate" was the word of the day on the vocabulary app his dad had made Abel download. It meant the dragon was too mad to feel, think, or notice the danger it was in. Insensate with rage was not a way you wanted a loose dragon to be. A word Abel knew that sort of meant the same thing was "berserk."

Carrot Soup Supreme had gone berserk.

"Look at its eyes," Roa whispered. They'd turned pearl white from lid to lid.

"Racing dragons are well trained," Abel said. "How could it just go berserk?"

"How could it come from behind to win that race?" Roa replied. "It wasn't natural."

At that moment, all three military Sawtooth pilots fired their missiles, which struck the orange dragon in the chest and in each shoulder. It roared and lashed out, tearing off a plate of one Reaper's armor and almost knocking the other two out of the sky.

"Those attacks should have taken it down!" Roa gasped.

The Reapers spat fire. One dragon alone probably couldn't hurt another dragon too badly just with their breath, but three at the same time could do some damage.

Apparently, Carrot Soup Supreme wasn't totally insensate, because when the flames hit it from all three sides, it shrieked. Then the wyvern above fired its poison breath, which mixed with the flames and ignited as green fire.

Carrot Soup Supreme unleashed a cry so loud and high-pitched that the glass of the luxury boxes cracked. People on the ground covered their ears and screamed. Even Dragon Safety Officers in their riot gear fell to the ground, their helmeted heads in their hands. Abel noticed Jazinda Balk being rushed from her box by her Red Talon bodyguards. Her son lingered a moment longer, looking back at the suffering dragon with disgust.

"They're torturing it!" Roa cried out. Roa was the sort of person who loved all dragons and hated to see one in pain. Roa respected a dragon's nature, even when that nature was destructive. "They're *killing* it!"

Abel dared to look up as the orange dragon went rigid in the sky. Wyvern poison filled its lungs, and the trio of dragons' breath burned its scales. Then, like a demolished skyscraper, it collapsed toward the terrified crowd below.

People scattered as the dragon's body crashed, cracking the concrete.

Roa had tears in their eyes, but Abel's parents were already looking at the Dragon Safety Officers staggering back to their feet.

"Mom," Abel whispered to his mother, who was still protecting him with her body, as if that would've mattered against a berserk Reaper or a riot police stun blast. "I think those cops are coming for me."

"For you?" she whispered. "Why?" But then she looked around and saw what Abel saw: riot police by the hundreds grabbing people, young and old, some dressed in the colors of different kins, some clearly in no way connected to any criminal gangs whatsoever, and some who might've been dressed in kin colors, but not on purpose. Maybe they just liked fashion. The DSOs were arresting people at random. They'd think of what to charge them with later. That's how the Dragon's Eye worked.

Of course, they had good reason to arrest Abel. He didn't know how yet, but the Sky Knights had rigged this race.

"It has to do with Lina," Abel said, which his mother immediately understood.

"You can tell me about it later." His mom met his eyes. "And you *will*. But for now, let's get out of here."

His dad helped Roa and Topher up, and they moved quickly through the aisle to one of the holes that Carrot Soup Supreme's claws had torn in the stands. Hopefully they'd be out before any of the riot police noticed where they'd gone. They blended into the fleeing crowd as quickly as they could, heading for the ramps and elevators, where the taxi-backed dragons had already lined up to whisk people away.

Before Abel slipped from the stadium on an overcrowded long-wing bus, he glanced back at the chaos; then he took another look at the account balance on his phone. The screen still showed $550 he didn't have before.

While their bus winged away between the glass skyscrapers and bright neon billboards of the Raptura District, Abel watched swarms of Dragon's Eye wyverns dive into the stadium. Huge long-wing prisoner transports landed to load the hundreds of civilians the police had arrested, while short-wing Blue Foots flapped in with ambulances on their backs to haul away the thousands more people who'd been injured. In Abel's head, the shrieks of the orange Reaper echoed.

Oh, Lina, he thought to himself, *what have you done?*

"**What has Lina done?**" **Silas** demanded the moment they walked through their apartment door. "And don't tell me she wasn't involved in this. We *know* she was involved in this!"

Abel's older brother had the television on. The City News Network showed images of Dragon Safety Officers at the raceway, arresting people who the caption on-screen said were "dangerous kin thugs."

None of them looked like a dangerous kin thug. The Wing Scout leader was there, handcuffed and being led onto the back of a long-wing Black Colossus prisoner transport dragon. So was the grandfather Abel had seen, now separated from his grandkids.

"Silas, honey, so good to see you!" Abel's mom hugged Silas while their father closed and locked the apartment door.

Silas had a new undercut for the coming school year; his long hair on top swept over the clean-shaven sides and back. He also wore his senior dragon cadet uniform, silver pants and a crisp green coat with medals and ribbons on the collar. Abel noticed that he wasn't wearing the Dragon's Eye pin he usually wore when he was on official secret police business.

Funny, Abel thought, *how the secret police aren't always proud of what they're doing. Otherwise, why would they keep it secret? Why would Silas pretend to be a cadet at the Academy if he had no shame about being a Dragon's Eye agent?*

Abel suspected the images of arrests on the news were part of the reason.

"We already know that the Sky Knights are responsible for the incident at the raceway today," Silas told his family. "And I know Lina was there."

"Why don't I make some dinner?" their dad suggested. "Will you be staying for dinner?"

"No," Silas grunted. "I'm too busy. We're all on high alert."

"So many more innocent people to arrest," Abel grunted back.

"I wouldn't mouth off if I were you," Silas snapped at him.

"Ep ep!" Abel replied with the traditional dragon cadet battle cry, though he was far from a cadet and his brother knew it. "No mouthing off, sir," he added. "I'll leave my mouth all the way on."

"Mom!" Silas groaned. He sounded just like he used to when he was Abel's age and his voice had started to crack. "This is what I'm talking about! If it weren't for me, Abel would be in juvenile prison for dragon battling!"

"We know, darling," his mother said. "And we're grateful."

"*He* doesn't sound grateful." Silas glared at Abel.

"I'm *super grateful*," Abel said, entirely unconvincingly.

"You're gonna be *super punched* in a second!" Silas moved for him, and Abel dodged behind the couch.

"Boys! Stop it!" their father yelled as best he could. His voice was still weak from the case of Scaly Lung he'd had last year. "It's been a long day, and I don't want you two fighting. You're brothers, and, Abel, Silas *did* keep you out of prison. It behooves you both to get along."

"Well, I saved Silas from the Red Talon kin!" Abel reminded everyone. "So he can *behoove* my butt."

Silas had been kidnapped and used as the prize in the dragon battle Abel and Karak had won last spring. Where was *his* "thank you"?

Instead of being thankful, Silas lunged at Abel. Abel dodged again, just as Percy, the family pangolin, came scuttling out of his room and rolled into a ball at Silas's feet.

No matter how much of a jerk Silas could be, he could never be a jerk around Percy. He squatted down to pet the little ball of scales, shaking his head. He even laughed a little. "Behoove your butt? Really?"

Abel shrugged and laughed at himself. "Okay, it wasn't my best comeback. But you were about to punch me."

"I wasn't really gonna punch you."

"You totally were!"

"I wasn't!" Silas sat on the couch. "Okay, maybe a little punch. But you deserved it."

Abel stuck out his tongue.

"So . . ." Silas looked from Abel to his parents; then he dropped his voice to a whisper so they couldn't hear. "I know you talked to Lina," he said.

Silence fell over the living room, as heavy as a wyvern sitting on a robin's egg. Abel's heart raced, but he kept his face calm. The first rule of secret keeping was to stay calm. Silas might not really know. He might be bluffing to trick Abel.

His brother let out a long, slow breath. "Lina is a dragon thief and a dangerous kinner. You shouldn't risk going to jail for her. Mom and Dad don't deserve to have *two* kids in jail."

"Mom and Dad don't deserve to have a son who's more loyal to the Dragon's Eye than his own family," Abel said.

"Watch it," Silas warned him. "The Dragon's Eye is here to protect our city and its way of life. You insult them, you insult our government, and *that* can land you in a world of trouble."

"He didn't mean it," their father told Silas. He'd heard everything somehow. "Just like you didn't mean to say no to your mother's dinner invitation, right?"

Silas was about to respond when his dad gave him one of those dad looks. Silas deflated. "Sure. Fine. I'll stay for dinner."

Their dad smiled. "Wonderful! I'll let Mom know." He scurried to the kitchen, telling Abel to wash his hands as he went.

"How does he do that?" Silas wondered.

Abel shrugged, standing up to make his way to the hall bathroom. "Just a dad thing, I guess. They probably teach it to you when you have kids." Abel paused for effect. "So you'll never know."

He shut and locked the bathroom door before Silas could throw a couch pillow at him.

Brothers, Abel thought. *At least when Lina nearly got me killed, she was trying to do something nice. Even when Silas is trying to do something nice, he's a jerk about it.*

Abel washed his hands, but after he was done, he pulled his phone out and checked the credit account again. The $550 from the race was still there, which made his entire fortune $567. He'd earned the other seventeen by helping out at the neighborhood laundromat.

If he kept the $550, did that make him a part of Lina's crime? And what *was* Lina's crime? Was it just cheating at the race, or did she and the Sky Knights have something to do with the orange Reaper going berserk?

He shuddered, remembering the sound that Carrot Soup Supreme made as it was blasted from the sky. He'd never seen a dragon hurt like that before, and he worried the sound was going to haunt him forever. It wasn't like in the action movies where dragons—and people—exploded all the time. And it wasn't like the dragon battles, where the different kins were trying to *win* each other's dragons, not destroy them. This was something else. This was an execution.

How could Lina be involved in something that led to the death of a dragon? And why?

When he stepped out of the bathroom, Silas was right in front of him, towering so close Abel could smell the coffee on his big brother's breath. Abel breathed back up at him. The dragon pepper sundae had done his own breath no favors. The two boys stood there breathing on each other like malodorous miniature dragons.

Finally, Silas broke the smelly silence.

"Lina was arrested an hour ago," he said. "They caught her hiding in a movie theater near the raceway."

"No," Abel said.

"She's already on her way to Windlee Prison," Silas told him.

Abel shook his head. His sister was too slick to get caught. She'd never been caught before.

"You're lying," Abel told him.

"I'm not," Silas said. "The Dragon's Eye thinks she's part of a terrorist plot."

"You have to help her, then!" Abel raised his voice. "She's not some hardened criminal!"

"Yes," Silas replied, "she is."

Silas was one of those people who believed there was such a

thing as criminals, but Abel knew better. There were people who did crimes, but that didn't mean that's who they were. Abel had eaten a spicy sundae; did that make him a sundaeist? Silas spent a long time on his hair; did that make him a stylist? The Dragon's Eye were the ones who decided what a crime was, and even that changed all the time. How could you describe someone with a label that meant so little but sounded like it meant so much? Everyone was more than the worst things they'd done.

Abel had to appeal to the parts that might still care about their sister more than he cared about the Dragon's Eye.

"Lina wouldn't hurt anyone on purpose," Abel said. "There's no way she would've made that dragon go berserk, and you know it."

"Someone did," Silas said. He glanced over at their parents in the kitchen, then leaned close to Abel. "Remember our agreement?" he whispered. "You spy for me and the Dragon's Eye and we keep your dragon battle with Karak out of the official records?"

"I remember." Abel had made that deal so Topher and Roa would stay out of trouble but also to keep the Dragon's Eye from going after Karak. The Sunrise Reaper had flown free and, as far as the government knew, had never existed at all. As long as Abel cooperated, no one would think to try to capture Karak again.

His brother could change that with a few entries into a computer. He could turn Karak into a wanted dragon, and Abel and his friends into fugitives themselves.

"What do you want me to do?" Abel sighed. "Spy on my classmates?"

"I don't need a spy to give me reports about who drew Thunder Wings graffiti on a locker, or who said the Sky Knights were 'cool.' You're not going to be a snitch. You're going to be an *operative*."

"A what?"

It annoyed Abel when his brother used a fancy word just to sound smart. Silas had aced his Dragon Rider entrance exam when he was eleven, the same one Abel had failed when it was his turn. Abel knew his brother was smart; he didn't have to show it off all the time.

"A secret agent," Silas said. "It'll be like one of your comics. You get to go undercover in the process, maybe clear Lina's name."

"Really?" Abel almost couldn't believe it.

"She's a crook, but I agree with you," Silas said. "She didn't make that dragon go berserk. I want to find out who is really responsible."

"And when you do?" Abel wondered.

"Then I make the arrests and get promoted, and Lina gets released from Windlee," Silas said. "And Mom and Dad never have to know their daughter went to jail at all. Like you said, they don't deserve that."

"How can I help?" Abel asked. This moment of generosity from Silas felt as flighty as a fledgling dragon, fixing to wing away at any sudden startle.

"By doing something I think you'll like anyway." Silas smiled. "You're going to race."

Abel's face became a question mark.

"Someone is messing with dragon DNA," Silas said. "That dragon at the races had been hacked, like a computer. It'd been made faster than a normal Reaper, and more aggressive too. You and I both know Reapers don't race like that. I think someone was controlling it somehow, and—"

"Lost control," Abel finished his big brother's sentence.

Silas nodded. "My theory is that they're involved in illegal dragon races before they test out the experiments at the professional races. So I want you to infiltrate the underground races and find out who's involved."

"Infiltrate?" Abel repeated quietly.

"When school starts tomorrow, I want you to find out where the illegal races are and challenge someone."

"Who should I challenge?"

Silas patted him on the shoulder. "That's your job to figure out . . . *Agent* Abel."

Abel had to admit, in spite of his brother's smug expression, "Agent Abel" sounded pretty cool. "Do I get a code name?" he asked.

"No," said Silas. "And if you get caught, I can't help you. You're my *secret* agent. The Dragon's Eye will deny all knowledge of your work; they'll say you're a criminal just like Lina."

"And I'll be thrown in prison just like her too," Abel said.

"Yep," Silas agreed. "Along with Roa and Topher. They're your known accomplices. I figure you'd tell them what you're up to anyway."

Abel was impressed. Silas was devious, but he was smart. He was using Abel's loyalty to manipulate him.

"If you want to," Silas added, "you can give them code names."

"Oh, thanks, that's so *generous* of you," said Abel. "I get all the fun of spying for my big brother but none of his help."

"That's not fair," Silas replied. "I *will* help you. You're going to need a new dragon to race, seeing as you let yours disappear." He rolled his eyes as he said it, but he also handed Abel a scrap of paper with an address on it. "Go there tomorrow after school."

"What's there?" Abel asked.

"Someone who can sell you an illegal racing dragon," Silas said. "Five hundred sixty-seven dollars should about cover the cost."

"What?" Abel gasped. "How did you know about that?"

Silas smirked. "The Dragon's Eye knows *everything*," he said.

"Except for what you need your little brother to find out for you," Abel reminded him.

Silas ignored his sarcasm and sniffed the air. A smile cracked his lips. "Is Dad making beefy curry noodles? They're my favorite."

He left Abel standing in the hall as he bustled to the kitchen table. Abel was stuck in an impossible position. He had to do his brother's dirty work and infiltrate an illegal dragon race in order to get his sister out of prison. But if she *was* involved in experiments on dragons, maybe she *deserved* to be in prison.

He hated that he had to keep all this from his parents too, who didn't even know Lina had been arrested. The Dragon's Eye didn't always tell families about their arrests, even for someone as young as sixteen. Sometimes, people just disappeared. No one knew if the kins got them, or the police, or if they'd just been eaten by a long-wing Rock Biter at a construction site. Drakopolis was a dangerous city. Now Abel would have to fly right into the middle of that danger.

Even though he liked beefy curry noodles too, Silas had ruined his appetite. He was going to have to get a new dragon. He was going to have *train* a new dragon. Part of him wished he still had Karak to fly with. The other part felt selfish for wishing he could put a free dragon back in a saddle.

He poked his noodles around in the bowl without touching them.

"Must be the dragon pepper sundae," his father said.

"Yeah, must be," Abel agreed. The others slurped their noodles and made small talk about anything but what had happened at the raceway or how Lina might be involved.

It was all Abel could think about.

• • •

At bedtime, he texted Roa everything Silas had said. He pretended like he was describing the plot of a comic book, in case the Dragon's Eye was snooping on his texts—which they probably were. Roa would understand.

Once he heard the little *whoosh* of a text sent, he leaned back against his pillow and stared at the billboard glowing across the street. Lane lights blinked, and dragon traffic bustled by. In his head, Abel was still watching Carrot Soup Supreme fall. He could still hear the sound it made, and his skin prickled with the memory.

Faintly, he heard Silas leave to go back to his barracks at the Academy. He heard his mother leave for the late shift at the feed plant. He heard his dad padding down the hall.

"You feeling okay?" his father asked, poking his head into the room.

"Mmm-hmmm." Abel didn't want to talk too much. He knew if he started talking about what had happened to Carrot Soup Supreme, he wouldn't be able to stop. He could never resist telling his parents the truth, but secret agents weren't supposed to spill their secrets to their mommies and daddies. Knowing too much would put his parents in danger too.

They worked so hard, and they didn't deserve trouble. Better to keep his mouth shut and handle this problem on his own. Once he'd cleared Lina's name, gotten Silas his promotion, and stopped the criminals who were messing with dragons, then he could tell his parents the truth. He told himself he wasn't going to lie forever, just for a little while longer.

Of course, he thought, *that's probably what all liars tell themselves.*

"Don't want to talk?" His dad sat gently on the edge of the bed. "That's fine. You know what I like to do when I don't feel like talking?" Abel looked at him, waiting. He knew his eyes were damp, and he knew his dad saw it too. He patted Abel's knee. "I like to hear a story," his dad said.

Without waiting for him to object, his father pulled one of Abel's favorite books from when he was a little kid up on his phone, *The Last of the Dragon Queens* by H. G. Sloane.

" 'It was the night before the great battle,' " he read from the opening. " 'And the Dragon Queen sat with her friends, wondering which would fly through storm and siege and which would fall . . .' "

Abel leaned into his father's shoulder, and he listened. Abel was thirteen years old, so he'd never admit it, but sometimes it just felt good to listen while someone you loved read you a story, even though you both knew how it ended already. A good story was so much more than its ending.

He let his father read to him until he fell asleep.

THE CITY OF DRAKOPOLIS WAS shaped like a huge spiral, with giant boulevards as wide as ten dragons across swirling out from the center. These boulevards were sliced through with thousands of smaller and smaller connecting streets and paths and alleys. There were more neighborhoods on any one arm of the spiral than any one person could ever know the names of. Usually, it was the graffiti on the walls that told you where you were at any given moment because the electric street signs were half-broken and half-wrong.

No one knew exactly how many people lived in Drakopolis. The population was in the tens of millions, at least, and it seemed like all of them were trying to go somewhere at all times, which meant none of them were going anywhere most of the time because they were all stuck in traffic.

Especially this morning.

Dragons lugged wagons and dragons hauled buses, dragons pulled luxurious private cabins and dragons flew with nothing more than a saddle and a dusty pilot. They flapped and screeched and roared at each other all the way from the lanes at ground level to the lanes 150 stories high, pinched between gleaming glass skyscrapers that jutted like talons trying to scratch claw marks on the sun.

And that was just on one street in Abel's neighborhood.

Abel's school was about as far from Abel's neighborhood as it could be. It would've taken a full day to fly there in city traffic if he had to take the public roads. Luckily for Abel, school buses had their own special lanes above the traffic. Only the huge military long-wings flew higher, keeping an eye on the city below.

Abel said goodbye to his parents on the rooftop platform of their apartment building just before sunrise, eyes all bleary with sleep.

"Did you have to wear *that* jacket?" his father asked, running his hand along Abel's patchwork leather jacket with the rainbow stitching of a laughing dragon on the back.

"It's the coolest thing I own," Abel answered, though that wasn't why he was wearing it. The laughing dragon was the symbol of the Wind Breakers kin. If he was going to stay out of jail, he had to keep his end of the bargain with Silas and get himself challenged to a race. The jacket was like an invitation to the kids who were trying to impress other kins. And the Wind Breakers were the only kin who wouldn't feed Abel to a wyvern for wearing their symbol.

Also, it was a *really* cool jacket.

As a green long-wing Cloudflayer swooped in with the bus on its back, his father gave him a hug that lingered just long enough for Abel to lose any cool he felt.

"Have fun," his dad said. "Stay safe."

Abel nodded and climbed the ramp into the passenger compartment. He hadn't even found a seat yet when the Cloudflayer flapped its wings and the building's platform dropped away. The long-wing rose above the blinking lights of the neighborhood, wings beating steadily.

"Stow your bag and take a seat!" a loud voice shouted. "Unless you want to be hauled to school hanging from the bus's claws!"

Abel looked for the shouter, a broad-shouldered man in Dragon Safety Officer armor.

Since when do Dragon Safety Officers ride the school bus? he wondered.

The DSO pointed a meaty finger at Abel. "Do not eyeball me, kid, or I will feed your eyeballs to the pavement!"

Abel didn't know what it meant to get your eyeballs fed to the pavement, but he didn't want to find out. He sat down in the first seat he found, next to a new girl with a ruby-red stud in her nose. She smiled and tapped the nylon safety harness on the seat, telling him to strap himself in.

The bearded Dragon Safety Officer frowned at him, then took his own seat in the front of the passenger compartment.

"Don't worry about him," Abel's new seatmate whispered. She looked about his age. "They're assigning added security to all the schools this year. My dad works in the dispatch office, so he told me all about it. You're Abel, right?"

Abel nodded, feeling a little proud that his reputation preceded him.

"Thought so," she said. "I heard about you when I found out I was transferring to this school. My name's Lu."

"Hi, Lu," Abel said. "So you've heard about me, huh?"

"I mean, it'd be hard not to have. All summer, everyone was talking about the kid who won a battle on the back of a Sunrise Reaper. Did you know that the Thunder Wings put out a reward for sucker punching you?"

Abel gulped. "They did?"

"And the Red Talons put out a reward for anyone who gives you a snapdragon wedgie. Five bucks per wedgie."

Abel's stomach sank. "What's a snapdragon wedgie?"

"When you pull the underwear so hard it tears off the waistband," Lu explained.

"Ouch." Abel winced.

"Yeah," Lu agreed. "Ouch."

"What about the Sky Knights? Did they put a bounty out on me too?"

"I haven't heard anything about that," Lu said. "Maybe because of your sister."

"Wait?! Everyone knows about her?" He couldn't believe all his secrets were out in the open like this. What had happened to privacy?

He was afraid Silas had something to do with it. If everyone knew Abel was a criminal with criminal connections, then the illegal racers would be more likely to trust him. And if *they* trusted him, he'd be a better spy for Silas.

The dishonesty made him a little dizzy. In movies and comics, spies were cool and heroic. In real life, he'd been a spy for only a few hours and he already had knots in his stomach.

"Everyone knows everything, Abel," Lu chuckled. "And sometimes what they know is true. There are even rumors your brother is a Dragon's Eye agent."

Abel tried to keep his face from revealing anything. That was not information *anyone* should know. "Silas?" he scoffed. "He's too lizard-brained to be a Dragon's Eye agent."

Lu snorted. "Ha. Though you probably shouldn't talk about him that way. He's pretty popular at the Academy."

"Silas? Popular?" Abel couldn't believe it.

Lu nodded. "I know he's your big brother and all, but a lot of the kids have huge crushes on him."

"Crushes? On Silas?" Abel shook his head. He couldn't imagine it.

"Wait . . ." Abel said. "You transferred *from* the Dragon Rider Academy?"

Lu nodded sadly. "Expelled," she said. "Not my fault! They'll expel you for tying your boots wrong at the Academy. So here I am. Municipal school."

"It's not so bad," Abel reassured her. "You can tie your boots any way you like here," he added, waggling his eyebrows in a way he thought made him look charming.

Lu smirked and leaned in to whisper, "So is it true?"

Abel's heart leapt. Was this the moment his popularity started? Would it feel different to be one of the cool kids? Would he walk differently and start calling things he liked "fire"?

He hesitated to speak. He didn't want to mess this up.

"Did you really win a battle against the Sky Knights, the Thunder Wings, *and* the Red Talons on a stolen Sunrise Reaper? And then let all the dragons you won *go free?*"

Abel met her eyes. They were dark brown and kind, and she seemed to know everything already. He wasn't sure why, but he wanted to impress this new girl.

He nodded. She smiled at him, patting him on the back. "I thought so."

And then, fast as lightning striking a cell tower, her hand dropped down behind him, snatched the top band of his boxer shorts, and yanked with such force he was flung hard against the safety straps that he now wished he hadn't clipped into. They locked him in place while Lu yanked again, forcing the treasonous cloth of his underwear into such a brutal wedgie he couldn't help but scream. The kids all around turned to look. Some of them burst out laughing, just as the fabric tore and the waistband ripped free.

Even some of the classmates Abel thought *liked* him laughed, like Tall Andi and Prentiss and Bo. Their betrayal hurt worse than the wedgie.

No, he thought through gasps, *nothing hurts worse than this wedgie.*

Lu held his waistband up like a trophy. "That's a snapdragon!" she shouted. "Anybody film that? I want my five dollars!" Lu tucked the shred of his waistband into the inside pocket of her jacket. A few kids had their phones up, taking video.

So much for starting the school year cool, thought Abel.

He glared at Lu with tears in his eyes.

"Jazinda Balk sends her regards," she told him. "The Red Talons don't forget their enemies." With that, she leaned back in her seat, crossed her arms, and closed her eyes to nap, though she opened one of them to glare sideways once. "And if you think about messing with me in my sleep, just know that I can do a lot worse than wedgies."

She closed her eyes again. Abel saw the Dragon Safety Officer staring at him but doing nothing to intervene. Was he on Lu's side, or did he just hate Abel?

How was this school year already going so painfully awry? It hadn't even started yet!

Abel shifted uncomfortably. He had to let go of his dignity to pick out the wedgie, which further amused the kids around him. At least Prentiss mouthed a silent "sorry" his way.

He glanced out the window to see if they were close to Roa's building yet. He'd like to have a real friend on the bus as soon as possible. As they flew, he dared a look at Lu again, sleeping soundly.

She wasn't even afraid of him getting revenge while she had her eyes closed, which made him think she wasn't really asleep, just taunting him.

He wouldn't fall for it. He'd bide his time.

Sleep well, he thought. *And go ahead. Underestimate me. That's the same mistake all my foes have made, before I vanquished every one of them.*

It was a cool line, imagining he had "foes" or that he'd "vanquished" them. He would've felt a lot cooler thinking it if he wasn't still trying to pick his boxer shorts out of his crack.

ABEL GAZED OUT THE WINDOW past Lu as they flew over Drakopolis. The spires on top of skyscrapers blinked with warning lights so that passing dragons didn't crash into them, and Abel saw the shadows of other school buses gliding lazily on the high winds. Military wyverns and police Reapers flew in and around and above the traffic, and others steered as far away from those dragons as they could.

In Drakopolis, most people viewed the military like the inside of a dragon's mouth: best avoided if you had a choice. Also, most people who found themselves inside didn't come out the way they'd gone in. Silas definitely hadn't. Before the Academy, he wasn't a bad big brother.

But that was a long time ago.

With a tight spiraling drop, the bus descended from the clouds, flapping between skyscrapers toward the landing platform at Roa's apartment building.

Abel sat up straighter and watched out the window. They flew past gleaming towers in colorful patterns of expensive dragon glass, then tall apartment blocks of yellow and red brick, then the gray cinder blocks and heavy steel of the cheaper buildings.

They were all tagged with huge amounts of graffiti, all sorts of colorful names and pictures and code words you probably had to live there to understand. There were beautiful murals of dragons and riders, odes to girlfriends and boyfriends, and murals of heroes and cartoon characters and even beloved teachers.

Abel's neighborhood graffiti mostly celebrated money and violence. And curse words. His neighborhood was controlled by the Red Talons, who loved power and wealth above all, while Roa's neighborhood was controlled by the Thunder Wings, who loved knowledge and science above all. Their values showed up in their vandalism.

In Roa's neighborhood, the Thunder Wings symbol was stenciled on walls and billboards and the metal grates over store windows: a lightning bolt with a dragon's head. The symbol made him tense. He was no fan of the Thunder Wings, and they were no fans of his. They'd taught Abel to ride Karak, and in return, he beat them in battle and set Karak free. They'd have happily fed him to one of their other dragons.

They loved knowledge, sure, but they used that knowledge to be better thieves and criminals. The Thunder Wings designed and sold most of the weapons systems that the kins used and trained most of the unlicensed dragon veterinarians. If someone was messing with dragon DNA, it was probably the Thunder Wings.

When the bus came to a hover just over the pickup platform, Abel kept his eyes on the boarding ramp, hoping to warn his friend about the wedgies.

When Roa got on, though, Topher was with them. He hadn't known Topher slept at Roa's or that they were hanging out without him.

Abel knew he shouldn't take it personally that his friends had arrived together, but for some reason, it irked him. He really liked the word "irked" because it sounded like what it meant, like an annoying noise from a neighbor's apartment when you were trying to sleep or like that one piece of your boxer shorts you couldn't quite pick out after a wedgie. *Irk*.

He felt irked.

His friends finding seats together without him? That *irked* him.

Topher lived way out in a distant neighborhood, and his family situation wasn't great. They weren't likely to help him get to the bus platform for the first day of school, so he'd probably stayed over at Roa's after the chaos at the racetrack. It made sense for him go to Roa's instead of to Abel's. Topher's neighborhood was also a Thunder Wings neighborhood, and in Drakopolis, you had to be careful about which neighborhoods you went to after dark, even if you weren't in a kin yourself. While the police enforced the laws of the city, it was the kins who enforced the way people lived.

They still could've told me, Abel thought.

Roa glanced his way from their seat and gave him a smile, but before they could even say "Hey," the Dragon Safety Officer was yelling at them to sit down and stay quiet.

"This is a school bus, not a social club!" he shouted. "My name is Officer Grallup, and I am the *Kin Intervention Safety Specialist* assigned to your school. My job is to monitor for kin activity and divert troubled students from a life of crime and despair." He sounded like he was reciting an employee handbook. "I am here to keep you safe, and I urge you to report any signs of kinship to me immediately."

Topher cleared his throat loudly. "Excuse me, sir?" he dared.

Abel willed his friend to keep his mouth shut but was also curious where this was headed. Topher had a way of irking adults like no one else could. It was a talent. "What are the signs of kinship?"

"What?" Officer Grallup snapped, rising from his seat.

"You said to 'report any signs of kinship' to you?" Topher made air quotes with his fingers. "What are the signs?"

"The wearing of kin colors or emblems," Officer Grallup said, glaring at Abel in his colorful jacket. "An interest in dragon battling or racing." He was still glaring at Abel. "A history of known kin activity." His face was turning red he was glaring so hard. "*Any* delinquent behavior," he added back to Topher. "If I catch it, I stomp it out!"

"Delinquent behavior like, um . . ." Topher mimed thinking hard. "For example . . . um . . ."

Roa glanced over their shoulder at Abel with a *can-you-believe-this-guy?* look.

Abel glanced back with a *please-get-him-to-be-quiet* look.

Roa shrugged. There was no shutting Topher up once he decided to annoy someone.

"Like not wearing your safety harness on a moving dragon?" Topher suggested cheerfully, adding a point of the finger at Officer Grallup, the only person in the bus's passenger compartment not wearing his safety harness.

"You wyrm-tongued little wart!" The officer rushed at Topher, but at that moment, the bus began its rapid descent toward their school, diving nearly straight down. Officer Grallup fell off his feet and sprawled against the front wall of the bus compartment like a bug splattered on a windshield.

Everyone burst out laughing, which made Grallup's face turn angry purple. As the bus swept in for a landing, he scrambled to his seat in the front and glared at Topher with fireball eyes. Then he glared at Abel again and shook his head, like he knew Topher was his friend and blamed Abel for it. Abel wondered if this bus ride was going to come back to haunt him.

Probably, he thought. *Grumpy men's grudges are like a sandwich left in the bottom of a backpack. They don't get better with time.*

Once the bus had landed, the kids jostled their way out. Abel joined the scrum, eager to catch up to his friends. Suddenly, he felt a breath on the back of his neck. He went rigid.

Lu was right behind him. There was nowhere to go in the crowded aisle.

"Relax," she whispered. "I can't snapdragon you twice on the same day . . . not until you put on new underwear." She patted his shoulder, then elbowed past him.

"And tell your friends they're next," she added, winking at Roa and Topher. "They better bring extra underwear from now on."

When Abel finally caught up with his friends on the landing platform outside school, Topher and Roa watched Lu saunter over to a pack of older kids.

"Who *was* that?" Topher asked. "And what did we ever do to her?"

"Her name's Lu," Abel said. "She's a wannabe Red Talon. Expelled from the Academy."

"What was that about my underwear?" Roa asked.

"There's a bounty on our butts," Abel explained. "Literally. Wedgies. Be warned."

"You just make friends wherever you go, huh, Abel?" Topher slapped his back, which was a very Topher way of showing affection.

They hesitated together on the front steps of the school. The last time they were here, Topher was still the class bully, their favorite teacher was secretly a Thunder Wings dragon rider, and Lina had staged an elaborate and dangerous prank to get the school shut down for the rest of the year. It was weird to just return like nothing had happened.

"I think Lu's the one," Abel said at last.

"The one what?" Roa frowned.

"The one I'm going to challenge to a race," he said. "If she's trying to impress the Red Talons, then she'll know about any secret dragon racing that goes on."

"You're really doing this?" Roa shook their head. "You're really going to infiltrate an illegal racing ring to spy for the Dragon's Eye?"

"It's not for the Dragon's Eye," Abel explained. "It's to help my sister get out of jail. And to prevent what happened to that orange Reaper from happening to any other dragon."

"Yeah, but what if we get put *in* jail in the process?" Topher wondered.

"We?" Abel said.

"Duh," Topher replied.

"Like we wouldn't help?" Roa shook their head at Abel. "We're your ground crew. Always."

Abel smiled at his friends, grateful he didn't even have to ask.

Silas had told him, if he got caught racing dragons, he was on his own. Abel could end up in jail by doing the job Silas had given him *or* by not doing it. It was a no-win situation, but at least he wasn't in it alone. Like Dr. Drago said in Abel's favorite comic, *When you're playing a game you can't win, you're gonna have to break the rules.*

WW3D, Abel thought. *If he were in my situation, what would Dr. Drago do?*

"Get to class!" Officer Grallup shouted, snapping Abel's attention back.

"I can't believe they assigned our school a Kin Intervention Safety Specialist," Roa whispered as they walked through the huge double doors into Municipal Junior High 1703. "They're like cops without the training and counselors without the kindness."

"Also their acronym is KISS," Topher said. "Get it? Kin Intervention Safety Specialist. K-I-S-S?"

Roa and Abel looked at him like, *So what?*

"It's just funny, is all," he said. "I would *not* want to kiss that guy."

"I'm sure the feeling is mutual," Abel told him.

They all laughed. Abel really missed when things were simpler, when he and Roa could spend recess joking around, daydreaming, avoiding Topher's bullying, and playing with their DrakoTek cards. Now they spent their free time plotting crimes, Topher had become their friend, and the dragons they played with were way scarier than anything on DrakoTek cards. The stakes of the game were higher too.

Abel didn't like the moral complications of being a thirteen-year-old criminal double-agent dragon rider, but he had to admit, it was kind of exciting.

When the first-period bell rang, Abel's mind was already racing with thoughts of . . . well . . . racing.

7

THE SCHOOL DAY WAS AS uneventful as a school day could be.

They met their new teachers, who talked mostly about preparing for the standardized tests and completing the necessary health and safety forms. They went over rules for the classroom, and rules for the hallways, and rules for the buses and the lunchroom and the Educational Resource Dragons in gym class. Rules, rules, rules.

At one point, they read aloud a short story they'd all read the year before with their last teacher. At another point, they did math that Roa had learned in third grade and that went completely over Abel's head. They didn't see Lu for most of the day. She'd made friends among the other wannabe Red Talons.

None of them were actually kinners yet; most kids were still trying on the identities they might wear for the rest of their lives. But once you put on the symbol of a kin, it was nearly impossible to get out—or at least to get out alive. Thunder Wings stayed Thunder Wings and Sky Knights stayed Sky Knights and Red Talons stayed Red Talons, and none of them could be friends with each other. This year was probably the last chance these kids would have to change their minds. In spite of the rules, the school was like a hatchery for nestling kinners.

All day, Officer Grallup paced the halls, ignoring Red Talon, Thunder Wing, and Sky Knights doodles on lockers but watching

Abel through his mirrored sunglasses, his thick beard hiding a scowl.

Abel couldn't get close to Lu and her pack of junior Red Talons until just after last period, as everyone bustled for the buses to go home. Grallup walked ahead, and no other adult paid Abel any mind.

He saw Lu headed for the front door, and told Roa and Topher to hang back. He didn't want them to get in trouble if he got caught.

"Get caught doing what?" Roa asked, but Abel was already weaving through students to catch up with Lu.

"Hey!" he shouted at her. "You're real tough when you catch a guy by surprise. How about when we're standing face-to-face?"

Lu whirled around. She was about his size but looked like she had a bundle of springs beneath her skin, ready to uncoil. Her feet shifted into a fighting stance. She knew exactly what she was doing.

"Fine," she said. "Bring the fire."

Oops.

Abel had never been in a fight before, not a fistfight anyway. He didn't ever want to be.

"I'm not gonna fight you," he told her, hoping that would be enough, though he wasn't sure the choice was his now.

"Scared?" she sneered.

Lu's friends all oohed and aahed. Other kids slowed down and circled them in the hall. They were drawing more attention than Abel had wanted. He had to be quick before a teacher came to see what the trouble was. Or worse, before Officer Grallup came. For the moment, he kept his distance.

"Scared of you?" Abel scoffed. "My pet pangolin, Percy, could pick you apart. But we both know that if there was a fight, I'd get blamed for it."

"Not my problem," Lu said.

"Oh, so you're on *their* side," Abel said. She'd walked right into his trap. "You want to do Officer Grallup's work for him? I thought you wanted to be a real Red Talon kinner, not a KISS snitch."

"OOOOO," the crowd moaned, like wind passing over an open sewer pipe. Being a snitch was about the worst thing you could be in Drakopolis, especially if you were trying to get into a kin.

"I'm no snitch," Lu said, glancing at her new friends nervously. The Red Talons fed suspected snitches to Goatmouth short-wings with dull teeth—and they made no exception for middle schoolers. Lu was on the defensive now.

Abel had her right where he wanted her. "So how do we settle this like kinners?" he asked. She had to think the idea was hers.

She thought a second. Abel worried he'd played this wrong or picked the wrong kid. He wondered if he was gonna get punched instead of challenged. He held his breath until Lu nodded. "This weekend. After curfew. A race."

"A race?" Abel exhaled and acted like he was surprised.

"Bring a dragon; short-wing only. It's not a battle."

"Oh, right." Abel smiled at her. "Because only the kin can battle and you aren't *really* in a kin. You're just a little wannabe, like a baby dragon who spits milk and thinks it's fire."

"Ooo, *ultra burn!*" Prentiss Patek whispered from somewhere behind Abel.

Lu's eyes flickered over Abel's colorful jacket. It was a gift from the Wind Breakers kin, and it was designed for dragon battling, with protective wrist cuffs and a reinforced collar. It not only had the Wind Breakers symbol stitched on the back, it had a few scuffs from the dragon battle he'd worn it in. It was the real deal from a real kin . . . kind of.

The Wind Breakers weren't like the other kins. They didn't control territory or recruit members or battle dragons like the Red Talons, Thunder Wings, and Sky Knights. They were more of an idea, dedicated to freedom, chaos, and embarrassing the powerful. Anyone who shared those beliefs could claim allegiance. Abel did. He'd won his battle in their name. But, because the Wing Breakers weren't organized—they had no leaders or meetings or money or power—they weren't exactly ordinary criminals.

All the kins broke laws, but without the laws, they wouldn't exist. Lawbreaking was how they got rich and powerful. The Wind Breakers, on the other hand, weren't rich or powerful. They just didn't believe in laws . . . *any* laws. They didn't try to cheat the system like the other kins; they tried to exist outside it. They were anarchists, which was a word Abel thought he'd understood until he met some of the Wind Breakers and realized they were just a community. Lawless, but not dangerous. They wouldn't hurt him for wearing their symbol. They wouldn't protect him either.

On the news, they were called terrorists, and he'd always believed it, but Abel found the more he learned about them, the less the label made sense. Part of being thirteen, he'd discovered, was that nothing was as simple as it seemed when you were twelve.

"I will be a Red Talon soon," Lu told him. "Once I beat you, they'll let me in and you'll regret talking to me like this."

"I already regret talking to you at all," Abel said, which earned another round of oohs and aahs from the crowd and another *"Ultra burn!"* from Prentiss, who must've just learned that expression.

They'd even used it in math class, when Bo Ryland forgot to move a decimal point two places. It had kind of lost its impact. Abel still gave Prentiss a polite nod. It was good to have allies.

"Just be at the Old Tail Factory District at midnight on Saturday," Lu said. "Ready to race. Winner gets the loser's dragon. And the loser gets an *atomic* snapdragon wedgie."

"Fine," said Abel, though he didn't know what made a snapdragon wedgie atomic. "But after *I* win your dragon, you have to atomic snapdragon yourself!"

Lu shrugged. "I don't plan to lose," she said. "Saturday night, we'll see who the *real* dragon rider is."

"Yes, we will," Abel said. Instead of waiting for her to leave first, he just cut right through her and her friends toward the bus. Roa and Topher ran to catch up to him.

"Do me a favor," Abel whispered as they walked. "Watch my back, please. I *really* don't want another wedgie today."

"I think you're in for worse than a wedgie," Roa said. "You don't actually *have* a dragon to race on Saturday."

"I will," said Abel. "I couldn't tell you in the text last night, but you two are going to help me get it."

"We are?" Topher cocked his head.

"Yep." Abel slipped Roa the piece of paper Silas had given him.

"You know where this is, right?" Roa shoved the paper in their pocket as they got closer to the bus.

"No," said Abel, "but I figured you would."

"It's the Burning Market," Roa whispered.

Abel tripped over his feet and had to catch himself from eating pavement. *"The Burning Market?"* he repeated. Abel honestly couldn't believe Silas would send him there, of all places.

"Is that place even safe for kids?" Topher asked.

Roa shook their head. "It's not safe for *adults*."

Topher nodded gravely. "Well, I guess we're going shopping!" he said with a confidence he was obviously faking. Abel was grateful. He couldn't even fake confidence. The Burning Market terrified him.

PART TWO

"WHICH WOULD FLY THROUGH STORM AND SIEGE AND WHICH WOULD FALL?"

THE BURNING MARKET WAS ON FIRE.

This, of course, was how it was supposed to be. The Market burned year-round, twenty-four hours a day, except for Saint George's Eve, the last Tuesday of every month, and an unofficial kinner holiday called Thieves Banquet, when all kin battles and grudges and schemes were put on hold and a citywide truce declared and no one tried to feed anyone else to a dragon.

Today was not that day.

The Burning Market was not, precisely, a *legal* market. It was like a mall for everything *illegal* in the city, from weapons and dragons to banned books and pirated games. It was not an honest place, nor an entirely safe one.

It was especially unsafe for three kids who had enemies in every kin in Drakopolis, did not know their way around, and were looking to buy an illegal racing dragon.

Abel wondered if this had all been a very bad idea.

"We're not old enough to buy a *legal* racing dragon," Roa noted. "So what difference does it make that we're buying an illegal one? We're notorious criminals now, Abel. Might as well lean into it. Let's get tattoos!"

Abel's and Topher's jaws dropped.

"Kidding!" Roa said. "I'm just trying to lighten the mood. You boys need to relax. If you look nervous in there, they're gonna smell it on you."

"All I smell is Topher's Wild Wingman body spray," Abel said.

"It's Knight's Armor scent," Topher corrected him. "It's supposed to make me smell metal."

"You smell mental," Roa replied, which made Topher raise his arms, waving his pits in their direction.

"Um, can you two please chill?" Abel asked. "We gotta go in there."

The three of them turned to look at the gate again.

Abel couldn't think of many places he'd like to be *less* than the Burning Market. Maybe the dentist's office. Or a broken public restroom during a neighborhood street carnival. Or the opera. But he did have to admit, the fire-shrouded building looked pretty cool.

"You've got to admit," Topher said. "The building looks pretty cool."

Abel smirked at his friend.

The Burning Market sat in the middle of a block of huge glass-and-steel skyscrapers. Its front was all sharp angles that pointed toward the sky, like a child's drawing of fire. It was covered in gleaming copper plates that caught the light and made it shine bright orange. But the most remarkable thing about it was how the entire copper front of the building was covered in flame, burning out of little gas jets that studded it from top to bottom. There was one tall gap for the heavy doors in the middle, the only way in or out. To get inside, you literally had to walk into the fire.

Abel didn't move from his spot on the sidewalk. If anything went wrong in there, he and his friends could vanish. He wondered if Silas would come looking for him, or if he'd at least tell their parents where he'd sent Abel dragon shopping. He wondered if Lina had been to the Burning Market before. She probably had. She was a dragon thief, and where else would a thief go to sell her stolen dragons?

On official maps, it was marked as a garbage incinerator, which made no sense, because dragons burned all the garbage in Drakopolis. The local Dragon's Eye agents and Dragon Safety Officer patrols were paid to pretend that's what it was.

Abel had realized that the things grown-ups believed didn't always have to make sense once other grown-ups had agreed to believe them too. Adult reality wasn't a set of true things; it was just a set of things adults had decided to believe at the same time. The Burning Market was only a real place to those who wanted it to be. Everyone else in the city just pretended it didn't exist.

As long as it stayed relatively peaceful inside and as long as the only people who got hurt, robbed, or killed there were other criminals, the city let the market run. It had been running for as long as Abel had been alive. It had been running since before his great-grandparents were born. It was part of the unofficial history of Drakopolis, the history you'd never learn about in school. Its slogan could've been: *If you ain't allowed to own it, you can buy it here.*

"You're doing that thing again," Roa told Abel. "That thing where you freeze up and get lost in your brain."

"Right, right, sorry," said Abel, glad to have a friend who knew him better than anybody.

"I thought he was just freaking out like I am," said Topher, and Abel was glad to have a friend like Topher too. They were a well-balanced crew. If he had to go into the Burning Market, there was no one else he'd rather go with than these two.

He led them toward the doors. The heat blasted him in the face as they stepped through and were hit by a wall of cool air on the other side of the dangling plastic curtain strips, which also slapped him in the face. The roar of the air-conditioning was so loud that, for a moment, Abel thought it was a dragon.

It couldn't have been a dragon, though, because there was no way to hear just one over the din of the market. Machines buzzed and beeped and whirled. Merchants and customers shouted and bargained and heckled each other. There was gambling and cheering; there were weapons going off and holograms dancing to every kind of music; and there were other dragons, of course, of every size and shape imaginable, roaring and screeching and cooing. The place was—to use a word Roa liked—cacophonous.

"This place is flamin' loud!" Topher shouted, much less poetically than Roa would've put it.

The three of them made their way from the front door, down a wide center aisle that was like its own street filled with stalls and booths. Merchants eyed passing customers.

"Baby pangolin?" one called to them. She was a sweet-looking older woman in a pink cardigan embroidered with flowers. "I've got rare breeds, genetic mutations. You want an oversized crossbreed to guard you while you sleep? You want a pet that glows? Good prices—come on over!"

"She's a cheat, kids!" a merchant across from that one yelled. He was dressed from neck to toe in spike-studded blue leather and had a blue mohawk to match. In his arms, he cradled an adorable baby pangolin that was bright pink, not a color the small ant-eating mammals took on naturally. "She uses paint and trickery. I can promise you, my breeds are all genuine mutations. They cost more because they're *worth* more!"

"Don't listen to that liar!" the old woman yelled. "He'd rob his grandma for her last dollar!"

"I told you I'd repay you!" he yelled at her.

"You're my least favorite grandchild!" she yelled.

"I'm your only grandchild!" he yelled back.

"Worse luck for me!" she moaned.

Abel's head ping-ponged between them. "Sorry," he said, finally interrupting their squabble. "We're not looking for a pet."

"Pfft!" The old woman waved her hands and turned away. Her blue-haired grandson just sucked his teeth and looked for new customers. A neon sign hanging over the center of the aisle said: DOMESTICATED FAUNA AND SUPPLIES.

"That means pets," Roa explained. "We won't find what we want here. Dragons are not pets."

Abel studied Silas's paper for the location of the stall he was supposed to find. Under the address for the Burning Market was just a name: OTTO VOORHEES.

"This is place is huge," Topher said. "How do we know where to go?"

"Hey, tadpoles!" the mohawk guy shouted at them. "Try the information booth."

He pointed the pangolin he was holding toward a metal cylinder in the middle of an intersection. Abel thanked him but noticed he had a small tattoo on his index finger: an infinity symbol with an armored helmet. He was a Sky Knight. Abel wondered if he knew Lina, but didn't want to draw attention to himself by asking.

They approached the information booth, and the cylinder projected a map in the air in front of them.

"That's convenient," Abel noted as he studied it.

The Burning Market had thirty-five different sections across six different floors. Each section was filled with stalls and shops selling a specific type of item. The one closest to the main entrance sold rare, exotic, banned, or stolen pets and pet supplies. The section next to it had twenty booths selling pirated movies and counterfeit DrakoTek cards (which Abel felt a moment of temptation to browse, even though he knew it was wrong). There were fortune-tellers and gambling parlors, unlicensed doctors and self-taught veterinarians, and an entire row of shops that sold only "data harvests," whatever that meant. Something to do with farming, Abel figured.

The sections got more strange and more illegal the higher one went in the market.

"There!" Roa jabbed their finger into the holographic map. On the top floor, there was a section selling dragon eggs—and an even larger one selling dragons. It was by far the largest section of the market. It took up most of the floor.

"There must a hundred different merchants up there," Topher said. "How will we find the right one?"

"Guess we'll just have to ask around," Roa said.

"Careful asking questions here!" The older woman had snuck up behind them, and all three startled. "The Dragon's Eye has agents lurking about. Kinners of every sort too. Ask the wrong questions and someone's as likely to take your tongues as to answer your questions."

"Take . . . our . . . tongues?" Topher was always a pale white color, but he went even whiter.

Before Abel could stop her, the old lady had snatched the paper from his fingers. She studied it and shoved it back at him.

"Otto? Hrmgf." She made a face like she'd just gotten a sour serpent candy stuck in her nose. "That old lizard's not worth the time it takes to bathe a basilisk. What do you want with him?"

"We need to buy a—" Topher began.

"Our business is our business," Abel cut him off. "You know where Otto is?"

She snorted. "All the way down the last aisle on the sixth floor, right next to the sign for the bathrooms. You can't miss it."

"Don't tell us what we can't miss," Topher said, trying to regain his cool and utterly failing.

The old woman just shook her head. She returned to her booth to yell across the aisle at her grandson some more.

The kids made their way to the escalators, past salespeople demonstrating every kind of illegal item, shameless scam, and sketchy deal imaginable.

On the second floor, there were sections for dragon riding armor, and dragon battling armor, sections for human-sized-weapons and sections for dragon-sized weapons. On the floors above, there were sections that sold poisons, and sections that sold antidotes, sections for dragon feed, and a section that sold dragon body parts.

Abel shivered and averted his eyes, trying not to see the wings laid out like rugs and baskets full of talons, horns, scales. Merchants and poachers haggled with each other in hushed and suspicious voices.

"Don't make eye contact with anybody," Roa warned.

That was fine with Abel. He didn't want to meet anyone who traded in dragon parts. Some mean-looking folks with Thunder Wings tattoos eyed the three as they passed, but no one tried to stop them on their way toward the sixth floor.

High in the rafters, over each floor of the vast market, kinners from the Sky Knights, the Thunder Wings, and the Red Talons were perched on dragonback, watching everyone below—as well as each other.

"Security," Roa said. "The merchants pay every kin to keep order. Having every sort of criminal watching every *other* sort of criminal keeps them all honest. Or at least at the same level of dishonest."

Drakopolis was like one of those dolls that you opened to find a smaller doll inside, and then a smaller doll inside that one, and on and on. You could live your whole life in the city and still discover strange and terrifying new things inside it every day. It was unsettling, Abel thought, but also a little exciting. It was hard to be bored in Drakopolis.

And it was impossible to be bored in the Burning Market.

As they stepped off the escalator onto the sixth floor, the smells hit Abel first, then the sounds.

"Whoa," Topher said.

"Whoa," Roa echoed, their vocabulary for once in total agreement.

There were dragons everywhere. Sleek silver Steelwings flew in circles just below the ceiling, and tiny multicolored dragonettes perched on neon signs. A five-ton baby Reaper with gleaming gold scales sat on a heap of fake gold, its wrists and ankles bound in magnetic cuffs to keep it from flying off. It watched them walk past with gold-eyed hunger.

There were short-wing, medium-wing, and long-wing dragons in every direction. All of them were tagged with wrist cuffs by their merchants, ready for sale, ready to be trained and raced and fought. And even—Abel shuddered to think it—*hunted*.

Each dragon dealer had a kind of gated area that held their sales table and rows of stalls behind them, just like in a stable. Some had their dragons displayed to be gawked at, while some kept them behind closed stall doors, which they only opened if they decided the buyer was serious and had money to spend.

There were a lot of people with money to spend. There were kinners in their kins' colors, and society people in elaborate fashions. There were shop foremen in overalls looking for cheap industrial dragons, and businesspeople looking to buy dragons low and resell them high.

And there were probably spies swirling among them all too, spies for the kins and spies for the Dragon's Eye and spies only out for themselves. There was no way to know who was who or what was what.

Abel realized he was getting lost in his thoughts again.

He took a deep breath and slowed his brain down.

They walked the aisles until they saw the neon bathroom sign with the image of a little green dragon perched on top of a flickering orange toilet. Just below the sign, a gray-scaled Ice Drake dozed in front of the door. It had a scanner around its neck to charge people twenty-five cents as they went in. When a nervous customer in a wide-brimmed hat tried to skip paying, the Ice Drake snorted frost and growled. The customer quickly took money hidden in the brim of their hat and gave it to the drake before it could encase them in a frozen coffin.

Even peeing had a price at the Burning Market.

In the area next to the bathroom, Abel spotted the dragon dealer they had come to find. The old lady had been right: They couldn't miss him.

Where the other market booths had neon signs or gleaming holo-grams, Otto Voorhees had a hand-painted sign that read: LEGACY DRAGONS. Though the paint had peeled a bit, so it looked more like LEG___ DRAG__S.

Otto himself sat on a rusty metal chair beside a rusty metal table in front of a row of rusty metal stalls, which were filled with a col-lection of the oldest, tiredest, most broken-down-looking dragons Abel had ever seen.

The dealer and his dragons were all fast asleep.

"This can't possibly be the place," said Topher.

Abel double-checked the piece of paper. "I'm afraid it is."

9

"Excuse me?" Abel called to the old man. "Mr. Voorhees?"

He didn't respond. A large magenta Infernal with one wing medical-taped to its body poked its head out of a stall and snorted sparks that showered the old man. Otto swatted at them without waking up, and the long-wing dragon lowered its head again, having lost interest.

"I'm not sure this guy is gonna be of much help," Roa suggested.

"I'm not sure these dragons are either," Topher said. In the second stall, a saggy-winged lump of gray scales with a mop of gray fur between its horns shook the floor with its snoring.

"EXCUSE ME!" Abel shouted. For added effect, he banged on the old guy's hand-painted sign.

"Huh? What's the noise, eh?" The old man wheezed, one eye popping open under his bushy eyebrows. The other eye followed like it was running to catch up. "Who is it? Godfrey? You back with the noodles?"

"Um, no, er, Mr. Voorhees," Abel said. "I'm . . . uh . . . I mean, like, we're here to—"

"Huh? No noodles? What?" It seemed like Otto Voorhees couldn't hear very well.

"NO NOODLES!" Abel shouted. "I'M HERE TO BUY A DRAGON! SILAS SENT ME!"

"Lower your voice, boy!" The old man popped to his feet like a sprung spring, leaping the distance between them and pressing a papery palm over Abel's mouth. His other hand wrapped around the back of Abel's neck with alarming strength. "Not wise to shout your business around this place, got it?"

Abel nodded. The man removed his hand from Abel's mouth, then released him and stepped back, straightening his frayed purple blazer.

Otto was much larger than he'd looked in his chair, and younger too. He had a shock of salt-and-pepper hair on his head, pointing in all directions, and his outfit was an odd mix of castoffs—a purple blazer paired with a black silk shirt and green tuxedo pants. His face had deep lines, but they looked like the kind that came from living hard, not living long.

A neck tattoo of a dragon wrapped around a stack of books suggested membership in a long-forgotten kin, and the big scar on his forehead suggested the kin was better off forgotten. He had the letters "RIDEFIRE" tattooed across his knuckles in faded blue ink. Abel had seen that tattoo on long-haul pilots who flew Goliaths across the Glass Flats.

How in the world did Silas know this man?

"So little Silas sent you?" Otto asked with a wheezing laugh. Calling Silas "little" made Abel smile. His brother would not like it. Abel couldn't wait to tell him. "I wondered when he'd call in the debt I owe."

"Wait, *you* owe *Silas*?" Abel found that hard to believe. What could this tattooed old dragon dealer owe Silas, of all people?

"He got me out of a jam some years back," Otto said. "I was a riding instructor at the Academy, and I was . . . well . . . *borrowing* supplies to sell to, er . . ." He looked around the market like he was searching for a word in the high rafters where smaller dragons perched. "Neighborhood organizations."

"You were stealing," Roa said flatly. "And selling the stuff to the kins."

Otto shrugged. "Teaching doesn't pay much, kid, and I liked to bet on the races. Anyway, Silas was only twelve years old at the time, but that little scamp caught me. Rather than turn me in, he suggested I resign quietly, and that I remember to whom I owed my freedom. The boy told me that one day he was going to be an officer, and that he might need a man like me to do him an unsavory favor. What kind of a kid talks that way?"

"Silas," Abel said, unsurprised by his brother's devious planning. Still, Abel was kind of impressed that Silas hadn't always been such a stickler for the rules.

The old man looked between Abel and his friends. "So who in the flames of Friday are you three supposed to be?"

"Doesn't matter who we are. We're here to buy a racing dragon from you," Abel said. "The fastest you've got."

The old dragon rider sucked his teeth and locked eyes with Abel. Then he cracked his R knuckle, then the I, D, and E ones. Before he made it to FIRE on the other hand, however, he burst out laughing.

"Why didn't you *say* so?! I know I have a racing dragon in here somewhere! Maybe I left it in my other jacket! Ha ha ha!" He slapped the pockets of his blazer theatrically. "Oh, that's good! I never took Silas for a joker, but this is a good one . . ." Otto waved his hands dismissively and went back to his little seat, putting his feet up on the rickety table, where he kept an old-fashioned ledger book and a mug of pens. The mug said: A KNIGHT

SLAYED MY HOMEWORK. "Tell him he got me. This was a good one."

"I'm serious," Abel said just as Otto's chair tipped too far and he toppled backward onto the big magenta dragon. The Infernal opened one eye and grunted out tiny blue flames from its nostrils but then went back to sleep.

Otto popped to his feet and brushed himself off. A few shifty-looking shoppers at other stalls glanced in his direction, then returned to their business. Though some, Abel noticed, kept looking over their way.

Abel double-checked that Roa and Topher were still standing behind him, watching his back. He didn't want a surprise snapdragon wedgie from one of these people pretending to be a customer. Nor did he want a knife in the spine.

Calm down, Abel, he told himself. *You're catastrophizing again. There are tens of millions of people in the city. You're not special. No one knows who you are.*

"You're Abel, aren't you?" the old man said. "Silas's little brother? The one who beat all the kins in a battle and let that Sunrise Reaper go free last spring?"

Okay, this *guy knows who you are,* Abel thought. He really didn't like when his catastrophizing leapt out of his head and into the real world.

"Look, mister, I have money," he said, with more confidence than he rightly should've given the small amount of money he actually had. "And Silas said you'd help me. But I guess I can tell him you thought it was all a joke. I'm sure he'd find that funny. You know he has a great sense of humor."

The old rider raised a bushy eyebrow. They both knew Silas had no sense of humor.

"You've got money?"

"Mm-hmm," Abel replied with as neutral a tone as he could.

Real racing dragons could cost tens of thousands of dollars. Even hundreds of thousands! With his $567, he knew one of Otto's motley menagerie was the best he could do; he just hoped it was enough.

"Well then, kiddos, meet the finest legacy dragons your money can buy!" He gestured broadly at the row of stalls behind him.

The magenta Infernal finally opened both eyes but didn't lift its head. The lump of gray in the next stall stayed fast asleep. Abel couldn't see into the rest of the stalls, so he had to walk forward to check them out.

"What's a legacy dragon?" Topher asked.

"It's a euphemism," Roa told him before Otto could answer.

"Oh, right, of course," said Topher. Then, after a breath, he asked, "What's a euphemism?"

"A euphemism is when you use a nicer word than the one you actually mean," Roa said. "Like, saying 'borrowing' when you mean 'stealing.' 'Legacy' here, I think, means 'worn out.'"

The old man snorted. "I pride myself on giving even the lowliest dragon a chance at rehabilitation. Surely, you, Roa, can appreciate that."

Roa froze. Otto knew who they were too and that they loved dragons—even the lowliest, most worn-out ones. How much did this man know about them?

"I think you'll be interested in this one," Otto said. He led them to the last stall in his row. They passed a wingless Educational Resource Dragon, the kind that schools used, who was pacing back and forth, and a Rock Reaper who was eating mush from a trough.

"Is that dragon toothless?" Roa asked, somewhat horrified.

"Don't judge," Otto snapped at them. "If you lived to nine hundred eighty-four years old, you'd have no teeth either."

Roa balked. Dragons lived a long time, but none of them had ever seen one *that* old before. In fact, Abel realized, he'd never seen an elderly dragon at all. He'd also never wondered what became of them when they could no longer work. He thought again about the dragon parts for sale downstairs and shuddered. Better a stall at Otto's than getting dissected by poachers.

They reached the last stall. Unlike the others, it had a door. Otto unlocked it with a scan of his phone. It slid open with a scraping sound. Flecks of rust fluttered to the floor, but it was dark inside.

There was movement in the darkness. Abel leaned forward to see better, when a face the size of his body lunged from the shadow, a full mouth of fangs open wider than Abel's whole height.

"Ahh!" He leapt backward into Topher and Roa.

There was a loud THUNK, as Otto tapped his phone, laughing again. The magnetic cuffs on the dragon's ankles locked it in place on the floor. The dragon was a pink-and-blue short-wing, some kind of combination breed. Its coloring was uneven over its scales, like someone had just tossed the scales on haphazardly. It had bright yellow eyes, and a pair of curled horns that wrapped from its forehead to the underside of its jaw. Its wings were a shocking bright green, folded at its sides, and its tail was long and smooth and ended in a sharp and fearsome hook of pearly white bone. The dragon looked wild, and smart, and deeply unhappy to have visitors.

"Her name's Brazza," Otto said. "Don't know how old she is, but she was a lightweight battler for a few years, judging by the scars on her flank. Until a . . . *friend* of mine won her and thought to race her. She was fast but had a bad attitude."

The dragon snapped her jaws, daring any of them to take a step into her stall.

"I see that," Abel said.

She opened her mouth like she was snarling and roaring, but no sound came out.

"Oh, and she doesn't make noise," Otto explained. "I think she worked for a ring of thieves for a while. Makes sense they'd train silence into her."

"That's not right," Roa whispered. "Dragons shouldn't be silent."

"Maybe it's her choice?" Otto shrugged. "Either way, with the right trainer, she could be a fine racer." He looked Abel up and down, rubbed his chin as he thought. "And I'd be happy to part with her for, let's say, two hundred thousand dollars."

Abel's heart sank. That was way more than he had or might ever have in his life.

Otto read his body language and sucked his teeth. "Well, since you're family to Silas, and since you made such a fool of Jazinda Balk and the Red Talons last spring, I suppose I could make some modest concession on price."

"What does that mean?" Topher cut in.

"It's another euphemism," said Roa. "It means he's willing to negotiate."

"What are you willing to pay?" Otto asked Abel.

"Three hundred," Abel tried.

"Three hundred thousand?" Otto laughed. "Kid, you're not supposed to negotiate yourself to a higher price!"

"No," said Abel. "I meant three hundred dollars total."

Otto sighed. He cleared his throat and made a great show of thinking, but he wasn't a good actor. "How about five hundred and sixty-seven?"

Abel gasped. "You . . . you knew?"

Otto smiled. "It's my job to know," he said.

"Then why go through this whole act with the two hundred thousand?" Abel wondered.

"To see your face!" Otto laughed. "I don't get a lot of customers. Have to make my own fun." He pointed into the stall where Brazza still thrashed against the magnetic cuffs, enraged. "You want her or no?"

"One condition," Abel said. "I have to see if there's a hope of riding her. If she and I don't understand each other, there's no sale."

He thought back to when he'd first met Karak in an abandoned warehouse. He'd nearly tried to incinerate Abel. It took time for them to trust each other, to become partners.

Not partners.

Friends.

He wondered if he'd be able to befriend a new dragon, if he even wanted to. He felt guilty, like he was betraying Karak's memory, but what choice did he have? Karak was gone, and Abel needed to race.

"You want a test drive?" Otto bowed, then pointed Abel to the stable. "Be my guest."

Abel took a deep breath. It was now or never. He had tamed a mighty Sunrise Reaper. He could tame this mixed breed. He would show no fear.

WW3D, he repeated in his head like a mantra. *WW3D. What would Dr. Drago do?*

He stepped forward into the dragon's stall, leaving his friends behind. When you faced a dragon, as friend or foe, you faced the dragon alone.

Brazza thrashed against the cuffs that held her feet to the floor, and she opened her mouth wide, right in front of Abel.

He froze, realizing he hadn't asked if the dragon had a breath weapon or not. He shut his eyes and winced, waiting to be engulfed in flame or ice or broken glass. The thing about mixed breeds of dragon was that you never knew what they could shoot from their mouths. That was part of the reason kinners bred them, and part of the reason it was illegal to breed them. The government had rules about the types of dragons that were allowed to exist; any that fell outside those rules were banned. No one talked about what happened when a banned dragon was caught. Abel feared they ended up in pieces for sale on the fourth floor of the Burning Market. The thought made his skin prickle.

That was a good sign.

His skin wasn't being fried off by dragon fire. His eyeballs weren't burned by poison breath, or his bones snapped by jagged shrapnel.

He opened one eye, then the other.

Brazza just stared at him. She'd closed her mouth to watch Abel with slitted eyes. He dared another step toward her, close enough that she could bite his head off if she chose to.

"What are you doing, Abel?" Roa asked.

"Showing her I trust her," Abel said. Then he sat cross-legged on the floor directly below Brazza's snout. "And doing something that helps me when I'm in a bad mood."

Very slowly, he pulled his phone out of his pocket, tapped the screen, and brought up his book.

"It was the night before the great battle, and the Dragon Queen sat with her friends, wondering which would fly through storm and siege and which would fall."

The dragon listened. Abel read.

He didn't know if she'd be any good at racing, but he knew he had found his partner.

10

TRAINING BEGAN IMMEDIATELY. THEY ONLY had four days to get ready for the race against Lu, and Brazza needed a lot of work.

After reading to the dragon for half an hour, Abel stopped in the middle of a chapter and stood up. The dragon's slitted eyes snapped wide open. Her body had relaxed while listening, but it tensed now. She raised the huge hook on her tail over her back like a scorpion.

"Okay, Brazza. Savvy, friend, savvy . . ." he cooed at her, using kinner slang to say that everything was okay. "I'll read you a little more *after* we get to know each other. Savvy?"

The dragon didn't impale him right away, which was a good sign.

"I'd like to work with you. With your permission, of course." Dragons were proud creatures, and this one had probably had her pride hurt for a long time. Dragons' bodies were tough and healed quickly, but their egos were fragile. Once pierced, they could be hard to repair. He had to try, though. Abel needed her. And from the looks of the stodgy stall where she was kept, she needed him too. "How would you feel about racing with me on your back?"

Again, the dragon didn't impale him or eat him.

"She must like you!" Otto called from the stall entrance. Brazza thrust her neck out and snapped at Otto, but she was too far away and the cuffs still held her in place. The dragon dealer laughed. "She's not fond of me!"

"These are my friends." Abel pointed at Topher and Roa. "They're gonna help us work together, okay? With your permission?"

The dragon swung her neck from side to side, considering the two nervous kids.

"Come on in," Abel urged them. "Brazza wants to meet you."

"Meet us or *meat* us?" Topher said. "Like, meat you eat."

"I get it," said Abel. "Just get in here and be polite, please." He turned back to the dragon. "Sorry, he can be . . . well . . . himself. But it's part of his charm. And Roa, well, they're going to look after your health. You'll be in really good hands. They've taken college-level Dragonistics classes. They know everything."

"Well, not everything," Roa said, stepping into the stall. "But it'll be a pleasure to look after you."

The dragon snorted.

"I'm a designer!" Topher blurted as he came in, not wanting to be shown up. "I know how to build cool stuff, see?" He pulled out the small notebook he always carried, where he wrote what he called lyrics but were really poems, and where he did sketches of his ideas for dragon equipment.

"We're young," Abel said. "But we're a good team. You won't regret flying with us."

"She won't be flying with you until I get paid," Otto called, not stepping a foot into the stall himself. Abel didn't know how much human speech dragons understood, but Brazza's lips curled from her teeth in a way that suggested a growl.

Abel pulled out his phone and opened the credit app; he clicked on the entire balance in his account, all $567 of it. He waited for

Otto's icon to pop up, then he swiped the money into it. There was a whooshing sound, and his balance dropped to zero. Otto's phone dinged. He smiled as he took Abel's meager life savings. Abel smiled too. He didn't like having the ill-gotten gambling money and was glad he'd put it to use for something good.

Or maybe good. There was still a chance his new purchase would eat him.

"You bought yourself a dragon," Otto said. "Now what are you gonna do with her?"

• • •

You would think transporting a dragon in a city full of dragons would not be that hard, but you would be wrong.

"First of all," Roa reminded them, "no one under sixteen years old is supposed to pilot a dragon on the streets without an adult. Secondly, no one under eighteen years old is allowed to own a dragon. And thirdly, Brazza is an unauthorized breed, which means if you're stopped by a patrol, she'll be seized by the government and—"

Abel put his hand up to stop Roa. He didn't want to think about what would happen to Brazza. He could still hear the shrieks of the orange dragon at the races echoing in his thoughts.

"Also, we don't know if she'll let you ride her," Topher pointed out. "And we don't have a stable to ride her *to*."

"Y'all didn't think this through very well, did ya?" Otto asked. He took his seat at the front of his market stall again. He started tapping his phone screen and speaking to them without looking. "This dragon is no longer my property nor my responsibility, but I'm not a heartless man. Back when I was a teacher, I was admired for my *fairness*, see? So I'll be fair to you now, give you some time to figure this out." He held up his phone to them: a timer counting down from one hour. "You've got an hour until the magnetic cuffs release and she's all yours. She won't have to go home with you, but she can't stay here."

"Okay," Abel said, thinking fast. "We can take her to one of the abandoned skyscrapers across town. She'll be safe there, and we can train her around the empty buildings."

"How are we gonna get her there, though?" Roa asked. "We can't just fly her through the main streets. We'll get pulled over for sure. She kind of stands out. And so do we."

"We'll need a disguise," Abel agreed. He looked around the vast building. "Luckily, we're in a place where you can buy anything."

"But we don't have any money left," Topher said.

"We have Roa." Abel turned to his friend. "And they're the best DrakoTek player I've ever seen."

"Wait, you want me to play a game of DrakoTek?" Roa's forehead wrinkled with deep and doubtful lines.

"I want you to *win* a game of DrakoTek," Abel said. "In one of the gambling parlors on the first floor."

"But we don't have anything to bet," they objected.

"Of course we do!" Abel said. "We have a dragon!"

• • •

Downstairs, Abel had found the most self-serious, grim-faced group of DrakoTek players any of them had ever seen. The cards were bright and colorful, but the players' faces were flat and dull, revealing nothing.

It hadn't been hard to find a game. The moment the gamblers saw three kids who'd just bought a dragon from nutty old Otto Voorhees, they thought they had an easy win. They hadn't reckoned with Roa's skill.

The bet was simple. All or nothing, winner got the loser's cards and, if Roa lost, their dragon too. If Roa won, they got the cards and a whole heaping pile of cash, which would easily be enough to buy a disguise for their dragon, a racing harness, and other supplies.

They'd been playing for half an hour and hadn't won yet, though two of the grim-faced players were already knocked out.

"Get 'em, Shanna!" one of the losers cheered. The best player among them, Shanna, laid down a silver-scaled wyvern card, with a double-point breath enhancer, a gas mask against reverse poison attacks, and a special "hold back" card that let her play the last card of her move *after* Roa went. It was a good hand. Abel had no idea how he'd beat it. Luckily, he wasn't the one playing.

"Wowee," Roa said. The others around the table laughed and patted Shanna on the back. Abel noticed that she had a kinner tattoo behind her ear, the lightning dragon of the Thunder Wings.

"Sorry, kiddo," Shanna said. "I'm gonna take that dragon off you. Hope you learned something about playing grown-up games."

Roa smirked. Sure, grown-ups could play DrakoTek, but that didn't make it their game.

"Sorry, you misunderstood me." Roa plucked the cards that they were going to play out of their stack. "I meant 'wow,' like 'wowee, that was a really dumb move my opponent just made.'" Roa gave Shanna an insouciant grin, which was Roa's favorite kind of grin. It was a grin that said *I've got nothing to worry about from the likes of you.*

Shanna grinned back, but her grin dropped as Roa laid down the card for a short-wing Swamp Wyrm, a kind of dragon that lives in the toxic water of swamps and sewers and, importantly, breathes poison. They had a plus-five defense against all wyverns, *and* when played with a spitting weapon card, they reversed any breath enhancer card's damage back onto its player. Roa played the spitting weapon card next, then dropped a cold-blood card, which made their dragon invisible to any dragon other than Frost Dragons. For their last card, they played a shining piece of gold.

"Why did you play *that*?" Abel wondered. The only reason to play a gold piece card was to try to bribe another team's dragon into doing what you wanted. It didn't work if they were in the middle of attacking you, and Shanna still had her "hold back" card left to play.

"Watch and see," Roa said. Shanna ran her hands over her deck, rummaging for the last card to play, getting madder and madder. The clock on the table was ticking down. She only had thirty more seconds to decide her play. "What's the problem, Shanna?" Roa taunted. "You noticing you're now at minus three? Unless you play a healing card, I win."

"Don't tell her what to play!" Topher objected.

"She doesn't have a healing card left," Roa said. "She played her last one two rounds ago to beat me with that Reaper. I knew she'd want to intimidate me with attack cards. All I had to do was inflict some damage to make her use them up. And then just wait."

"Wow, you're a genius," Topher said.

"I'm not a genius," Roa replied. "I just pay attention."

"You're an ankle-chewing kin traitor!" Shanna erupted. She threw her cards down to lunge across the table at Roa.

The other players caught her and yanked her back. "Whoa! No violence at the Burning Market!" they yelled.

Suddenly, one security kinner from each of the three kins rushed over, and three more circled above on short-wing Gull Stalker dragons.

"Problem here?" the Sky Knight asked.

"Nobody fights in the market," the Red Talon said.

"You have a problem, you can settle it outside however you choose," the Thunder Wing reminded Shanna. "In here, we'll have peace."

Shanna settled down and flopped into her seat. She shoved the cards toward Roa. "You win, kid. But I'd watch your back."

Roa shrugged. "I've got friends to watch my back for me," they said. "And you owe me some cash."

Abel patted his friend's shoulder, proud of Roa for keeping their cool, though his heart thundered in his chest. "Told you Roa had us covered!"

They had twenty-five minutes left to get a disguise for their dragon and get to Otto's.

"I got this part," Topher said. "I know just what Brazza needs."

• • •

With only minutes to spare, they stood in front of Brazza's stall, ready to take their dragon out.

"Okay, I have to admit," Roa said. "This disguise is genius."

"Not genius." Topher grinned. "I just pay attention."

"I think you're both geniuses," Abel told his friends from atop the pink-and-blue dragon's back. "But I still have to fly her."

"We'll stay on the phone the whole time," Roa said. "And we'll meet you at the empty skyscraper with the ad for Peanut-Butter-and-Pickle Wyvern Wafers on the side."

"Wish I could fly you there with me," Abel told them. "But I don't think Brazza will let anyone else on."

At the mere suggestion, Abel felt Brazza's back tense. Some people thought dragons were just dumb animals, the best of whom could follow commands and fight like demons, but Abel knew they were so much more than that. They had complicated ideas and emotions and desires—and they all had a lot of pride.

"It's better this way," Roa said. "We'll take separate buses so no one can follow us."

"But we've got money now!" Topher objected. "Let's take a cab!"

"Then the *cab* will know where we've gone," Roa said. "And cab pilots turn their flight plans in to the Dragon's Eye for review every day. I swear, Toph, you make a lousy criminal."

"Thank you," he said.

"Okay, kids, time's up," Otto announced. "Be on your way. Follow the exit signs for Dragon Riders. And let your brother know we're even now. Thanks for shopping at Otto's."

Abel tugged the reins to nudge Brazza forward out of her stall. She hesitated, but he didn't yank again. He figured she needed time to decide if she wanted to follow his suggestion. If he tried to force it, she was likely to resist. After a count of ten, she stepped forward, out of the stall and onto the main floor of the Burning Market.

Folks turned to look at the kid in the brand-new riding saddle atop the notoriously difficult dragon. Then they turned away, just like Topher had said they would.

They'd wrapped Brazza up in an advertisement for "low-interest home loans at variable rates with zero processing fees." Abel didn't have a clue what any of those things meant, but that, Topher had said, was the point.

"No one else does either!" he had explained. "No one pays attention to these ads. It's better than an invisibility cloak!"

"What is an invisibility cloak?" Roa asked.

"Who cares?" Topher replied. "This is better!"

Sure enough, not even the security goons up in the rafters looked his way. When he reached the exit, his phone rang. He tapped his earbud.

"Don't get pulled over," Roa warned him.

"Don't get followed," he warned Roa.

"Savvy," they agreed together.

Abel gave one quick shake of the reins, asking Brazza to fly.

She turned her head to look at him, perched in his saddle at the base of her neck. If she chose to take off now, this would be their first flight together. He had no idea how it would go.

She snorted soundlessly, set her gaze straight at the fire gate to the exit platform, and hesitated. She took a long look back at her stall and then at Abel. He felt her body relax.

Then she ran!

The wall of flames loomed larger in front of them, then larger still. Brazza unfurled her wings and leapt from the ground the same instant a circle of clear air opened in the flames.

They launched into the dusk over Drakopolis, leaving the Burning Market behind. Brazza flapped hard for the ragged edge of the city, where ruined skyscrapers loomed. A list of fixed-rate home loan prices fluttered behind her, and not a soul paid any attention to the boy and his dragon at all.

11

BRAZZA FLEW SMOOTHLY, KEEPING TO the edges
of the city traffic. She moved up and down between the flying-drone
lane markers and flapped with a steady beat that made riding a
pleasure. Abel enjoyed the peace and calm as he let her stretch her
wings.

The sun was dipping in the sky, lighting the clouds brilliant
orange against crisp blue. The silhouettes of high-flying long-wings
sliced this way and that as the medium- and short-wing traffic bustled around them. Other dragons roared and screeched in traffic,
but Brazza flew steady and silent toward the outskirts of the city.
She was, Abel thought, not the least bit stubborn or difficult to fly.

Until he tried to make her speed up.

The traffic had thinned as they turned onto a long stretch of
open lane, not another dragon around for hundreds of feet above
or below. There were nothing but warehouses and vertical farms,
all the lane-marking drones hovering in bright green. This was
the perfect place to see what kind of racer Brazza could be.

He gave a quick jiggle of her reins, just to warn her something
was coming; then he leaned forward so his face was almost against
her neck. He squeezed his legs tight and let the reins fall loose.

A well-trained racing dragon knew that loose reins meant it was
time for speed. A well-trained racing dragon stretched its neck and
plunged forward at the first opportunity. A well-trained racing

dragon was a ballistic missile that the best riders simply clung to, doing their best to steer and trust the dragon to do the flying.

Brazza was not well trained.

The moment Abel let the reins loosen, the dragon twisted her head sideways, giving him a look down the length of her neck that reminded him of his mom when he hadn't cleaned his room after he'd promised that he would. It wasn't angry or mean, just "disappointed." He didn't even have time to apologize or explain, like he would to his mom. In this case, the eight-ton dragon wasn't interested in words.

Brazza let her flying do the talking.

She rolled her entire body to the right and snapped her wings in sudden fury, flying sideways with her back toward the buildings along the avenue. She was going to scrape Abel out of his saddle like gum from the bottom of a shoe.

"No, Brazza!" Abel shouted, tugging on the reins, trying to straighten her out. He had to slow her down, to regain control.

She ignored him. Abel learned quickly that a ninety-pound boy could not force an eight-ton dragon to do anything it didn't want to do.

"Please!" he begged.

The buildings beside him rushed past in a blur of glass and stone and steel. He clung as close as he could to Brazza's neck. If he could have crawled into her mouth at that point, he might've found it safer than on her back. He just missed being brained by a flagpole. They zipped so close to a landing platform, he felt his jacket brush against concrete.

"I'm sorry!" he yelled. "Please stop!"

A two-hundred-story soybean farm loomed ahead, the lush

green plants stacked atop each other, bursting from vertical irrigation pipes. Abel was a heartbeat from being impaled on them.

Please don't let me die on a soybean, he prayed. *Not on soy.*

He'd never been a fan of tofu, even though his parents loved it. He shut his eyes, pictured his mom and dad and Percy. His friends. Lina and Silas too. He thought about how much he'd miss them all. There was so much more living he wanted to do, but this was it. He'd made the wrong dragon angry, and it was over for Abel.

Just before a fatal impact with the farm, Brazza looped straight up, sparing him . . . sort of.

Abel's feet pointed at the sky, and he felt like his stomach had fallen into his nose. He was suddenly looking down at the building that had nearly killed him. Time froze. He hovered upside down for a breath; then Brazza dropped like a stone into a sewer, straight for the solar panels on the farm's roof. She skimmed over them upside down, so close that Abel's hair streaked their hot surface, even as he clung to the dragon's neck. He shut his eyes again, feeling the g-forces pulling him from the saddle, pulling his soul from his body.

"I'm sorry!" he repeated. "I'm sorry! I'm sorry! I'm sorry!"

His world lurched, and he was upright again. The wind was no longer pulling his lips from his teeth, and his stomach settled back to its usual spot. Brazza was in the center of the empty avenue once more, gliding along between the green-lit drones with languid flaps. She was smooth as a noodle sliding through broth.

Abel loosened his cramped hands on the reins and unclenched his legs from the sides of her neck. He slumped in the saddle and exhaled, staring up at the orange-and-pink sky, where the first stars were just popping out. He breathed in through his nose and out through his mouth, trying to calm down, slow his heartbeat, and keep from throwing up.

His hands shook, but he had survived. And he'd learned a valuable lesson: Brazza was in charge.

One glance back over his shoulder taught him a second lesson, and this one actually made him smile.

They were *very* far from where he'd first loosened her reins for speed.

Brazza was *fast*. Like, really, really fast.

If he could figure out how to train her without getting himself killed, she might just be an unbeatable racer.

That was, at this point, a big *if*.

He had no idea how to train a racing dragon, but he started to think that might be an advantage. Brazza had no desire to *be* a racing dragon.

• • •

"What took you so long?" Roa asked the moment he'd landed on a crumbling platform halfway up the ruined skyscraper. The sun had set; the city's neon lights gleamed and blinked like humanity's own starlight. Roa and Topher were impatient after a long, long wait.

"Brazza has her own pace," Abel explained. After her deadly burst of speed, she'd decided to fly extra slowly, daring him to try speeding her up. Unlike the dragon pepper sundae, this was a dare he did not take.

"Well, I hope she's faster in a race, because that took *forever*," Topher groaned.

"My parents called, like, four hundred times," Roa said.

"What'd you tell them?" Abel asked.

"As little as possible. Just that I'd be home late and they needed to trust me. How about yours?"

Abel pulled his phone out to check. He had thirty-seven missed calls. "I just didn't answer," he said meekly.

"Brave," Roa grunted. "You better call them back."

"Your parents are chill, though," Abel said. "My parents will want to, like, get *involved*."

"They were helpful the last time we had a dangerous dragon and a kin battle to fight," Roa reminded him. "And your mom does work at a feed plant. I'm not sure how else we're gonna find food for Brazza."

They all looked around the empty space, windows broken and open to the autumn air. The paint had peeled from the walls, and whole sections of the floor and ceiling had collapsed. At some point, squatters had lived here and built fires that left round scorch marks on the floor. Someone had spray-painted the laughing dragon symbol of the Wind Breakers kin on a few support pillars. Someone else had painted a large mural of a fancy ball, but instead of people all dressed up in expensive clothes, it was dragons.

Other than vandalism, artwork, and time's decay, the building was empty.

They all looked at the colorful dragon, who had shimmied out of her advertisement disguise and proceeded to shred it with her long gray claws. She sat on her haunches now, head rising above the broken ceiling and resting her chin on an exposed steel beam. Her back legs were splayed open at odd angles, and her belly was thrust forward. Abel had never seen a dragon sit that way. It was not a flattering look.

"You hungry?" Abel asked.

The dragon rested her front claws on the steel beam on either side of her face and licked her lips. She'd looked small next to the larger and better-fed dragons on the sales floor of the Burning Market, but on the eighty-seventh floor of a ruined skyscraper, she looked huge and she looked hungry.

"What do you think she eats?" Abel asked.

Roa studied the dragon, poking their tongue from the side of their mouth as they thought. That was Roa's thinking face, ever since they were little kids. Their eyes darted up and down and side to side over Brazza's scales and wings and claws. They studied her tail and her horns, her snout and her eyes.

Brazza twitched, then leaned her neck way down to meet Roa's gaze and did the same inspection to them. Roa didn't flinch. They just nodded and let themself be inspected.

"Fair's fair," Roa said, opening their arms so the dragon could get a better look. Brazza seemed to like that. She spread her wings for Roa to see.

The two spent a long time studying one another.

"So . . . any ideas?" Topher's patience for the long silence ran out. He was not a boy who did quiet waiting very well.

"A lot of ideas," Roa said.

The dragon snorted and rested her head back on the beam. "She's got the snout shape and the horns of Steelwing, but her wings are shaped like a Reaper's. They're too long for her body, and they aren't even with each other. Her shoulder muscles look more like a wyvern's, but she has four legs, not two, and she's smaller than a wyvern, so all that extra muscle must give her more power. Her scales are octagonal, which makes me think of a Drake, but her coloring is like a cross between a Widow Maker, a

Moss dragon, and a Goatmouth. Maybe with a touch of Steelwing and Blue Foot in there somewhere."

"Okay, so she's a mutt," Topher said. "We knew that."

"The problem is, some of the breeds I just mentioned are charivores, only eating food they've burned; some only eat live prey; and one of them is a vegetarian."

"So we test it out," Topher suggested. "Call your mom and tell her to bring a little of everything."

Abel had pulled out his phone, but his thumb hovered over his mom's number. Could he really ask her to endanger her job?

"If we offer the wrong food, she might get offended," Roa said.

"So we apologize." Topher shrugged. "I offend people all the time."

"We know," Abel and Roa said simultaneously.

"If she gets offended, we say sorry and do better next time," Topher explained. "That's my approach. If we're sincere and *actually* do better, can she really stay mad?"

"She doesn't need to stay mad," Abel said. "She could kill us all even if she's only mad for a second." He shuddered at the memories of the soy farm looming up at him and the solar panels streaking by. "Also, I really don't want to get my parents involved. Silas and Lina might not care when they put our family in danger, but I do. Someone's got to look out of for my mom and dad."

"But they're the adults!" Topher threw his hands up in the air.

"Exactly," Abel said. "They have their own problems. They don't even know that Lina's in jail. They still think she's on the run. I won't add to their problems." He put his phone away. "I saw a noodle shop a few blocks away. Roa, why don't you use some of the money you won at DrakoTek and order . . . everything. Get it delivered, then tip really well so they keep quiet." He turned back to Brazza. "We're gonna get you a ton of noodles and stuff," he said. "Maybe you'll like some of it? Spicy miso ramen?"

The dragon cocked her head at him.

"And if you don't like it, we'll do better tomorrow," he added.

She rested her head on her paws, blinked at him. Her expression was inscrutable.

"What is she saying?" Topher asked.

"I don't know," Abel said. "Her expression is—"

"Inscrutable," Roa said.

"Yeah," Abel agreed. He looked back up at Brazza. "I know you understand me," he told her. "The thing is, it's late and we have to get home. So . . . um . . . we're gonna get this food and then leave you to rest. But we'll be back. You're not our prisoner, okay? If you fly off and leave tonight, we won't stop you. But if you're still here tomorrow afternoon, we'd be pretty happy." He looked at his friends, then back to the dragon. "And please don't try to kill any of us?"

The dragon dropped onto all four of her legs, coming down so hard that the floor shook and dust rained down all over Abel. She sneezed. The sudden burst of wind and dragon snot knocked Abel off his feet and slid him back in a streak across the dusty floor. He was gonna have a bruise on his backside. Another one.

When he looked up, Brazza's head loomed over him, lips curled to show her jagged teeth. Some were longer than Abel's entire body. He did his best not to flinch. He really hoped he hadn't just made a wild miscalculation about what the dragon understood.

After a single heartbeat that felt like a year, Brazza's pink tongue shot out and licked him from the tips of his shoes to the top of his head. She cleaned the dust off like he was a hatchling freshly popped from the egg. It was a sopping, sticky sign of affection, but it *was* a sign of affection.

"Noodles it is, then," he said, dripping dragon drool.

After the food arrived and they tipped the delivery rider double the cost of the huge meal (which was already a lot), they left Brazza to claw through the bags and cartons.

Abel and his friends said their goodbyes, then made their long and winding ways on the public buses, bound for home.

Abel didn't know he was being followed, but he'd find out soon.

12

WHEN ABEL ARRIVED, HIS MOTHER was already at work and his father had fallen asleep on the couch. Percy was curled in the crook of his elbow. They were watching the news.

"The riot at Windlee Prison ended with no law enforcement casualties," the newscaster said over images of the huge concrete prison.

A riot? At Windlee? What about the prisoners? Abel wondered. *What about Lina?*

The newscaster had already moved on to a new story. "Now let's hear from our own Ella Ortega all about the latest trend in fine dining—charcoal tastings!"

"That's right, Wyatt. Diners are just burning to get their tongues on these charred treats . . ." the other newscaster blathered. Abel's father sat up, bleary-eyed.

"Abel?" His voice came out scratchy, like it always did since his recovery from Scaly Lung. "There's dinner in the microwave for you."

Abel went right to the kitchen to heat it up. He was starving.

"You're home late," his father called from the couch.

"Roa and Topher and I had some after-school stuff to do," Abel said. It wasn't a lie, exactly, it was just leaving things out. He had decided not to lie to his parents. He just wasn't going to tell the whole truth either.

"After-school stuff?" his father said. "Is that how you tore your favorite jacket?"

Abel hadn't realized his brush with death had been so bad for his clothes, but he saw it now. There was a big gash on the shoulder of the leather jacket. Thankfully it hadn't gone through enough to cut him, which he figured was why dragon riders wore leather in the first place.

"Dad," he said. "If I tell you that you don't want to know, would you not ask any more questions?"

"I'm your father. It's my job to know."

"But . . ." Abel tried to imagine what his dad was thinking right now. His youngest child comes home late with a slash in his jacket, probably smelling of dragon and sweat and take-out food. Then he doesn't even bother making an excuse. What could his dad possibly hear that would keep him from asking more questions? "A disagreement with some other kids," Abel said. "I need to handle it on my own."

His father pursed his lips, nodding his head a little as he thought. Finally, he asked, "If it gets to be *more* than you can handle on your own, will you tell me or Mom?"

Abel promised he would.

"And if it's not safe, will you tell me or Mom?" he asked.

"Well," Abel sighed. "I mean . . ."

"It's already not safe," his father finished the thought for him.

"Sorry," said Abel.

His dad nodded, frowned, but then took a deep breath. "I trust you, Abel," he said. "Don't make me regret that trust."

"I won't, Dad, I promise." Abel suddenly wanted to give his father the biggest hug in the world. He wished he could tell him everything: about Lina being in Windlee Prison, where there were now riots; about spying for Silas to uncover who was messing with dragon DNA to clear Lina's name; and about racing an illegal dragon he'd bought with illegal gambling money.

Knowing anything about any of that would make his father an accomplice. He could end up in Windlee Prison too. So, instead, Abel took his steaming Pineapple-and-Pepperoni Pizza Pouch out of the microwave and sat at the kitchen table. His dad kept him company.

"Did I tell you about the book I'm listening to?" he asked Abel excitedly. "It's by that comedian with that show about the assassin who inherits an antique shop? It's really funny!"

They spent the rest of dinner talking about TV shows they liked and about Abel's comics and about nothing at all. It felt really good not to think about dragon racing until bedtime.

Which was why it came as such an unpleasant surprise when he got to his room after brushing his teeth and Lina was waiting for him.

• • •

"Don't race on Saturday," she told him.

"Um?" He looked around at his bed, his posters, his binders of DrakoTek cards spread out on the floor, reassuring himself that he was actually in his room. "You're supposed to be in prison!"

"I wouldn't say I'm *supposed* to be there, little brother," she replied, casually running a finger over the poster of the All-Star Teen Dragon Dancers he had up. Suddenly, Abel found it very embarrassing. "Anyway, there was a riot."

"I saw."

"So I broke out," she added, like she was merely telling him what she'd had for dinner.

"And you came to *my* room?" Abel asked incredulously. He was tired of his brother and sister thinking they could rope him in to whatever schemes they had going, just because he was the youngest. It wasn't fair.

"No," she said. "I'm not even here."

"Okay, whatever," Abel grunted. "How did you hear about my race? And why shouldn't I do it?"

"You're middle schoolers, not secret agents," she said, apparently unaware that Abel was both. She didn't need to know everything he was up to. He certainly didn't know everything *she* was up to.

"You still didn't answer my second question," he said. "Why shouldn't I race?"

"Because I'm not the only one who knows about your challenge," she told him. "And there are some bad people interested."

"People like who?" Abel asked. Maybe his sister could tell him what he needed to tell Silas. It would be a lot easier that way.

"You don't need to know," she said. Lina wasn't the sort to make things easier for her brothers. "It's just better that you don't race your little school friend at all."

"Lu is not my friend," Abel said, offended.

"You know what I mean," said Lina.

"No, I really don't," said Abel. "Why don't you explain it? Because after what happened to that dragon at the raceway . . . If you were responsible—"

"I'm not," she cut him off. Her voice sounded urgent, and apologetic. "I swear on a secret, I had nothing to do with what happened to that orange Reaper."

"Then how'd you know it would win?"

"I knew it had been . . . altered," she told him. "Something with its DNA to make it faster."

"Like how they made dragon peppers," Abel observed.

Lina shrugged, and Abel didn't explain.

"How'd you know when it would try to win?" he asked.

"Part of the DNA alteration was computer code," she said. "So that an operator could give instructions by remote."

"Like flying a drone?"

Lina nodded.

"But it didn't work how it was supposed to?" he asked. "They lost control?"

She nodded again, and Abel moved in for the kill—at least, conversationally.

"You sure know a lot about what happened to that Reaper for someone who says she doesn't have anything to do with what happened to that Reaper," he said.

Lina grunted. He'd caught her. "I don't have to explain everything I do to my little brother."

"Like how you cheat," he snapped.

"You're such a kid." Lina waved her hand at him dismissively. "The world isn't one of your comics. There are no perfect heroes. Everybody cheats, even the good guys."

"I've noticed cheaters always *think* everybody else cheats," Abel said. "That doesn't make it true."

"Believe what you want," Lina said. "Did you pay back the money you won at the raceway?"

Abel stiffened his back. He didn't answer.

"Of course you didn't," she said. "You used it to buy your racing dragon."

"How'd you know that?"

"Again," Lina groaned, "you're middle schoolers. You kind of stood out in the Burning Market, and the Sky Knights have eyes everywhere."

"It's my money," Abel said. "I can do what I want with it."

"I'd hoped you'd use it to help Mom and Dad pay a bill or something," Lina said.

"I'd hoped my big sister wouldn't be a thieving, cheating kinner," Abel snapped at her. "If hopes were halos, we'd all be angels."

He'd read that line on the label for a box of tea. He liked getting the chance to use it.

His sister laughed. "Seriously, little brother, don't race this weekend."

"Tell me why."

"Because I actually do care about you," she said. "Bad things happen at these illegal races."

"Bad things happen at the legal ones too," he said. "Your little experiment went wrong and drove that dragon berserk."

"I told you, it wasn't my experiment."

"But you profited from it," he said.

"I do what my service to the Sky Knights demands," she said. "We are fighting to create a more just Drakopolis for everyone. Sometimes unpleasant things happen in that fight for justice."

"Yeah, but the unpleasant things didn't happen to you," Abel told her. "They happened to that dragon. You feel good about that?"

"Of course not."

"So who's responsible?" he demanded. "Whose experiment is it? The Thunder Wings'?"

"The Thunder Wings would never," Lina scoffed. "They don't

want dragons to be— Wait." She caught herself and narrowed her eyes at him suspiciously. "Why do you want to know so badly?"

"Because—" Abel only realized after he started talking that he didn't have an answer he could tell her. The truth was that he was spying for Silas. For the Dragon's Eye. She would never cooperate. She would never *snitch*.

Lina drummed a rolled-up comic on her knee. Abel wasn't one of those collectors who kept their comics all neat in plastic and perfect mint condition, so he didn't mind that she'd rolled it. He minded that she wasn't telling him the whole truth.

Just like I'm not telling her either, he thought. Or Dad. That made him mad at himself. Even though he knew it was unfair, he had to take the anger out somewhere. He aimed it right at Lina.

"If you know who's responsible for an innocent dragon's suffering and you do nothing about it, you're not a good person," he snapped. He crossed his arms for emphasis, which didn't look as intimidating as he'd wanted it to, but now he couldn't uncross them again without being awkward.

He looked around for something to pick up, to make it seem less weird, but all he saw was his school tie on the dresser, an armed Battle Wyvern he'd made out of Blox when he was eight, and a stack of DrakoTek duplicate cards that he'd been hoping to trade at school but had forgotten to bring. The first day of school seemed like years ago now, but it was just that morning.

"Hey," Lina said, jolting at him from the bed. "You're doing that thing again, letting your brain flap away without you on its back."

"Am not," he told her, though he was very much doing exactly that. "Anyway, you broke out of prison and into my room. You don't get to boss me around."

"I just want to warn you not to race," she said.

"Message received," Abel told her. "And request denied. I'm racing. And I'm gonna win."

His sister stood up slowly, looking at him for a long, uncomfortable time. "I remember when you'd do anything I said, just because I was your big sister." She smiled sadly. "You ever miss being little?"

Abel laughed. "Sometimes. But I don't miss *that*. Or Silas flicking boogers at me."

"He also held you when you cried, you know," she told him. "When you were a baby, Silas was the best at calming your tantrums. He was very protective."

"I didn't know that." It was hard to imagine his big brother being anything other than a self-righteous bag of dragon farts.

Lina crossed the room suddenly and gave Abel a surprising hug. He tensed at first, then relaxed into it. It felt really nice to let his sister hug him.

Then, just as suddenly, she let him go, cracked the door into the hall, and peeked out. "I'm going to get some clothes from my room," she whispered. "At least think about what I said. Don't race. And also, don't tell Silas you saw me."

"Because you're an escaped fugitive?" Abel asked.

"Because I love knowing something he doesn't." She laughed and slipped out to the hall with silent footsteps.

Though he listened for her to come back, Lina left the apartment again without a sound, like she'd never been there at all. No wonder she was such a good dragon thief. Abel just prayed she was nothing worse than a dragon thief.

No one should own dragons anyway, he thought. *So stealing them isn't the worst thing you can do. Hurting them, on the other hand . . .* He wasn't sure he'd be able to forgive his sister for being involved in that.

Abel was alone again in his dark room; Lina was probably creeping back to the Sky Knights, while Silas slept in his barracks. Mom was at work and Dad sound asleep. The whole family was scattered into their own little worlds, part of their own little plots. The thought made him sad.

Yeah, he thought, *I guess I do miss being little sometimes.*

But little kids didn't get to race dragons, and Abel wasn't gonna give that up.

IT WAS HARD TO PAY attention in school for the rest of the week. Instructor Shrank droned on and on about the history of the first settlers of Drakopolis and how they trained the last wild dragons in the Glass Flats not to fight each other but to do cooperative work.

"And as the city grew and thrived, the dragons' fortunes improved as well," she said. "They multiplied, grew stronger, prospered into the countless breeds you see in our city today. Now they work in everything from sanitation and transportation to entertainment and law enforcement. The dragons serve humanity so that they themselves may prosper."

As she went on and on, Abel thought about the orange Reaper at the raceway: how it had shrieked. That didn't seem like a dragon prospering. That seemed like a dragon being used up and thrown away. Abel was starting to think the history they learned in school wasn't totally honest. It wasn't a lie, exactly, it was just leaving things out.

In math class, they talked about math. In lit class, they talked about literature. In Life Skills, they learned about the different jobs they could get with a degree from high school. And in Dragonistics, they read literature about using math to figure out how much weight different dragons could carry on their backs for the companies that hired people with degrees from high school. In gym class, they ran laps.

It was all rather dull.

Lu and her friends sneered at him when they passed in the hallways. Abel was careful not to let her get behind him. He would *not* be wedgied again.

"Heard you bought a broke-down dragon," she said. "Good luck beating us."

"What are you racing, your grandma's pangolin?" Topher mocked her.

"Pangolins don't race," Lu replied, not really getting the putdown, which wasn't that good anyway.

"Neither do you!" Topher replied, which Abel admitted was a pretty good setup.

Topher looked satisfied with himself, but Lu kept her sneer on Abel.

"While you try not to lose control of that discount mutt you bought," she said, "you'll be sniffing the tail end of a retired Dragon's Eye wyvern." Her friends laughed. "Just kidding," she added, and then delivered her own killer line: "You won't even be close enough to smell its backside. Loser."

She walked away before Abel could object or Topher could insult her. Roa, however, looked pleased.

"She's not too smart, is she?" they asked as they made their way out of school. "She just told us the kind of dragon she's racing. Now we can plan strategy based on what a wyvern can do. Meanwhile, she has no idea what our dragon can do."

"Yeah," said Abel, "but neither do we."

"That's why we need training. We can—" They fell silent. Officer Grallup stood between them and the exit, arms crossed, glaring down from behind his mirrored sunglasses.

"Where are you three off to?" he asked.

"The school day's over," Abel said. "We're leaving."

"Mmmm-hmmm," he said. "Talking about wyverns?"

"You shouldn't eavesdrop on other people's conversations," Abel said. "It's rude."

"It's my job," Grallup replied. "I'm here to stop any kin activity before it starts. And you three sound like maybe you're starting something."

"We're talking about DrakoTek cards," Abel offered. "You see, Lu has a rare Moonglow Colossus card that I want, and she wants to trade me, but she's asking for three Reapers, a Ruby Widow Maker, and a half dozen equipment cards, which is way too much for just one Colossus, even a Moonglow. But she says it has a special breath weapon, and I say that's not worth three Reapers and a Widow Maker, so we're talking about which of my cards I should offer in return, although Roa thinks that—"

"Enough!" Grallup raised a meaty hand to silence him. Abel had found that he could wear out just about any adult's attention span if he talked fast enough about DrakoTek or comics or any of the things adults decided to think were silly. They never realized he could use their own impatience against them. Boring adults with his passions was Abel's very own breath weapon.

"I know you're up to something," Grallup declared. "I hear the rumors. Racing and the Burning Market and your no-good kinner sister . . ."

"If you have proof, you'd already have arrested us," Roa told him. "So unless you do, we're gonna go." They walked right up to Grallup and stood directly in front of him. "Excuse us."

Grallup snorted but stepped aside, gesturing for them to pass.

"Watch yourselves," he told all three of them. "Because I'm watching you too."

Abel was in awe of Roa. They generally liked school and followed most of the rules. (Except for the ones about illegal dragon possession, kin activity, and dangerous racing . . . but those were more like laws than rules, a difference about which Roa could talk for hours if given the chance.) When Roa believed they were in the right, they were unflappable and unstoppable.

"Let's change buses in Center City," Roa suggested in a whisper. "In case Grallup is following us."

"But that'll take twice as long to get there," Topher groaned. "Why is being a covert agent and criminal mastermind so time-consuming?"

"Who said you were a mastermind of anything?" Roa shoved his shoulder, laughing.

"We all know I'm the brains of this operation," Topher joked, self-aware enough to know that none of them thought that.

"So what am I?" Roa laughed.

"You're like the spokesperson," Topher said.

"Our secret criminal plot needs a spokesperson?" Roa rolled their eyes but rested their hand softly on Topher's shoulder. "Maybe we need a new mastermind!"

"Hey, what am I?" Abel jumped in, wanting to be a part of the joke.

Both his friends stared back at him, dead serious. "You're our dragon rider," they said in unison. None of them joked about that.

They rode the rest of the way in near silence, though Abel saw Topher and Roa keep stealing looks at one another. After they were the last riders on the bus, they saw the fading paint of the Wyvern

Wafers ad up the side of the half-ruined skyscraper. They had to walk awhile to get to the building, because there weren't a lot of bus stops in this neighborhood.

Abel stopped at the entrance to stretch; they had a lot of stairs to climb before they got to Brazza.

"Come on, team." Topher started up. "Last one to her has to shovel dung!"

That got Abel and Roa moving. Even so, Topher was faster and called to them from each floor's landing, taunting about how slow they were and how much dragon dung could weigh.

"He knows he still has to do it even if he wins," Abel panted at Roa when they took a rest on floor fifty-one.

"Don't tell him that," Roa replied, just as breathless. "He'd never go upstairs at all if we weren't chasing him. He needs to think it's a competition."

They both laughed and started up again. When they finally reached the eighty-seventh floor, though, there was no more laughing.

Abel's heart sank.

Brazza was gone.

14

"OH NO." ABEL SLUMPED AGAINST a broken piece of wall and dropped his face into his hands. "Oh no, oh no, oh no."

"You probably shouldn't have told her she could leave," Topher suggested. Abel glared at him.

"Not helpful," said Roa.

"What? Now he's mad at me, not at himself," Topher said. "That *is* helpful."

"I'm not mad at anyone." Tears pressed on Abel's eyes. He did all he could to hold them back. "I just didn't think she'd actually leave. I thought we—" He considered how to say this without sounding ridiculous. Dragons didn't have the same kinds of emotions that people did. They were not sentimental. Whatever he'd started to feel about Brazza, she did not and could not and would not feel the same. But he at least thought they understood one another.

"At least she liked the food." Roa pointed at the carnage of delivery cartons strewn around the floor. There wasn't a scrap of noodle or dumpling left. She'd even eaten the limp lettuce from the bottom of the take-out containers that no one ever eats. "She's not flying through the city hungry, devouring civilians."

"If she gets caught out there, they'll destroy her," Abel said.

"And if you don't show up at the race on Saturday, you'll look like a coward," Topher added, earning another glare. "Sorry, sorry . . . I mean, yeah . . . um . . . how can I help?"

Abel just shook his head. He had no idea what to do.

He didn't care what Lu and her friends thought of him, but if he didn't infiltrate the races, Silas wouldn't be able to clear Lina's name. Whoever was hacking dragon DNA would keep doing it, hurting more dragons and more people in the process.

"I'm not giving up on Brazza," Abel declared. "We just have to find her and convince her to come back."

"Find her?" Topher pointed to the sky. "There are probably ten million dragons in the city! How do we find one?"

"There are twelve point three million registered dragons in the city at the time of the last dragon census," Roa said. "And that doesn't count all the ones the kins have illegally, or the strays and feral dragons that the counters couldn't tally. Also, the last dragon census was four years ago, so there are definitely more by now."

Topher threw his arms in the air. "See? More than ten million! You know I think you're great, Abel, and I really like our little crew here, but we can't do *everything* we set our minds to. This isn't some made-for-TV movie about kids with pluck and gumdrops."

"Gumdrops?" Abel cocked his head.

"He means gumption," Roa said. "It means spirited initiative and resourcefulness."

"Right, that," said Topher. "Gumption!"

"I won't give up," Abel said. "If she wants to be free, I'll release her. But safely, outside the city. Like I did—" His voice hitched at the memory. "Like I did with Karak."

"That is *very* moving," a voice said from the shadows. A figure emerged, doing a villainous slow clap as they stepped into the light.

Abel, Roa, and Topher whirled around, fists balled. "Take it easy," the voice said. "I'm not your enemy."

From the shadows stepped a tall kid in a Dragon Rider Academy uniform, his long green coat neatly tailored, his silver pants pressed with a crisp pleat over his thick boots. He wore the same undercut in his dark hair as Silas and all military recruits, but he had bright red streaks dyed in it too. He looked about Abel's age, though a neck tattoo peeked out over the high collar of his coat: the dragon sun of the Red Talon kin.

"You're Arvin Balk," said Abel.

The boy nodded.

"Wait, like as in the son of Red Talon boss, Jazinda Balk?" asked Topher.

"Yep," said Arvin.

"The same Red Talon boss whose dragon Abel's sister stole, who Abel then used to beat them in a battle and release into the wild?" Topher asked.

"Yep," said Arvin.

"The same Red Talon boss whose kin runs a few hundred neighborhoods, steals *whatever* they want from *whoever* they want, and bribes half the Dragon's Eye so they can keep brawling, battling, and murdering their enemies as the most powerful kin in the city?"

"That sounds like Mom," Arvin said, almost bored by it. It was as if Topher had just described his mother's dentistry practice, not her criminal empire.

"Oh, great! Hi. Nice to meet you." Topher opened his arms wide to emphasize his sarcasm.

"Why are you here?" Roa demanded of the young kinner.

"How did you find us?" Abel asked, which seemed like a more pressing question than why. If a teenager they'd never met before could find where they were, who else could?

Arvin smirked. "Your brother hid a tracking app on your phone," Arvin told him. "And I hacked his."

"Wait, you—" Abel was confused.

"Your brother still pretends to be a cadet major at the Dragon Rider Academy," Arvin explained. "Even though we all know he's really a Dragon's Eye agent. I am an *actual* student at the Academy, and as you mentioned, I'm my mother's child. I learned how to pick a pocket before I learned how to use the potty."

"TMI," said Abel.

"The point is, the only people who know where you are right now are me and your brother," Arvin said. "And if you give me your phone, I can change the app so he loses your trail too. He's an okay hacker, but I'm much better."

"Okay," Abel said, *not* giving Arvin his phone. "Now I need you to answer Roa's question. Why are you here?"

"To help you," said Arvin. "Your dragon's upstairs."

"Did you *kidnap* her?!" Topher moved forward threateningly. He was the closest their little trio had to "muscle." Arvin didn't look at all worried.

"Did I *kidnap her*?" Arvin scoffed. Abel and Roa looked at Topher.

"Toph," Roa said gently. "I don't think he could kidnap a dragon."

"I brought more food for her," Arvin told them. "She's eating. Like I said, I want to help you."

"So you came to feed our dragon," Topher grunted. "Thanks a lot. See ya."

"I came to warn you," Arvin said. "You need to lose your race on Saturday."

Abel shook his head. "Why would I do that? Are the Red Talons worried about some school-kid race? Does your mom actually care if Lu wins or not?"

"I'm not here for the Red Talons, my mom, or Lu," said Arvin. "My mom doesn't care who wins your race, though she'd love it if you were humiliated or killed during it."

"Nice lady," Topher grunted.

"I'm here because I heard how you let those dragons go free, but I wasn't sure until I saw you at the raceway. When I saw how you reacted to that orange dragon going down and, well . . ." He rubbed the back of his neck. It looked to Abel like heir to the Red Talons was nervous. "I think I'm like you."

This led Abel and his friends to raise their eyebrows like characters in one of Lina's young adult novels, who were always raising their eyebrows at each other. Sometimes, a raised eyebrow said a lot more than words could.

"I care about dragons," Arvin explained. "And whichever one wins the race on Saturday is in danger."

First Lina, now this guy. Abel wanted to know what was going to happen at this race more than ever. "Danger from what?" he asked.

"I'm not sure," Arvin replied.

"Oh, good; thanks for the big tip." Topher pointed toward the stairs. "*Now* you can go."

"All I know is that the winning dragon from every recent kin race and kin battle has disappeared," Arvin said. "They're illegal dragons doing illegal things, so no one can report their disappearance to the police. But someone is taking them, and I think it has something to do with what happened at the raceway. My mom's lost half a dozen top dragons just this month. She's put out rewards for information but gotten no answers. It's like the dragons just vanish."

"Dragons don't just vanish," Roa said.

Except, Abel thought, *Karak did. Dragons could vanish if people helped them to.*

"They do," Arvin said.

"Even more reason to win," Abel explained. "If I'm going to find out who was behind Carrot Soup Supreme going berserk, winning this race might be the best way to do it."

"You don't know what you're up against," Arvin sighed. "If they can outsmart my mom and the Red Talons, there's no way you can—"

Arvin's phone dinged in his pocket, and he pulled it out without finishing his thought. "I have to get back to campus before they know I'm gone. Just . . . trust me, Abel. Lose."

He turned to go, and Abel called out to him, "Wait! Take the tracking app off my phone!"

The boy looked back over his shoulder with a sideways smirk, his hair flopping over his eye. "Next time," he said. "For now, it'll be nice to know where you are." He winked at Abel and ran a hand through his hair. "Bye-bye, dragonflies," he added with a grin. Then he slipped back into the shadows.

Abel's heart was suddenly racing, and he wasn't sure why. He went to follow Arvin, but a loud thump boomed overhead and a loose ceiling tile fell in front of him. There was a floor-shaking shuffling of feet above. Suddenly, Brazza's head appeared over the open side of the building, upside down and looking in.

She snorted.

If she could roar, Abel imagined she'd be roaring.

If she could talk, Abel imagined she'd be asking, *Where have you been?*

If she had a breath weapon, Abel imagined he'd be toast.

She was ready to fly, and Abel knew better than to keep an eager dragon waiting.

• • •

They started by taking Brazza's saddle and harness on and off a few times, to get her more comfortable with the process. She didn't seem to mind and even offered a helpful wing bend or shoulder shift from time to time. She let Abel lead her to the edge of the building and, with a squeeze from his legs at the base of her neck, she leapt into the evening air, flying lazy circles among the crumbling skyscrapers and abandoned factories.

"You're doing great," Abel murmured at her as they flew. "Thank you for letting me fly with you."

He held the reins firmly so she could feel he was still there, but he didn't try to steer her; he just let her do what she wanted. He needed her trust him and to feel like they were real partners before he started asking her to do things.

Roa's voice whispered in his earpiece, offering advice as they watched through the fancy binoculars they'd bought at the market.

"There's a freight dragon coming across from the left. A Rainslicer straight ahead. Maybe take a hard right at that graffiti mural of a funeral?"

"I think that's a dinner party," Abel said, seeing the massive artwork looming ahead, all along the side of a windowless brick building.

"Whatever," Roa told him. "It looks like death. Just turn there if you don't want the freighter to see you."

"Okay, Brazza, here we go," Abel announced, preparing to turn. He leaned to the right and gently pulled the right rein so that she knew what he wanted. With an equal amount of pressure, she pulled the rein straight again, yanking him forward in the saddle. She didn't turn.

"Um, anytime now," Roa said in his ear.

"Come on, please." Abel tried pulling again, and again she yanked the reins back through his hand. "Okay, how about this?" he tried.

He leaned to the left and pulled harder on the left rein, signaling he very much wanted her to turn sharp left.

Brazza turned her body sharp right, exactly opposite the direction he'd pulled with exactly opposite the amount of force. They zipped below the huge dinner/funeral mural and slid between the buildings.

"Oh, that's how it's gonna be?" Abel laughed a little.

"Perfect!" Roa exclaimed in his ear. "Did you see how sharp she took that turn? And it looked like she picked up speed! I've never seen a dragon who can accelerate on a turn like that!"

"Yeah," Abel said. "And all I had to do was ask her to do the opposite."

"That's interesting," Roa said.

"She's *constitutionally defiant*," Topher piped in over his own mic. "The school counselor said that about me once. I always do the opposite of what's asked of me, like I'm programmed that way. Even if I want to do what I should, I won't if someone tells me I'm supposed to."

"So I have to fly her by giving the opposite command for what I want?" Abel wondered.

He took a deep breath and leaned back, telling Brazza to rise.

She sank. He leaned back harder; she sank faster. When he leaned forward, she rose. This was the opposite of the way other dragons flew. It was the opposite of the way Karak flew.

I have to stop comparing them, Abel thought. *I have to let Brazza be her own dragon.*

"It's working," he said. "Get ready."

"You talking to us or her?" Roa asked.

"All of you," Abel said. "If this doesn't work, I might need an ambulance."

With that, he pulled the reins and loosened his legs, asking her to slow down.

She shot forward like a laser beam. Abel did his best to hang on.

The city was a blur of lights and sounds; the wind whipping over his ears as they burst from the district of empty skyscrapers and abandoned factories into a neighborhood of tall apartment blocks and sprawling shopping centers. They streaked past hospitals and schools, under pedestrian bridges and through traffic circles. Dragons snapped at them as they passed, but the sounds were snatched away into the night.

"Abel!" Roa shouted into his ear. "I clocked you over two hundred miles per hour before I lost visual contact! Where are you?"

Abel didn't know; he was doing his best to steer up and down and right and left through the buildings and the traffic at faster speeds than he'd ever flown before. He had no idea how he'd find his way back or when, but he didn't want to stop. His mind was focused, his body fully tuned to his dragon's, and he knew even without Roa's speed measure that this dragon was breaking records.

He couldn't help but let out a massive "WOO-HOO!"

If he could keep her under control on Saturday, there was no way he'd lose the race.

He pictured the shock on Lu's face. Prentiss saying, *Ultra burn!* He imagined Silas shaking his hand afterward, saying, *Wow, little bro, you may be smaller than me, but you are ten times the dragon rider I am.*

He'd reply with something magnanimous, which was a word he quite liked, because it sounded like the boiling rock that comes out of volcanoes, magma, though "magnanimous" meant something like being kind and generous to those who are lesser than you, weaker than you, and maybe don't even deserve your kindness. So he'd say something magnanimous to Silas, like, "I can teach you how to ride a dragon if you're willing to learn." Or maybe something like, "I may be the best dragon rider in the family, but you have a cool haircut." Or maybe just, "PULL OVER!"

Wait.

That last one wasn't his thought.

Suddenly, his focus snapped back to reality. He'd gotten distracted and flown Brazza straight through the Central District Shopping Plaza. As he streaked past the five-story-tall Blue Wing Booksellers and the giant Locke & K's Department Store, the red-and-blue flashing lights of the Traffic Patrol blazed behind him.

He'd gotten into a police chase without even noticing.

Oops.

15

"**LAND IMMEDIATELY, AND PUT YOUR** hands up!" a mechanical voice blared over a loudspeaker. A bright spotlight suddenly enveloped him from high in the clouds. Abel knew a surveillance long-wing was somewhere up there, agents on its back recording him, running his image through a database to match his identity and classify his dragon.

They'd fail, at least with the dragon.

Abel was pretty sure they'd know exactly who *he* was any second, even with his helmet on. There were files on his whole family, thanks to Lina's criminal activity, and his patchwork leather jacket from the Wind Breaker kin. He suddenly realized why kinners wore the same colors and got similar tattoos—it made it harder to tell who was who. They didn't just identify what kin they were a part of; they made it so you couldn't easily tell them apart. The same with the green coat and silver pants of the Dragon's Eye. The uniform erased the individual and made him one piece of a much larger whole.

Abel, with his signature look and one-of-a-kind jacket, had made himself stand out.

"LAND NOW OR YOU WILL BE FORCED DOWN!"

Three wyverns fanned out behind him. The lane-marking drones in front of him flashed red and blue. They began to move, forming a blockade.

"What's going on?" Roa's voice came into his ear. He'd forgotten they were there. He really should've been paying better attention.

"Just a little trouble with the law," Abel said.

"If you get arrested, you know what they'll do to Brazza!" Roa warned him.

"I'll take care of it," said Abel. "They'll never catch us."

He leaned back hard in the saddle and let the reins go slack for speed, but Brazza slowed down.

"Oh no . . . not now," he pleaded. "Please. We gotta fly! Fast."

He looked in the saddle-mounted mirrors. Behind him, all three of the wyverns had gleaming orbs of poison gas forming in their mouths. It'd probably be enough to knock his dragon out—and definitely enough to knock out Abel. If he was lucky, he'd wake up in a cell. If he was unlucky, he wouldn't wake up at all.

As for Brazza, there was no good outcome. She couldn't get caught.

"I'll keep reading you the story we started once we get back!" Abel promised her, hoping she'd understand. "I know you want to hear the next chapter! There's romance and kissing!" He didn't know if dragons liked romance and kissing in their stories, but he had to get her interested *somehow*.

The dragon turned her head, eyes narrowed. She had a keen intelligence in her gaze, like when you look at a wire that's fallen in the street and you just know, without any proof, that it's live and sizzling with electricity. He thought he saw a grin creep up at the corners of Brazza's mouth, but that might've just been how her jaw was shaped.

She suddenly changed the angle of her wings and snapped them down, launching herself forward. At the same instant, she rolled to the left in a corkscrew dive.

"AHHH!" Abel clutched her neck for dear life. He locked his legs as tightly as he could in the saddle.

Brazza slipped out of the beam of the spotlight, moving faster than the Dragon's Eye could keep up. Behind him, the wyverns spat their poison, but Brazza, without any instruction from Abel, dodged the first blast, then the second, then the third, without slowing in the slightest.

Four more wyverns dropped down from the wide-open air in front of them, and two more were racing up from ground level. The shopping center blocked them in on either side. They were being pinched in from three directions. The lane markers had been reprogrammed to form a hovering net behind the police wyverns. More drones closed in, blocking every alleyway and turnoff.

Brazza, however, had the motivation she needed now. She was not going to let a bunch of attack wyverns and flying traffic lights stop her from hearing the rest of Abel's read-aloud.

She dove to the landing platform of the nearest parking lot and hit the pavement running. She smashed through the guardrail, slashing the hook on the end of her tail into the little guard booth. The unfortunate attendant dove for cover.

The bored dragons who were parked in their stalls while their owners shopped poked their heads up to watch Brazza run past. She was faster on her four feet than the two-footed wyverns following her.

She would've gotten away, except more armored Dragon's Eye wyverns arrived at every possible exit to the parking lot, sirens blaring, poison breath building.

Brazza, however, wasn't going through any of the exits. She pointed her head right for the double doors to Locke & K's

Department Store and burst through the glass-front lobby into the outerwear department. Customers fled, screaming, before her clattering claws. She tossed well-dressed mannequins in every direction with a thrash of her head. A woman in a dragon-scale winter coat froze in fright just in front of her, holding her credit card up like a shield.

Brazza showed her fangs. She still didn't make a sound, which made it easy to hear the woman squeak when she turned and ran, high heels clicking across the tile like tiny, scuttling claws.

Abel watched it all through his fingers over his face. He'd covered his head with his arms to avoid the broken glass, even though he had a helmet on, and he decided to keep his hands there for the duration. The leather jacket had protected his back and reminded him that it wasn't just a fashion statement.

Brazza crashed through the perfume section, huge claws smashing the cases. She broke open a fortune in fancy scents, filling the air with so many different smells, it might've worked as a poison breath attack. Only one of the wyverns followed them through.

"Okay, partner, how do we get out of here?" Abel asked. The wyvern behind them was fast on its feet. It gained on them with every bounding step.

Brazza's answer was to speed up her run, aiming straight for a solid concrete wall. "Um . . . I know you're strong and have dragon scales to protect you," Abel said. "But I'm just made of, like, meat and bones. I'd rather not have them all broken against a solid wall?"

At the last instant before impact, Brazza turned sharp left, tucking her shoulder and her front legs so she fell and rolled in the air. Abel's helmet sparked against the tiles but did its job protecting his head.

The wyvern couldn't turn as fast and ran at full speed into the wall. The twelve-ton attack dragon in police assault armor smashed its helmet directly into the plaster. It burst through the cinder blocks, tearing a hole in the wall that Brazza simply turned around and leapt through. She dove away as the stunned wyvern rider struggled to regain control of his stunned wyvern.

Brazza used the distraction to plummet between two more shopping center buildings, picking up speed as she weaved into a commercial district. She was going faster and faster, so fast that Abel couldn't even keep his hands on her body anymore. The safety harness on his saddle was the only thing keeping him tethered to her. His vision blurred with every breath-breaking, blood-swirling, bone-shaking turn she made.

On the Dragon Rider Academy entrance exam—the one Abel had failed at age eleven—there were questions about what happened to the human body at top dragon flying speeds, questions about "blood pressure fluctuation" and "cascading organ failure" and "maximum survivable g-force." He didn't understand the questions, let alone know their answers, but he had a feeling he was discovering what they meant right now.

His eyesight narrowed to a tunnel, heading toward darkness. His ears hummed. The world was turning gray.

"Abel! Abel!" Roa's voice called in his ear. "You okay? I've got a visual on you! You look limp in the saddle. Say something! Abel!"

Abel tensed and pushed against his narrowing vision, forcing his eyes open. He saw their ruined skyscraper in the distance, the Wyvern Wafer ad winking in and out of color as it grew larger. He feared he was either losing his mind or losing consciousness.

And then Brazza slowed.

The breath came back into Abel's lungs. The world returned to full-color focus. He gasped.

There were no other dragons around, no sirens, no chase. Brazza had left their pursuers completely in the wind. No one could possibly have kept up. They'd escaped, and Abel hadn't had to do anything more than offer her what she wanted: the promise of a good story.

She flapped leisurely in toward the eighty-seventh floor.

"Abel! Talk to me!" Roa pleaded over his earbuds. "You hit nearly three hundred miles an hour!"

"I did?" he croaked out. His mouth was dry, and his throat felt like he'd chewed on broken glass.

"You're on the news!" Topher exclaimed. "Your police chase was live on every network."

Abel didn't think that was nearly as cool as Topher did. But he couldn't answer because he was busying throwing up over the side of his dragon's back, seven hundred feet in the air.

16

"YOU WERE ON THE NEWS!" Silas snarled at him from their couch, where he'd been waiting when Abel got home. "Your police chase was carried live on every network."

Abel had liked it better when Topher said it. His brother did not mean it as a compliment.

Abel had gotten home pretty late. He'd had to stay for another hour after feeding and cleaning Brazza so that he could read more to her. He read to the part where the Dragon Queen disguised herself as a lowly swamp dragon to walk among her soldiers the night before the big battle. In the movie version, it was one of the funniest scenes, but in the book, it was a deeply sad moment. She shared her soldiers' fears and hopes and knew that she would be sending some of them to their deaths in the morning. She began to doubt there was justice in war and to wish she was not a ruler at all.

Abel liked the book better than the movie, even though the movie had great special effects. No special effects were as good as what his imagination could do. Brazza seemed to love the sad part, and Abel stopped reading just as the trumpets sounded for battle. He needed to keep his partner interested, at least until after Saturday's race. He promised he'd read Brazza a little more every day until they were finished, but he explained that he had to leave. It was late, and his father would be worried.

The dragon didn't seem to understand about that—dragons

probably didn't struggle with anxiety—but she let him leave without eating him, which he counted as a friendship win. He spent the whole bus ride home thinking of excuses about why he was *so* late on a school night. He hadn't expected to find his brother alone in the apartment when he walked through the door.

"Do you realize what I had to do to cover for you?" Silas scolded him. "First I had to access your file from another officer's account—which is illegal for me to do, by the way—then I had to delete your description and any mention of that *very* recognizable jacket of yours. Then I had to get here, to make sure no one had figured it out anyway and come to arrest you. I sent Dad for groceries with the promise I'd stay for a late dinner, even though Mom's at work and you know how Dad uses too much pepper when he cooks. It upsets my stomach!"

"Sorry about your stomach," Abel grunted. "I forgot how sensitive you are."

"A 'thank you' would be nice," Silas said.

"You're welcome," Abel replied.

Silas threw his hands in the air. "A 'thank you' from *you* to *me*!"

Percy came padding over and sniffed at Abel's pant leg until he picked him up. The little pangolin curled into a ball in his arms.

"I was only flying around on that dragon *because* of you!" said Abel. "I've got a race on Saturday that you told me I had to do! Have you forgotten that I'm your spy?"

"Have you forgotten that I can't help you if you get arrested?" Silas snapped back. Then he relaxed and softened his expression, letting his shoulders sink. "Well, at least we know your dragon is fast."

"What do you think will happen after I win?" Abel asked, remembering Lina's and Arvin's warnings.

"The real bad guys will notice you," Silas said. "And when they reveal themselves, I can make the arrests."

"And become the big hero?" Abel asked.

"And clear Lina's name," Silas reminded him.

"What if I don't win the race?"

"How could you not?" Silas said. "I just saw on TV how fast your dragon is."

"She does what she wants."

"Well, she better want to win," Silas said. "I can easily put your info *back* into the system. The Dragon's Eye would be knocking down this door to arrest you in minutes."

"You wouldn't do that to Mom and Dad," Abel told him. "Two kids wanted by the police? Even you're not that bad of a son."

Silas flinched, but then set his face into a hard expression. "I do whatever my service to Drakopolis demands."

"You sound just like Lina," Abel told him. "She said kinda the same exact thing."

"Don't compare me to my criminal sister. And— Wait—" Silas caught himself. He lowered his eyebrows and eyed Abel suspiciously. "*When* did she say that?"

"What?" Abel felt his voice catch in his throat. "When did she say what?"

He wasn't a great liar, and he'd just revealed too much. Silas was onto him.

"When did Lina say '*kinda the same exact thing*' I said?" Silas demanded, stepping over to Abel. He towered above Abel in that way he had, the way that reminded Abel his personal space and physical safety were entirely at his big brother's mercy.

He wasn't a little kid anymore, though. He didn't back down. He stepped right up against Silas's chest and looked straight up at him. "I don't know what you mean," he said.

"You've seen her," Silas said. "Where? When?"

Abel clamped his lips shut.

"Where?" Silas repeated. "She's an escaped fugitive. If you know where she is, you have to tell me."

"So you can arrest her too?"

"So I can *help* her," Silas said.

"I'm infiltrating the illegal racers for you," Abel told him. "But I won't spy on our family."

"You spy on who I tell you to," Silas told him back.

"Make me," Abel said, clenching his fists.

"Maybe I will," said Silas.

"Maybe you can't," said Abel.

"Maybe you're gonna find out," said Silas.

"Maybe you better not try," said Abel.

"Maybe you *both* better calm down!" their father barked from the doorway. He was holding a bag of take-out tacos under his arm.

"I don't know why you two are always at each other's throats, but I've had enough of it." They hadn't even heard him come in. Some secret agents they were. "This city is tough already without family making it harder for each other. Growing up, I wished I had siblings that I could talk to, though your grandma told me I was lucky to be an only child. Maybe she was right, if *this* is how brothers treat each other."

He shut the door and crossed into the kitchen without looking at them. Abel and Silas stood chest to chest, fists clenched, frozen.

Abel didn't want to back down first. Neither, it seemed, did Silas.

Their father started setting take-out containers on the table. "It's too late to cook," he said. "So I got each of your favorites from the taco truck before it flew to the next neighborhood. Mild salsa for you, Silas. And, Abel, dragon pepper for you?"

Abel flinched at the memory of his sundae.

"Just kidding," his father said. "Come on. Both of you wash your hands, and let's eat. Whatever's going on between you will keep warm longer than these tacos."

He sat down at the table and waited for the boys to break apart. Finally, Silas did.

"And, Abel," his dad called. "Maybe throw on some extra deodorant? You smell like a gym sock doused in every kind of perfume they sell at Locke & K's. Too bad they'll be closed for renovations for a while, huh?"

He quirked an eyebrow. Their dad must've seen the news and recognized Abel's jacket.

"Dad—" Abel started, but his father raised his hand to silence him.

"You promised to tell me when it was more than you could handle," he said. "You promised not to abuse my trust." He folded his fingers in front of him and then looked at Silas. "And you promised me you would look out for your little brother."

"I know, Dad." Silas suddenly sounded much younger than he was. "It's just that—"

His father shushed him. "I'd rather hear no excuses at all than hear my sons lie to me. So unless you're ready to tell the truth, Abel's gonna rinse off, and we're going to eat dinner in peace. If either of you feels you can be honest with your dad, who truly does love you more than his own life and safety, then you can tell me anything."

Silas hung his head and looked at his feet.

Abel hesitated, his heart breaking for his father's sadness. He *wanted* to tell him everything, but his dad's heart would break even more if he knew how all three of his kids were using each other and playing dangerous games with the city's most dangerous criminals. It would hurt him worse to know the truth.

So instead, they ate dinner quietly, listening to the roar and screech of the dragons outside, father and sons sharing a table, but each nursing his own private hurt and hoping someone else would speak first.

Stubborn as they were, none of them did.

17

AN UNEASY TRUCE SETTLED OVER Abel's family for the rest of the week. Silas went back to his barracks; Abel's parents talked to him about practical things, like remembering his lunch and homework. None of them mentioned Lina, though all of them were thinking about her. Abel went to school and did his best to avoid Officer Grallup, who eyed him suspiciously every time they passed in the halls.

"Hey, where's that fancy jacket of yours?" Grallup asked him on Friday morning. Abel hadn't worn the orange leather jacket outside since the police chase.

"What jacket?" Abel shrugged, flipping up his green school hoodie and walking right on by.

"Impressive display of insouciance," Roa whispered when they were out of Grallup's earshot.

"What they said," Topher agreed.

"Watch out!" Roa suddenly barked, and Abel whirled around just in time to catch Lu reaching for his waistband. She'd snuck up from an intersecting hallway.

"Nice try," he told her.

"Whatever," she grunted. "Who needs to wedgie you, when I can make you eat wind tomorrow night."

"You're pretty sure of yourself for someone with a sauce stain on her shirt," Abel said.

Lu looked down at her spotless white school shirt. Topher put his hand up for a high five, which Abel returned without looking. He felt, for a fleeting moment, perfectly and untouchably cool.

"Childish," Lu grunted. "Anyway, I'm pretty sure my wyvern will destroy your cut-rate Burning Market mutt," Lu said. "Felix is a champion."

"Then what's he doing letting you ride him?" Topher asked.

"Greatness sees greatness," said Lu.

"Maybe get his eyes checked," said Topher. Then he wrapped a protective arm around Abel and led him toward the front door. "Come on, I got your back."

"*We* got your back," Roa said, flanking him.

"Thanks." Abel glanced over his shoulder.

"See you tomorrow night!" Lu shouted. "Losers!"

Once they were clear of the school, his friends gave him some space.

"You sure you're gonna be able to get out tomorrow?" Roa asked. "You said your parents are pretty mad."

"They are," Abel sighed. "I'm gonna have to sneak out, but Lina used to do it all the time."

"No offense, Abel," Topher said. "But she's got, like, ridiculous stealth skills and you, um—"

Roa jumped in to rescue Topher. "Have other skills."

Topher grinned. "That's what I meant."

"Guess I'll need to count on luck, then, won't I?" Abel said.

"*That* you've got!" Topher agreed. "How else would we be friends unless you were very, very lucky?"

They all laughed as the bus landed. Officer Grallup boarded first. They spent the rest of the bus ride joking around and talking about

DrakoTek cards and Dr. Drago comics and nothing at all to do with illegal racing or drama at home or the kins. Officer Grallup looked disappointed when Roa and Topher exited the bus, having said nothing incriminating.

"Have a nice, quiet weekend," Grallup told Abel as he got off at his own landing platform. "Hope I don't see you before Monday."

"Why would you?" Abel asked innocently.

"Why, indeed?" Grallup snorted. He stood in the doorway as the bus flapped up and away, but he didn't take his eyes off Abel until the long-wing flapped around the corner of the next building.

Inside their apartment, Abel's mom was just getting ready to go to work and his dad was looking through take-out menus.

"Get something with vegetables tonight, please?" his mother said. "The onions in those mystery meat dumplings do not count."

Abel and his father shared an eye roll, which was as close to bonding as they'd come since the night of the police chase.

Abel knew that it was wrong to keep secrets from his parents like this, but he also knew he was doing it for the right reasons. He wondered if that made it okay. Did good intentions excuse bad actions, or would bad actions poison even a good result?

He really didn't know. He didn't have the answers to life's complicated questions.

What he did have was an eight-ton racing dragon waiting for him. After his race was taken care of and Lina's name was cleared, then maybe then he could come clean with Mom and Dad, but he feared he wouldn't be able to even then.

Lying was like riding an untamed dragon. You were safe from its bite as long as you stayed on its back. But once you got off . . . well, you couldn't control what would happen.

Stop it, Abel, he told himself. *Stop making up dragon metaphors to excuse yourself from lying to your parents. Just admit you're a spy and snitch and liar.*

Also, he heard Roa's voice in his head, *that was a simile, not a metaphor.*

• • •

Saturday night came fast, and Abel was a jumble of nerves. His mom didn't have work on Saturday, so they ate dinner together, no screens allowed. She immediately knew something was wrong between Abel and his dad.

"Okay, you two, what is going on?" she asked.

"That's a question only Abel can answer," his dad said.

Abel was in the process of filling one of the famous thin rice-flour pancakes with the spicy veggie-and-meat mixture that his mom only made on weekends. He overstuffed his pancake and took a too-big bite, buying time. He pointed at his mouth and made apology eyes at her.

"Mouth's full," he mumbled.

She folded her fingers and waited while he chewed as slowly as possible.

He swallowed slowly too and took a long drink of water.

Still, she waited.

"Nothing," he finally said, which earned him raised eyebrows and still more waiting.

In a recent issue of Dr. Drago, the heroic dragon veterinarian was framed by a devious kin boss. The Dragon's Eye arrested him for murder. He was interrogated by a clone of his own daughter, who became a homicide investigator after he freed her from the Neon Apocalypse Cult in issue #837. During the interrogation, his clone daughter never asked him a single question, just sat with him in silence for days. Dr. Drago eventually broke and confessed, even though he didn't do it. Silence from someone you love, he pointed out, can be worse than any torture device. Only the truly loveless can endure it.

Abel didn't last thirty seconds.

"It's a race!" he blurted. "I'm infiltrating an illegal racing ring for Silas to clear Lina's name and find out who is hacking dragon DNA, and it was me on the news the other night who wrecked that department store and I'm sorry, and I didn't mean to cause trouble, but also I have to race tonight if I'm going to help anybody, okay? I just have to!"

He sucked in a breath as he collapsed back in his seat, relieved and disappointed in himself at the same time.

His parents stared at him in frozen shock. A glob of meat plopped from his father's wrap onto his plate.

"Oh, Abel," his mother sighed.

His father set his dinner down and rubbed his face with both hands. His mother looked like there were three hundred different thoughts tripping over each other inside her mouth, so that none could get out. Abel knew that feeling.

"It'll be okay," he tried reassuring them both. "I can do this."

"And this was Silas's idea?" His father clenched his jaw as he pulled out his phone.

"Don't call him!" Abel pleaded. "He can't know I told you!"

"Oh, he's gonna know a lot of things real soon," his dad growled.

"Dumpling, wait." His mom put her hand on his father's phone. She only ever called Dad *dumpling* when he was getting worked up or they were getting romantic. Either way, it was embarrassing for

Abel to hear. She looked back at Abel. "This isn't a dragon battle?" she asked.

He shook his head. "Just a race."

"Against the kins?"

He shook his head no again. "Another student. She wants to be a Red Talon, but she's not yet."

His mom looked at his dad. They had a whole argument with their eyes right in front of Abel, but he didn't know how it went or who was saying what. He figured that's something parents just learned how to do. Maybe they took classes on their honeymoon or something. They reached some kind of decision, though, because they both nodded and looked at Abel in eerie unison.

"All right," his dad said. "You can go to this race, tonight," he announced. "BUT—" He knocked on the table.

"I am coming with you," his mother said.

"What?!" Abel shot up to his feet so suddenly he knocked over his water. "I can't bring my mom to an illegal midnight dragon race!"

"You can't go to an illegal midnight dragon race if you don't," she said calmly. The water spread slowly across the tabletop, but no one moved to clean it up. His parents stared at him.

"Ugh!" He threw his hands up. "Fine. But we can't show up together, and you have to wear a disguise and pretend you don't know me."

"You're worried I'll embarrass you?" she asked.

"What? No!" Abel grabbed a rag and began sopping up the water he'd spilled. Percy had come over to lick at the puddle on the floor, then padded away to the couch when he realized it wasn't soda. "I'm worried someone will try to kidnap you or something. Bad people go to these races."

"*You're* going to this race," his father pointed out. "You're not a bad person."

Abel thought about the Burning Market, the horrible things he'd seen there and how he'd kept walking right past them. He thought about making Karak battle and, even though he'd let him go, how cool it had made Abel feel. He thought about the terrible thrill he got slicing through the streets on Brazza's back, even as she left mayhem in her wake, and the lies and half-truths he'd told to everyone along the way. He told himself he did it all to help his sister and to help the dragons, but these weren't the sorts of things a good person did.

He met his father's gentle look. The faith his dad had in him hit harder than a blast of wyvern breath. He wanted so badly to be the person his parents thought he was, but he had done so many things a good son would never do. He burst into tears.

"Maybe I am bad," Abel said, his whole body shuddering with ugly tears. He didn't just feel like a villain; he felt like a baby too. The shame made him cry harder.

Finally, his mother put her hand on his, even though he was holding a sopping-wet rag. She locked eyes with him. "You're not a bad person," she said. "You're in a hard situation, but don't let that harden your heart, okay? Especially against yourself."

Her eyes were damp, which made Abel's eyes damp. He looked over at his father, who was full-on crying. He added his hand on top of theirs, over the rag. It made a squishing sound that made them all laugh, and suddenly they were crying and hugging and laughing around the kitchen table.

"I've got just the disguise for tonight," his mother finally said, getting up from the table. She sounded—*Abel couldn't believe it*—excited. "I haven't worn it since before your brother was born! You won't even know I'm there."

He smiled at his mom through his tears. "I mean, if you wanted to give me a signal from the crowd before we start," he said. "It'd be nice to know someone is rooting for me . . ."

She smiled back at him. "We are always rooting for you, Abel. No matter what."

PART THREE

"DON'T THREATEN YOUR
SIBLINGS WITH A KILLER
DRAGON."

18

THE MOON'S SLICE OF SILVER was no match for the blazing neon signs, the blinking billboards, and the flashing lane lights of Drakopolis on a Saturday night. Even in the desolate district where the race would start, the city's lights outshined anything nature could create.

Abel glided down with Brazza and landed in the middle of the quiet street, waiting for Lu and her wyvern to arrive. When he'd woken Brazza up for the race, she'd nearly bitten his head off. He had to promise he'd spend the whole day tomorrow reading to her if she'd race tonight. With that promise in her head, she got so excited, she flew to the starting line much faster than necessary. Roa and Topher weren't even there yet.

But that didn't mean Abel was alone.

A small crowd of nighttime ne'er-do-wells had gathered for the race. Abel recognized some faces in the crowd. There was Shivonne, a hostess at the all-night laundromat-casino in his neighborhood; and there were Sax and Grackle, Red Talon goons who'd happily have turned Abel into dragon feed. There was Jusif, one of the Thunder Wings Abel had betrayed to win his battle last spring; and Ally, Jusif's boss and Abel's old homeroom teacher. She'd been fired from their school for being a kinner, harboring stolen dragons, and battling against her own students. If Abel hadn't won, she might still have her job. He'd probably have been eaten, though.

She waved at Abel when their eyes met. If a wave could say, *I hope your dragon splatters you on the pavement like a clumsy toddler's ice cream cone*, that's what hers would've said to him.

Teachers are just like other people, Abel thought. *They can be as wretched or as wonderful as anybody else. Sometimes a bit of both.* Ally had been a great teacher, but, unfortunately for him, she was a better gangster.

There were spectators in the colors of each of the kins scattered in the crowd. Some had tattoos with the Thunder Wings' lightning dragon, and some with the Red Talons' dragon sun, and some with the Sky Knights' armored infinity symbol. There were even a few whose tattoos matched the symbol on the jacket Abel had put back on, the laughing dragon of the Wind Breakers kin.

It was amazing that no fights had broken out so far, but sometimes curiosity got the better of animosity. Grudges were put aside in the general excitement to see two kids race.

There were also regular civilian-type people, some of whom were probably Dragon's Eye agents themselves. Eager-eyed gamblers stood next to tired-looking panhandlers and late-night preachers and shift workers on break from the loading docks. There were Saturday-night partiers who'd probably just followed a rumor from one nightclub or another. Abel was, by years, the youngest person there. He scanned the faces, trying to pick his mother out of the crowd, but whatever disguise she'd worn was a good one. He didn't see a friendly face anywhere.

Abel checked the time on his phone, wondering where his friends were and when Lu would show up. It was 11:57 p.m.

"Abel, I can't say I'm surprised to find you here, but I sure am shocked!" a man called cheerfully from the back of a colorful Serpentine Reaper. People parted to let him trot his dragon's long body through the crowd.

"Fitz!" Abel grinned, glad to see a friend of sorts—if a middle schooler could consider the sometimes-helpful anarchist owner of a twenty-four-hour bookstore a friend.

Fitz owned Chimera's All-Night Coffee + Comics, where Lina had pretended to work while she was really out stealing dragons for the Sky Knights. Fitz was a legend around Drakopolis, liked and trusted by everyone he knew, fair and generous to anyone he met.

Most thought he'd been in a kin at some point, but no one knew which one. He had tattoos for all of them on the knuckles of one hand, and the word "UNITY" on the knuckles of his other. He had tattoos that told stories up and down his arms, some from the other side of the Glass Flats, where he'd traveled while in the Dragon Corps, and some from Windlee Prison, where he'd volunteered as a nurse in the hospital . . . or maybe been an inmate? No one could say for sure. He had one tooth made out of gleaming dragon glass, and it shimmered whenever he let out one of his thunderous laughs, which was often. He sidled his dragon up to Abel.

"I should've known when they hired me to referee a race between two kids that one of them would be you!"

"Who hired you?" Abel asked. Brazza eyed the long purple mane of silken hair on the other dragon. Fitz's dragon lowered its snout in respectful greeting, which satisfied Brazza enough that she didn't lash out.

Fitz shook his head. "Sorry, kid, I can't share my business. Otherwise, I wouldn't *stay* in business." He looked around at the crowd on the sidewalk. "Nice turnout you've got, though. People are excited to see you fly. Rumor is you were the one who gave the police all that trouble on Wednesday. That true?"

Abel shrugged. "Sorry, Fitz, I can't share my business either."

Fitz let out another belly-deep laugh, nearly falling out of his saddle in genuine delight. "You've got wit, Abel. I sure hope you've got your wits about you. There are all kinds of folks with an interest in this race, and not all of them have *your* interests at heart." He nodded toward Grackle and Sax, and then Ally and Jusif, and then to a face Abel hadn't noticed: Arvin Balk, heir to the Red Talons, standing by himself in the crowd and watching Abel with a blank expression.

Just then, a bright yellow Blue Foot short-wing with a taxi on its back flapped down to the street, screeching once as its passengers climbed down.

Topher and Roa ran over to Abel.

Fitz winked and walked his dragon up the street alone. He released a small red drone that hovered about a hundred feet above him. That would be the starting line. He sat below it, closed his eyes, and danced in his saddle to music only he could hear.

"Sorry we're late," Roa apologized.

"They just *had* to fly around in circles for forty-five minutes," Topher grumbled.

"We were scouting the course," Roa said. "Looking for places where you might run into trouble. It's called being a good ground crew."

"It's called a waste of time," Topher replied. "Brazza's so fast, it doesn't matter what the course looks like."

"That's hubris," Roa said.

"No," Topher snapped back. "Her name is Brazza. Did you hit your head or something?"

"'Hubris' means foolish arrogance and overconfidence," Abel said. "And don't worry, Roa. I'm not overconfident. I'm hardly confident at all." He nodded toward the unfriendly faces in the crowd.

"Just ignore them," Roa said. "Focus on what you do best. Flying. Nothing else matters right now."

"I wish that were true," Abel said.

"Don't worry—we got your back!" Topher grinned. "I designed this for you! Been working on it all week."

He pulled a contraption out of his backpack that looked like a bunch of stretchy black fabric with blood pressure cuffs on it, like the kind they put around Abel's arm at the doctor's office during his checkups.

"He's really proud of it," Roa noted.

Abel's blank expression deflated Topher.

"He doesn't get it," Topher sighed.

"Maybe explain it to him?" Roa suggested. "He hasn't been hearing you talk about it all week, like I have."

"Right, right,'" Topher said.

Abel didn't like that they had been keeping secrets from him, but Topher said he didn't want to bring it up in case he couldn't finish it in time.

"But I did!" He beamed.

"Okay, but what is it?" Abel asked.

"I call it a g-rig!" Topher said. "These are blood pressure cuffs—like they put on at the doctor's office?" Abel nodded. No surprise there. "You just put them on your ankles—do the belt up, the shoulder straps and the biceps go, like, under your jacket—and it will adjust your blood pressure for you when you start hitting the *really* high g-forces. I read about it online. When long-wings dive from super-high altitudes, the speed creates so much force, their riders lose control, lose vision, pass out, and even die. All because their blood gets pushed to the wrong parts of their bodies by the g-forces. They have special flight suits that help them stay conscious at like eight g's. I think *my* suit could make it up to twelve."

"That's just a theory," Roa added. "It hasn't been tested."

"But it could be today, right?" Topher nodded eagerly.

Abel took the strange tangle of straps from his hands and studied them. "You really think this will keep me from passing out?"

"It can't hurt to try it," Roa said.

"I signed up to race," Abel told them, "not be a test pilot for Topher's weird design ideas."

"Hey, my weird design ideas might save your life!"

"Don't be stubborn," Roa told him.

It stung to feel like his friends were ganging up on him, but they *were* trying to keep him safe. He knew he shouldn't be annoyed about it, but he was anyway. Still, he took off his jacket and put the contraption on.

"Twelve g's?" he said. "You think?"

Topher nodded eagerly. Roa just raised their eyebrows, like, *maybe.*

"It'd be pretty cool to see if Brazza could go fast enough for that," Abel said, tightening the last straps and putting his jacket back on over it. It fit so well, he barely even knew he was wearing it. Everyone underestimated Topher, but he really was very clever.

"Thanks, Toph," he added.

Finally, just a few minutes after midnight, with a chorus of shrieks and snarls, Lu's wyvern flapped in for a landing.

Abel saw right away that Felix was a retired fighting wyvern, just like she'd said. One of his eyes gleamed gold, but the other was milky white from lid to lid. There was a huge scar on that side of his face, where a talon had blinded him. His scales were black but faded, like a T-shirt that had been washed too many times. The ruff of his neck was hung with little tendrils like an old man's beard, and one of his feet was mechanical up to the ankle. Whatever fights this wyvern had been in, he had survived, but not unharmed.

His expression was as vicious as his wounds, and when Felix roared, the entire crowd on the sidewalk flinched. Abel and Brazza did too, which made Lu smile.

"Wow," Lu sneered as she guided her dragon toward him with smooth steps. "What a colorful mutt you've got. Too bad this isn't a beauty pageant. You'd win for sure."

"Well, your dragon looks like something another dragon already ate!" Topher shouted up at her.

She pulled the reins and brought the wyvern's face level with Topher. The dragon opened his mouth to show a ball of green poison growing in his throat.

"Ah!" Topher yelped. Abel noticed that he pushed Roa out of the way before diving to the side himself.

"NO!" Fitz bellowed from down the street with so much strength in his voice that the wyvern snapped his jaws shut. "Any attack on a spectator *or* on each other will result in immediate disqualification," he said.

Fitz trotted swiftly over to them, putting his long dragon in between Brazza and the wyvern, shielding Topher and Roa in the process. "If you break my rules, I will make sure that no kin *ever* allows you to ride a dragon under their colors for the rest of your mortal lives. Savvy?"

He glared at Lu until she looked down at her hands on the reins. "Savvy," she muttered.

He turned to Abel, almost as an afterthought, maintaining his impartiality as a referee.

"Savvy," Abel agreed.

"Good!" Fitz smiled, his old cheer pasted back on. "Well, it's twelve fifteen in the morning, the skies are clear, and it's a fine night for juvenile delinquency!" He clapped his hands once. "You will each line your dragons up below my drone. When I send the signal, take off. I've placed checkpoint drones throughout the city in a loop, each blinking purple, orange, purple, in this pattern—" He clapped twice, paused, then clapped once more. "Short, short, long. No other lights you see will be those colors in that pattern. The drones are at different heights in different streets, and you can travel any way you choose between them. But you *must* pass each checkpoint drone or you'll be penalized with five seconds added to your time. Fastest one to reach this finish line"—he pointed up at his hovering drone above him again—"without disqualifying violence or cheating, wins the race. That's it. Those are the rules. Savvy?"

"Savvy," Abel said.

"Savvy," Lu said.

"Then to the starting line!" Fitz announced.

Abel steered his dragon beside Lu's. He looked up at the drone.

"You got this," Roa said through his earbud.

"Just go really fast," Topher added.

He glanced back at them, then searched the crowd one more time for his mother's face. His eyes went right past her, then doubled back in disbelief when she smiled at him. She'd been standing front and center in the crowd the whole time, dressed like a nightclub performer! He'd been looking for some hunched-over-in-a-heavy-coat-and-hat-disguise-type outfit, but there was his mom in an opulent sequined gown, slathered in multicolored makeup. She wore a tall red wig, looking just like Dragon Queen herself, hiding in plain sight.

He laughed when she blew him a theatrical kiss, and felt his whole body relax.

"Here we go," Roa said.

Fitz pulled his dragon's reins, tilting its thin face to the sky. It launched a purple fireball, which burst into rainbow sparks high above. With that, Lu's dragon sprang from the ground. Abel shook the reins and squeezed his legs on Brazza's neck, but she just cocked her head and watched the gorgeous sparks fall.

"Um . . . I think you're supposed to race now?" Topher's voice crackled in Abel's ear.

"I'm trying!" Abel replied. "Come on, Brazza!"

He jostled the reins some more. He tugged and leaned. He patted her neck and kicked gently with his heels.

Nothing. She was mesmerized.

Lu was getting smaller and smaller as her dragon flapped furiously away. Every second that passed would make catching up that much harder.

In the crowd, people whispered and smirked. His mother looked worried. Arvin, on the other hand, looked pleased.

"Come on!" Abel bounced in the saddle.

Brazza just watched the rainbow sparks fall, until the last one fizzled out. When it was gone, she let out a silent sigh that Abel felt roll through her ribs. Then, without any warning, she bent her legs and jumped, wings snapping open with a FWOMP!

They were up and racing, and the best Abel could do was hold on tight and aim for the checkpoints.

In an instant, the ground was far below him, the crowd and their cheers lost on the wind. All that existed now was him, and his dragon, and the thrill of furious speed.

19

ABEL SAW THE FIRST BLINKING checkpoint ahead, hundreds of feet above him. He leaned back so that Brazza would go up, forgetting for a moment that she always did the opposite of what he asked.

She went down.

Fast.

"Ahh!" he yelled as the ground loomed. He leaned forward, flattening himself against her neck, and she pulled up, curving her wings, shooting skyward. They sliced below the checkpoint, missing by an entire dragon's length. He looked over his shoulder. It flashed red.

"Ugh," he grunted, but resisted the urge to blame Brazza. Never blame a dragon for the roughness of the ride; thank them for letting you ride at all. "We'll still get 'em," he encouraged her.

The red flash meant a penalty, and a penalty meant five seconds would be added to his finishing time. Even if they caught up with Lu and won, they'd have to win by more than five seconds. A close finish would mean his penalty cost him victory, unless she'd also missed a checkpoint. If he missed more, it wouldn't be enough just to catch up with Lu and win; he'd have to win by enough time to make up the difference.

That was how the race prevented cheating. You could cut across the city and circle back to the finish line, but you'd have the penalties for all those missed checkpoints added on. Fitz had probably calculated how many he needed to place to make sure both dragons had to fly the whole course.

Brazza sped up, her wings bending into a tight V, then slashing down. It wasn't a graceful motion, and it thrust her spine with each flap, lurching Abel forward in the saddle. But it made her fast. They crossed the next checkpoint another two hundred feet above them, picking up speed as they rose, and then the next one another hundred feet above that. They were above most of the neighborhood rooftops now. Looking down, Abel could see the purple-and-orange pattern blinking in a dozen drones, mapping the course ahead.

The drones were scattered on opposite sides of the widest streets and at different heights. One was barely hovering above the pavement. The next was close to it but five hundred feet higher. Fitz had set a punishing course for them, and Abel smiled. All the zigzagging and quick climbs were gonna be fun.

Lu and her wyvern were already as small as a dragonfly in the distance. They popped over a rooftop, then took a sharp turn out of sight into a new neighborhood.

"You're just kind of hovering," Roa's voice crackled in Abel's ear.

"Brazza does things her own way," he replied.

"There are a lot of different ways to lose," Topher said. "Just one way to win, though."

"Savvy," Abel confirmed. He patted Brazza's neck. "Hey, how about we finish this race so we can finish reading that book, huh? Just aim for the purple and orange lights."

The dragon turned her head to look at him. Then she looked straight ahead, rearing back so that Abel was looking straight up at the starry sky. With a lunge, she dove.

Both his hands clutched the saddle with white knuckles. He didn't dare even hold the reins, lest Brazza think he was telling her what to do. He could steer her just by leaning and squeezing his legs, which she found much less annoying than having her head yanked this way and that. He hardly had to steer at all, though. She understood exactly what needed to happen.

They sped past the last warehouses in the district, weaving through the checkpoints, up and down and side to side without missing a single one. The city was a blur as they turned sharp left, into a neighborhood of massive apartment buildings. Abel was nearly tossed out of the saddle by the turn. Then another quick one almost bashed his head into a bright yellow wall. He caught a glimpse of Thunder Wings graffiti as it brushed past his face.

"Hey, I'm still on here!" he shouted.

"Good to know," said Roa.

"I'm talking to the dragon!" Abel replied.

They slid underneath a billboard for Limelight Dance Hall, which had a Red Talon symbol spray-painted across it. One of Fitz's drones hovered just below. As the racecourse went on, Fitz got cleverer in placing the checkpoints, making them harder to spot and harder to get to. It would slow the racers down, make it more competitive. It wasn't all about speed, but smarts too. This was where the ground crew came in.

"I don't see the next one," Abel said. "I'm just past the Limelight billboard."

"Deep dive, then a right on Crescent and Third Streets," Roa said. "It's hovering just above the ground outside a store called BeDazzlers."

"They only sell bedazzled phone cases," Topher said. "How do they stay open?"

"I'm not really interested in their business plan right now, Toph," Abel replied. He leaned back to suggest Brazza dive.

She "obeyed" and swooped, her claws sparking against the pavement as they hit the street, weaving in and out of parking pods where dragons slept. He heard some of the dragons growl as Brazza blazed past.

"Got a visual on Lu," Roa said. "She just came up over the top of the Chainani Global Entertainment building. You're gaining on her."

"Savvy," Abel confirmed, focused on the next checkpoint. It was high above. He had to lean so far forward his head was almost below Brazza's neck, but she understood and turned straight up. Abel felt like his heart had been tossed into his toes. His vision blurred as they passed the drone, then turned for the next one, picking up even more speed.

He felt the pressure cuffs on Topher's g-rig tighten and loosen in a pulsing pattern—and his vision cleared. Abel's stomach still clenched against the speed, but the thing was working. His head stayed clear even as Brazza really let her wings unfurl with long sweeps through the air, every muscle working beneath her scales like rivers of lava beneath an erupting volcano. Before he could count to ten, he saw Lu and the wyvern up ahead. But Brazza flew so silently, they didn't know he was there yet.

"You're over three hundred miles per hour!" Roa cheered. "How do you feel?"

"Like a guy with really smart friends," Abel replied.

"Okay, good. Now it's strategy time," Roa added.

"I thought the strategy was to go really fast until I get to the end and then stop."

"Brazza's stubborn," Roa explained. "If she thinks she's winning she might slow down, not try as hard. Like Topher on the stairs."

"Huh?" Topher added, but this wasn't the time to let him in on the joke.

Lu's wyvern was only three dragon lengths ahead. They were below her by about two stories of the office buildings they were slicing between. A turn was coming up in front of a huge glass-fronted hotel.

"Stay behind her a while longer if you can," Roa explained. "Until you're closer to the finish line. Don't pull out in front until there's no time left for the wyvern to catch you."

"I'm not sure Brazza will like that," Abel said.

"This is where you prove you're a dragon *rider*, not a dragon passenger," Topher said.

"Ouch," Abel grunted.

"He's right," said Roa.

Abel would've had a comeback—something like *I'm the one three hundred feet in the air at three hundred miles per hour*—but his voice was stuck in his throat because Brazza pumped her wings, hitting what must have been four hundred miles per hour. Still, Topher's suit worked. Abel had to clench every muscle in his body against the g-forces, but he was hanging on at speeds that would've otherwise knocked him out.

The glass building straight ahead filled their view, and Abel saw Lu's reflection shimmering above his own. She saw him too.

Lu glanced over her shoulder. Her shining race helmet reflected the dancing neon lights of the city around them. Then she turned around, leaned to the right, and took the hard turn fast, accelerating through it.

But her wyvern was no match for Brazza.

Abel's dragon took the turn nearly sideways, pressing Abel down into the saddle and rising to the wyvern's inside, just out of reach of its grasping claws. They were literally neck and neck, and Brazza started gliding. The next flap of her wings would put her in the lead.

"Pull back!" Roa warned.

Abel dared to take the reins. It took all his strength and focus just to lift them. He wondered if Brazza would throw a tantrum the moment she felt him pull, but how else could he ask her to slow down? He didn't quite understand why he had to, but he trusted Roa's brain for strategy a lot better than his own. He'd never beaten them at DrakoTek since they'd started playing together in pre-school. Not once.

"Okay, Brazza," he said softly, his words snatched away by the wind. "Let's ease off a little."

He pulled gently, and Brazza answered by thrusting her neck forward, flapping once, and lunging a full body length ahead of the wyvern. Then another.

"SCREEEEEEEEEECH!" cried the wyvern as they passed. Abel looked back and saw Lu frantically waggling her reins, urging more speed. Felix strained to obey with bulging eyes and jaw clenched tight. Brazza glanced back and, sure enough, decided to gloat.

"Oh no," Abel sighed. Brazza rolled upside down with her neck bent so she was looking over her own stomach at the wyvern chasing after her.

"AHHHHH! BRAZZAAAA!" Abel's safety harness caught him, but he was hanging upside down, hundreds of feet in the air. His feet dangled over the city. Abel grabbed the strap with both hands, kicking uselessly to try and climb back up. The nylon harness that kept him from falling was now riding up on him painfully and yanking on Topher's g-rig too. Ironically, he was getting a brutal wedgie from his own dragon!

Brazza slowed, and Lu gained on them. Abel hung down in front of her wyvern's face like a roast duck in the window of a noodle shop. He worried the enraged wyvern would be tempted to turn the race into snack time. A dragon's desires were pretty simple: treasure, food, and pride, in that order. The wyvern might give up his chance at victory in exchange for a morsel like Abel. His shiny helmet would make a nice addition to the wyvern's horde too.

He pulled as hard as he could on the safety strap, arms burning with the effort to climb. He lifted himself up enough to grab the saddle with one hand, then the other. He kept pulling, but suddenly, Brazza rolled again, turning upright so fast, she flung Abel straight over her back and off the other side.

The harness caught him again with a quick jolt of nylon. The wedgie worsened.

"Ow!" he yelled, bouncing off Brazza's scales.

His arms ached, his legs prickled with pins and needles, the two accidental wedgies had nearly split him in half. But he pulled himself into the saddle and took the reins again. Brazza sped up. The wyvern fell behind.

And then dropped away. He dove down to a low covered alley, leaving Abel and Brazza high in the air.

"Abel, the course!' Roa yelled. "You just missed a checkpoint through the covered alleyway, and there's, like, ten more you'll miss if you don't double back and get inside!"

Abel saw the end of the wyvern's tail as it vanished. The alley was like a tunnel halfway up the buildings around it. These midair alleyways were all over this part of the city, spiderwebbing between the buildings, branching off from each other, going up and down in gentle slopes and tight twists, with countless unmapped openings. He'd have no way of knowing where the racecourse came out again. He could spend forever looking for it while Lu went ahead and won.

Roa didn't add the "told you so" that they were surely thinking.

"Told you so," Topher said without the slightest hesitation.

Abel ran his fingers along the smooth pink-and-blue scales of Brazza's neck. They were warm but not hot. She hadn't yet given all the speed she could. She had more race left in her yet.

"Okay, Brazza," he told her. "You like being counted out, huh? Coming from behind? This is your chance, but I need you to trust me. You're gonna have to let me steer, okay?"

He decided that a ripple of muscle along her spine was as good as a nod, and leaned hard to the right and back. Brazza obeyed, in her way, turning sharp left in a half circle and diving down toward the opening of the alleyway that Lu had taken.

The speed of it pushed Abel back even farther in the saddle, until he was bent so far at the waist that getting upright again was like doing every sit-up he'd ever been forced to do in gym class at the same time. He had to accomplish it without ever letting go of the reins, without pulling on them either. He didn't want to slow Brazza down or make her angry.

He got himself upright and nearly passed out from the effort, hanging his head to catch his breath. Brazza sped for the purple-and-orange checkpoint at the alley's opening, a perfect rectangle of concrete between two skyscrapers. A neon sign for a fortune-teller nearly took his head off as the dragon sliced into the enclosed alley, reminding him to focus. Dragon racers had to keep their eyes forward at all times, but also their minds.

They blazed past junk shops and pawnshops and shops that sold only used clothes and others that sold only used jewelry.

Up ahead, another checkpoint hovered at an intersection. He leaned all the way right, and Brazza turned all the way left, her wing grazing a laundry line hung out to dry along a wall. As they zipped past the checkpoint, something weird happened: It stopped blinking. The lights went off.

Abel didn't have time to think about it, though. There was immediately a hard right, then a straightaway, and then a sudden dive where the alley split into two levels. He nearly lost his head again on a dangling wire strung between shops. Brazza had to do a high-speed corkscrew to keep from missing two checkpoints hovering close together on opposite sides of the alleyway.

She passed the checkpoints perfectly, but again, their lights turned off.

After a series of hairpin turns and dizzying switchbacks that tossed Abel's dinner around inside his stomach and his brain inside his skull, he saw an opening up ahead. The purple-and-orange checkpoint blinked against the starry sky behind it.

He pulled the reins just a little, enough pressure to tell a normal dragon to slow just a tiny bit but which told Brazza that she should speed up.

Her neck thrust forward again, her wings forming almost straight walls on either side of her. They thrashed down so hard that the junk all around the alley swirled in twin tornadoes in their wake.

Abel laughed. He really liked this contrarian dragon of his. She flew on her own difficult terms. In a world where dragons were trained to be obedient and dutiful, he admired her unapologetic refusal to do anything the way she was supposed to.

A burst of cool night air hit him the face as they erupted from the tunnel, speeding in a high arc past Fitz's line of check-points. The flight through the alley had been dizzying, but now he saw they were over the neighborhood where they'd started.

"You made it out!" Roa cheered in his ear. "We see you up ahead! It's a straightaway to the finish line. You just go over the farm building in front of you and dive to just above ground level. Lu's pace is fast, so you'll need to be faster!"

"No other brilliant strategy?" Abel asked.

"When all else fails, fly as fast as you can," Roa replied.

He wrapped the reins around the palms of his hands. If Brazza only went fast when you tried to slow her down, he was going to pull her back with all his might. Hopefully she'd unleash all of *hers* resisting him.

He pulled hard, and Brazza's head tilted up a little in surprise, slowing her down. She glanced down her neck at him, slowing even further. He pulled harder, leaning back, and she narrowed her eyes. Had she figured out his game? Was she going to defy his reverse psychology just to be difficult? Had he made her mad enough that she'd try to splatter him on the pavement again?

Or was that the curve of a dragon's smile on her face?

Brazza straightened her head and snapped her wings wide.

That's when Abel found out what "fast" really meant.

THE CITY BLURRED. SINGLE DOTS of light became long streaks as Brazza blew past them. Abel pulled the reins against the strain of Brazza's power. She pulled so hard in return that Abel was lying down on her neck, mostly out of the saddle, his arms pinned underneath himself. He pulled with everything he had, and she flew with everything *she* had.

Through the leather of his jacket, he felt heat radiating from below her scales. He looked up the length of her neck, focusing on the point of her head between her horns and on the orange-and-purple drones that zipped past her so close he heard their motors whistle by his ears.

Everything else vanished. He was not distracted. He was not thinking about winning or losing or about Lu or the Red Talons or his family or even himself. He and the dragon were one being, a laser firing at the finish line.

He barely registered in his ear when Roa told him breathlessly, "You just crossed five hundred miles per hour! Five fifty!"

Lu's wyvern appeared ahead, weaving from side to side to block them from passing. Abel felt Brazza slow, just enough for him to suck a desperate breath into his burning lungs. Then, when Lu's wyvern was at the far side of a sideways swoop, Brazza burst forward and slipped past. Abel felt the sharp tip of the wyvern's wing brush his shoulder, but then Lu was behind him; the wyvern roared with the strain, but there was no catching Brazza now.

She snapped her wings open and closed and dove toward the last drones just over the street, twirling her body in a gleeful spin as they went. Abel saw the ground spinning up at him, and he closed his eyes tight to keep from throwing up. He'd never felt g-forces like this before. Even with Topher's rig pulsing and adjusting his blood pressure, he felt like he was going to pass out.

"Six hundred!" Roa's voice said in his ear, though they sounded four thousand miles away.

"That's gotta be a least ten g's!" Topher added.

"Slow down now, Abel!" Roa warned. He wasn't even sure his friend was talking to him. He felt sleepy. His vision tunneled, started to turn gray.

"SLOW DOWN!" Roa and Topher warned.

Abel felt his hands drop the reins, though he still felt their echo burning his palms. A calm feeling overwhelmed him.

It didn't last.

BOOM!

His entire body rattled when they hit the ground. Brazza had spread her wings out like parachutes to slow them down, all four claws clattering across concrete. She left a trail of sizzling furrows in the street, so hot they smoked, and then she came to a peaceful stop.

Fitz's dragon launched rainbow sparks into the sky to signal the race's end. They gleamed brighter than the lights of the city and showered the street in color. Brazza strutted back toward the crowd, eyes wide. She snapped at the falling sparks like they were candy. Fitz's dragon let out a few extras for her, which she quickly devoured. Her hooked tail swiped gently under the other dragon's chin as she walked past.

Was Brazza . . . *flirting*?

Lu's wyvern stumbled past them for a landing. The metal claw threw up white-hot sparks as it slowed itself, then half collapsed from exhaustion. Even coming from behind, Abel had beaten them by almost a minute.

Abel's mom came running from the crowd to cheer for him and his victory, forgetting all about her fabulous disguise. Roa and Topher strolled over, looking glum.

"What's wrong, team?' Abel yelled down at them, his voice hoarse. "You look like you were rooting for the other side! And, Toph, your suit was amazing! Look! I'm still alive!"

Arvin joined them before Topher or Roa could respond. He'd traded his cadet uniform for a muted red-and-maroon jumpsuit with black metal clasps and buttons. It was fashionable and more subtle than the other Red Talons in the crowd, who wore their kin colors bright and clear. They *wanted* to be noticed. Arvin didn't need to be. Everyone already knew exactly who he was.

He looked up at Abel and winked, like he was pleased, before he walked over to Lu.

"What was that?" Abel asked his friends.

"Congratulations!" Arvin called to Lu.

Lu flinched, stunned, then looked over to Fitz.

"Wait, what?" Abel shouted, also looking to Fitz.

Fitz was tapping his phone screen; then he held it up. "We have a revised winner!" he announced. "Abel, your time was fifteen minutes, twenty-three point two seconds; Lu's was sixteen minutes, eight point one seconds. She missed zero checkpoints. Abel, in spite of your amazing speed—really, I don't think I've ever seen a faster dragon—you missed nine checkpoints. At five seconds apiece, that's a penalty of forty-five seconds added to your time—"

"No one told me there'd be math!" Topher groaned.

"Which means—" Fitz confirmed with his calculator, but Roa had already done the math in their head.

"Lu wins by one tenth of a second!" they groaned.

A smile blossomed over Lu's face. The Red Talons cheered. Arvin gave her a fist bump. Another of the Red Talons handed her a patch with their symbol on it. She was getting everything she'd wanted: She was going to become a kinner. She looked over at Abel and made a claw with her hand and then gripped her throat with it. She mimed ripping it out, an unmistakable gesture that did not mean *Great job, kiddo.*

In the crowd, Abel's old teacher Ally and her Thunder Wing crew laughed and turned their backs on him, melting away again into the night. Clearly they were satisfied with Abel's public humiliation. He'd snatched defeat from the jaws of victory.

"You lose," Lu mouthed at him from the center of her adoring crowd.

"WHAT! NO! I DIDN'T! I WON!" Abel shouted. Brazza stopped flirting or whatever she was doing with Fitz's serpentine dragon and swung her head around to look at him. Then, seeing him upset, she swung her head around to find out why. Her eyes locked on Lu. She showed her teeth.

Brazza, it turned out, was an excellent judge of character.

She took a step toward Lu's wyvern, readying to attack. Abel was tempted to let her.

But Fitz rode his dragon in between them and raised his arms for an announcement.

"Congratulations to you both for a well-flown race," he said. "In the interest of a peaceful transfer of ownership, it's tradition for the winner to present the losing dragon with a token of thanks for worthy competition. So, Lu?"

Fitz gave Lu a very stern look, the kind he used at his bookstore to prevent shoplifting. He never had a problem with a kid taking a book if they couldn't afford to pay, he just wanted them to ask first. No one *ever* defied one of his looks, no matter how tough they thought they were.

Without further ado, Lu dismounted her saddle, slid down her dragon's wing, and approached Abel.

Brazza tensed. Abel felt her muscles ripple, her scales growing hot again. He still wasn't sure if she had a breath weapon, but this wouldn't be the place to find out.

He dismounted too and slid down Brazza's wing, intercepting Lu.

"Nice race," she said. "Too bad you lost."

"On a technicality," Abel said. "Too bad you weren't faster."

"A win is a win," she said. "And now that I'm officially a Red Talon, I'm going to own your dragon, and you are going to pay me some respect."

"I only pay what I owe," Abel told her.

She grunted and took out a smooth piece of colorful glass the size of her fist from her pocket.

"Lightning-forged glass from the flats," she said. "Unless your dragon doesn't like pretty things." She eyed Abel up and down. "I wouldn't be surprised."

"Why don't you throw it to her and find out?" Abel suggested. "See if *she* thinks you own her now?"

Lu looked back at Fitz, who shook his head at Abel just enough to warn him to be gracious in defeat.

"Ugh, fine," Abel grunted, and took the glass. Then he turned and showed it to Brazza. "It's for you," he said. "From her."

Brazza looked between the glass and Lu and back to the glass. She licked her lips. No dragon could resist a pretty piece of treasure, even a contrarian dragon like Brazza. She raised a claw and took it from Abel's hand. Then she settled down right there in the middle of the street, turning it with her sharp claws to see how the city lights danced on its surface.

Lu went back to the Red Talons to accept congratulations while Abel's mother and friends stood around him, looking at the dragon enjoying her prize.

"She won't go with Lu," Abel said. "No matter how much she likes that gift."

"She's not gonna have a choice," said Roa. "You can't just ignore the rules. People who ignore the rules end up eaten."

"But I didn't really lose," Abel argued. "I did *not* miss nine drones. Some of them just, like, shut off!"

"I know," Roa told him. "I think somebody hacked them so that you'd lose."

Abel gasped. "A hacker like—"

Abel looked over Arvin, who stood in the throng of Red Talons around Lu. He raised his eyebrows, signaling something, but Abel had no idea what. Then he bulged his eyes, but Abel shook his head.

"What?" he mouthed.

Arvin rolled his eyes and gave the quickest of gestures toward Lu's wyvern. Abel turned and saw it had a new rider, dressed in black.

Lu noticed a heartbeat later.

"My dragon!" she yelled, but the rider had already gained

control and spurred the dragon to take off. "They're stealing my dragon!"

"No!" someone in the crowd wearing Sky Knights colors yelled at her, laughing. "They've *stolen* your dragon."

The wyvern was airborne and, though weary-winged from the race, flew fast into the night.

Lu ran on foot, like she could catch up, shouting curses and pleas. Then she collapsed to the concrete after about a hundred feet. "Stop! Please! Come back! Help!" she cried out. No one moved to help her.

The Red Talons weren't about to go chasing after some school-kid's stolen dragon. Lu looked around desperately, pleading. Tears streaked down her face. "That was my uncle's dragon," she cried. "He . . . didn't know that I . . . borrowed it."

"Racing on a stolen dragon." Topher shook his head. "What'd she expect to happen? It's Drakopolis. Fire burns, smoke rises, and thieves steal."

Lu looked to Fitz for help, but he shook his head. "No way my dragon could catch that one," he said. "Sorry, kid."

There were a few people with their own big dragons who'd come to watch, but they all avoided eye contact, pretending to be busy on their phones or checking their saddles.

And then her eyes landed on Abel. He knew already that his was the only dragon fast enough to catch up with the thief.

Lu was already walking toward him.

"Please," she said simply. "You can keep your dragon if you help me get mine back."

"You've got nerve," Roa told her. "Looking to us after all your threats. We know you cheated to win."

"I didn't cheat," she said. "I swear."

"*Someone* cheated," Roa said.

"It was Arvin," Abel whispered. He met the boy's eyes across the street. "He knows how to hack phones; if he could hack my brother's, he could probably hack Fitz's too. He wanted you to win."

"But why?" Lu said miserably.

"I guess I have to find out." Abel turned to mount Brazza again.

"No!" Topher objected. "She doesn't deserve our help."

Abel shook his head. "No, but we're gonna help anyway. WW3D, right?"

Topher groaned. "This is hardly the time to act like a comic book hero!"

"WW3D," Roa agreed with Abel.

"This city teaches hard lessons," Abel said. "But they won't make less of me." He patted Brazza's neck. "Hey, pal, can you give that glass to my mom? I swear she'll take good care of it for you."

The dragon eyed Abel's mom suspiciously. She looked like a fabulous Dragon Queen in her high-heeled boots, sparkling makeup, and mirror-scaled coat. The shine of the lights off her outfit made her look like a valuable treasure herself. Maybe that's why Brazza decided to trust her. Or maybe she sensed Abel's trust. Or maybe she just felt like flying some more. Whatever her reason, she set the glass down at Abel's mom's feet and took a running start after Lu's stolen wyvern.

"Be careful!" his mom shouted after him "I lo—"

He didn't hear the rest of what she said because they were airborne and flying like winged fury. He barely had time to lock in his safety strap and realized—much to his chagrin—he *still* hadn't picked out his racing wedgie.

Who knew that being heroic would involve so many underwear malfunctions?

THIS WAS A DIFFERENT KIND of race. There were no checkpoints, there was no racecourse, and there were no rules.

Abel had no doubt he'd catch up to the dragon thief—they were flying an exhausted wyvern and Brazza still had energy to spare. He did, however, wonder what he'd do when he caught them. The wyvern had poison breath and plenty of battle scars. The dragon thief would probably be armed too. Brazza was fast and grumpy, but neither of those things were weapons.

He saw the wyvern and the thief up ahead, wings beating hard toward the entrance to one of those same alleyways he'd just raced through.

"We're gonna have to chase them low," he said, both to the dragon and into his earbuds.

"Be careful," Roa warned. "There are police patrols out, and they're looking for someone matching your description. As far as I know, you're the only person in Drakopolis with a pink-and-blue four-legged racing dragon and a patchwork leather jacket with a laughing dragon embroidered in rainbow thread on the back."

"A life of crime, but make it fashion," Topher joked.

"I'm diving now, Topher," Abel said. "Please kindly zip your lips."

With that, he leaned back, and Brazza dove into the narrow avenues between tall buildings. It was late enough at night that there was very little other dragon traffic flying around, but the wyvern was still ignoring all the lane signals. It flapped through bright red stoplights, dove, and rose between lanes without warning and made sudden unannounced turns that left taxis and freight dragons snarling.

Abel weaved among them, gaining on the wyvern with every flap. Brazza was so fast that traffic was a blur, the lights mere streaks in his peripheral vision. The holographic ads they flew through barely registered at all.

"There!" He patted Brazza's neck and pointed three lanes up and two over on a big avenue. The stolen wyvern was flying toward a huge billboard for a new live show featuring the performer Raina Terror and a hundred acrobats. The wyvern slipped into a garage just below it, and Abel followed. The narrow opening forced Brazza to slow down. Her claws clattered across the scuffed landing platform, and they proceeded inside on foot. Brazza walked with her head low, eyes scanning the rows and rows of stalls where dragons slept. The dragons snored loudly, but the human attendant in the booth was sound asleep, so Brazza crept on undisturbed.

From the corner of his eye, Abel saw the wyvern between two pods. The rider jumped down and scanned their phone on a stall door, which slid open to what looked like a normal overnight dragon parking stable. There was a hard floor giving off steam, a trough for food and water, and a screen at the far end that showed images of treasure in a huge underground lair. The screen created an illusion for the parked dragons that they were in their own caves, watching over a precious horde.

Usually, a rider settled their dragon in and left, closing the door behind them and locking it with their own unique code to prevent theft, but this dragon thief closed the door and stayed inside. Abel watched, but they didn't come out again.

He led Brazza over to the stall as quietly as he could and slid off her back. He peeked inside.

The stall was empty.

"It's some kind of trick," Abel said into his earbuds. "We're in parking lot number . . . um . . ."

"3-8-1-7-5-2 on Leviathan Avenue and Burner Street." A voice cut in over the phone line, but it wasn't Roa's or Topher's.

"Arvin?" Roa asked. "How did you get on this line? And how do you know where—"

"I'm better with computers than any of you," Arvin answered. "And we don't have time for me to go into a whole lesson about network security and tracking software. That's not a normal parking spot."

"Yeah," said Abel. "I figured that out."

"Oh, you've got everything under control, then? Don't want my help?" Arvin snapped.

"Some help," Roa snapped right back. "It was you who hacked the drones so Abel would lose."

"I did what I had to do," Arvin said. "I warned you not to win the race."

"I'm warning *you* I'm gonna punch your face," Topher replied.

"Don't threaten me in rhyme," snapped Arvin.

"The rhyme was accidental," muttered Topher. "I'm still gonna beat you down."

"I'm not your enemy," said Arvin calmly. "But I'm also not an enemy you'd want."

"You don't scare me," said Topher.

"I should," said Arvin.

"HEY!" Abel whisper-shouted over the mic at all of them. "Can y'all save it for later, please? I'm kind of in a situation here. And Arvin hasn't lied to us. Let's hear him out."

"Thank you, Abel," said Arvin. "Like I was saying: That's not a normal parking spot . . ."

Just as the door to the parking spot slid open.

"Did you do that?" Abel asked.

"Is 'Two-Hearted Dragon' the banger of the year?" Arvin replied. None of the others answered. Abel knew it was a pop song, but that was about all. He was into comics and DrakoTek, not pop music. "Yes," Arvin answered his own question with a sigh. "Now get inside."

"What about Brazza?" He looked back at his colorful dragon, peering into the spot over his shoulder with a large amount of skepticism. She even flinched when her eyes rested on the trough. "I think I better leave her out here."

"Are there security cameras?" Roa asked.

Abel looked around. It hadn't occurred to him that he was being watched. His colorful jacket was on a crime spree, and there were probably alerts going up about him all over the city.

"I'm on it," Arvin said. "Hacking in now. I'll run a loop from before you got there and send the live feed to our phones. No one but us will know you're there, and we'll keep an eye on Brazza while you're . . . inside."

"Inside," Abel repeated, looking at the parking stall again.

"I can't do this forever, savvy?" Arvin said.

"Roa? Suggestions?" Abel asked.

"I don't trust him," they said. "But I trust your gut. What's it telling you?"

Abel thought about Arvin showing up with more food for Brazza, and about his look of horror when Carrot Soup Supreme fell from the sky at the raceway. He thought about Arvin's bright-eyed wink after the race, and how he'd tracked Abel's location on his phone but apparently never turned any of that info over to the Red Talons.

At the same time, this kid was a hacker and the heir to a dangerous criminal empire. Abel knew he shouldn't trust him, but, in spite of himself, he wanted to.

"I trust him," Abel announced.

"Good enough for me," said Roa.

"Fine," said Topher unconvincingly.

"I'm touched," said Arvin. "Now get going? I can't stay inside this security system forever."

"Savvy," Abel answered with a quiver in his voice. He stepped into the parking stall.

The door slid shut behind him. Inside, the stall was quiet and hot. The treasure on the screen at the far end sparkled and gleamed. There was a soundtrack of wind whistling through caves. It was supposed to be so comfortable that dragons slept through the night. Parking lots didn't want grumpy dragons waking up and trashing the place.

"What now?" Abel asked.

In answer, the floor moved beneath him.

Then it dropped away from the walls.

Abel fell to his knees as the floor on which he stood became a moving platform. Overhead, a new floor slid into place in the stall, replacing the one that he was on.

The platform was now a high-speed elevator inside the walls of the parking lot. If anyone had peered into the stall, it would look empty. His surprised scream didn't even make a sound through the heavy concrete.

As far as the world above knew, Abel was gone.

THE FLOOR WAS NOW A moving platform, zipping underneath the huge garage, sideways, then down, then sideways, then down. It whizzed past sewer lines and fiber-optic cables, and all the hidden guts that make a city building work. It went so fast, Abel had to lie flat and grip the tiles with his palms, trying not to throw up or get thrown off.

"Hello?" he said into his earbuds. "Where is this thing going and when is it going to be over?!"

"Er . . . fit . . . gar . . . un . . . bree . . . hel . . ." he got in reply.

"You're breaking up! Hello? Hello!" He'd lost his connection. Wherever he was heading, he didn't have a signal. The platform sped up. It spun sideways and the g-forces of the spin were all that kept him from flying off into a concrete wall. Then it dropped straight down, so suddenly he couldn't help screaming.

"AHHHHHHEEEEEE!"

The platform slammed to a bone-rattling stop. Abel knocked his mouth shut hard. He ran his tongue over his teeth to make sure they hadn't shattered. He was actually glad he'd lost his phone connection because he didn't want his friends or Arvin to have heard him screaming like that. It was not a dignified tone.

Once certain that he'd neither shattered his teeth nor wet his pants, he stood up and brushed himself off. He was in a huge windowless corridor; he guessed it was underground. Then again, it was hard to judge distance when you were screaming at the top of your lungs and clenching your bladder shut.

The corridor was big enough for three dragons to walk side by side on the floor, and nine more to fly side by side above them, like a giant trapezoid. There was a track down the center where the platform could slide, though in this case, it stayed put and he had to hop off and walk.

There were glowing arrows painted on the floor and walls, with different instructions for dragon riders and work crews. As Abel stepped from the platform into the hallway, the signs sprang to digital life, showing 3D hologram maps and exit signs and even the universal symbols for the bathrooms.

"This is some kind of base," he said, just in case his friends could still hear him. He didn't receive a response. "I'm going farther in."

After he passed each sign, it flattened again into normal-looking paint. The movements kept making him spin around, nervous that he was being followed. Abel didn't like walking through an interactive building. He actually missed his school building, where the signs were faded and didn't move when you weren't looking.

More technology just makes things creepier, he thought.

He reached an intersection where the huge hallway kept going, but two human-sized hallways branched off on either side.

As he considered which way he should go, the painting on the floor projected a hologram in front of him: an orange arrow shimmered, pointing left. Then it turned purple and blinked on and off, shifting back and forth between orange and purple, just like the drones in the race: short, short, long. It repeated the pattern over and over.

Roa, Abel thought.

Arvin had hacked the system, so even though they couldn't talk, they could communicate through the building itself. Roa would know that Abel didn't have a mind for secret codes, but he'd just finished a race following this pattern, so of course they knew he'd recognize it. His friends were talking to him!

He followed the arrow down the corridor. The walls were metal and smoother than the ones in the big hallway, where dragons had cracked and scratched them. Humans couldn't do the kind of damage to a building that a dragon could.

There were metal doors all along the corridor, but none were labeled. They all had red lights above them, and small viewing windows. As he walked by, Abel peered inside and saw stalls and stalls of sleeping dragons, just like at the Burning Market. Each dragon wore electromagnetic cuffs on its wrists to hold them in place. As he went down the hallway, he could only just make out their shapes in the dim stalls, but he was pretty sure none of them was Lu's.

There was one more door at the end of the corridor, but this one had no viewing window. No lights blinked over it either.

"Little help?" he said, but still got no answer.

A metal plate said the door was exam bay 7b. There was a keypad next to it. Abel waited for it to spring open, but nothing happened.

"Come on, Arvin," he mumbled. "I'm here . . ."

Still nothing. He was on his own.

Maybe Arvin had lost contact with him, or maybe he'd reached the limits of his eighth-grade hacking ability. Maybe Abel had been wrong to trust Arvin at all, and this was a trap to get rid of him. It was definitely an underground lair, and if comics had taught Abel anything, it was that nothing good ever happens in underground lairs.

Or maybe . . . Abel touched the handle with his fingertips and gave a gentle push.

The door cracked open.

It wasn't locked to begin with.

Sometimes, the obvious answer to a problem was also the best one.

He slipped through and found himself on a high catwalk above a huge industrial veterinarian's office. Bright white lights blazed down, keeping Abel hidden in total darkness above.

He recognized some of the equipment from his Dr. Drago comics. There was the special sonic heart monitor that could take readings through a dragon's scales. There was a big machine with high-powered syringes that could inject medicine between a dragon's scales. And there was a tray of surgical tools that could, if necessary, slice and dice and remove a dragon's scales altogether.

A chill ran along Abel's spine. He thought about the section of the Burning Market that sold dragon parts. Had he just stumbled into a "chop shop," where stolen dragons were dissected and sold off in pieces?

Lu's wyvern, Felix, was strapped to a large metal plate on the floor in the center of the room. His wings were bound to his body with huge restraints, and one of his legs was locked in a cuff. The mechanical claw on the other leg had been removed and sat on a table off to the side, hooked up to computers. There were extra cuffs too, enough for a four-legged dragon.

Like Brazza, he thought. They were ready for whichever dragon won. This was the place Silas had wanted to find. This was where someone was hacking dragon DNA.

Lu's wyvern's head and neck rested flat. His body rose and fell with deep, steady breaths. His eyes stared at nothing. All around the weary dragon were lab technicians in heavy leather smocks and big rubber gloves. Abel recognized a few of them by their infinity tattoos.

Sky Knights.

Then he saw something that turned the chill on his skin into a burning rage:

His sister, Lina, was standing beside the dragon, dressed in all black. *She* was the dragon thief!

No wonder she'd told him not to race. As much as Silas had wanted him to find this laboratory, Lina wanted him not to. He'd been caught up in a game between his brother and his sister— between the Dragon's Eye and the Sky Knights. And the biggest losers in this game were the dragons themselves.

Of all the kinners Abel could've found down here, why did it have to be Lina?

Beside Lina stood another figure, one that made Abel grind his teeth on sight: Officer Grallup.

What were his sister and the KISS officer from his school doing in an underground laboratory with a stolen dragon?

"Will it work this time?" another man asked. Abel recognized this one too. Captain Drey, boss of the Sky Knights. He'd met Abel before. He'd stolen Karak, and Abel had taken the dragon back. Drey had vowed revenge, and only Lina had protected Abel from the Sky Knights' wrath. If he got caught here, she probably wouldn't be able to protect him any longer.

Abel took a deep breath to calm himself, and he listened.

"Science is a process, not an end point," a lab technician in a shiny neon-pink rubber smock told Drey.

"It'll be *your* end if you don't start getting this right," Captain

Drey answered coldly. Officer Grallup laughed, but the Sky Knights boss hadn't said it to be funny. He meant it. Lina wore a blank expression on her face, like she wasn't listening at all, like she didn't want to be there.

Is this why you warned me not to race? Abel wondered. *Because you wanted to protect me from the Sky Knights' dragon theft? Or because you wanted to keep me from knowing about it?*

The lab technician in the pink smock lined up a giant needle at the wyvern's side, using a laser to aim it between two scales. Then, with the press of a button, the needle shot forward and pierced the wyvern, who didn't even flinch.

Abel did.

He watched, skin prickling, as the technician pressed another button and drew the dazed dragon's steaming hot blood.

When the syringe was full, the technician put it in a different machine, and they all watched as swirling strands of DNA projected above it.

"This will do nicely," the lab technician said. "We can use the wyvern DNA to improve speed, strength, and docility."

Abel didn't know what "docility" meant, but he repeated the word to himself three times to force it into his memory. He could look it up or ask Roa what it meant when he had service again. *Doss-ill-ity. Doss-ill-ity. Doss-ill-ity.*

"Why didn't you get the faster dragon?" Grallup grumbled at Lina.

"My orders were to bring the *winning* dragon," Lina replied. "Which I did."

"Or were you just too sentimental to steal from your scrawny little brother?" Grallup snarled.

"Insult my family again and see what happens." Lina glowered at the much bigger man.

"Lina follows orders," Captain Drey defended her, forcing Grallup to back down. Then he turned to Lina and spoke gently. "But, Lina, we're designing something never before seen in the world. Some creative thinking on *all* our parts is necessary. A good soldier isn't just an order-following robot. She can improvise and adapt to achieve her mission objectives, understand? We're trying to free Drakopolis from a corrupt and cruel government. We can't afford to let family sentimentality slow us down. The oppressed of Drakopolis are *all* our family, yes?"

Lina nodded. She looked like she did after getting scolded for wasting water in the shower, annoyed but also knowing she'd been wrong.

It was weird for Abel to hear his rebellious big sister described as a soldier, especially since Silas actually wore a military uniform. Out in the world, his siblings were so different from how he saw them at home. Lina, the rebel, was a good soldier committed to a brutal cause. Silas was a loyal soldier, breaking the rules to try to clear his sister's name. His siblings were so much more complicated than Abel had thought they were. Perhaps the same was true of him.

Maybe we're all complicated, Abel mused. *My friends, my parents, even my enemies. Even Grallup.*

"Come on, Drey, just order her to steal her brother's dragon," Grallup said.

Okay, so not Grallup, Abel thought. *He's just a goon.*

"We could integrate its speed into the program," one of the technicians said. "But its temperament would need adjustment."

Drey looked at Lina. Abel held his breath.

"I'd really rather not steal from my own family," she said, and Abel exhaled. Maybe his sister wasn't a total Sky Knights fanatic yet.

"He bought that dragon with the race winnings *we* gave him," Drey said. "It's hardly stealing."

"I've already brought you dozens of dragons," Lina objected. "Are you telling me that that's not enough?"

"Progress demands sacrifice," the lab technician said. "We've used up the dragons you brought."

"Used up?" Lina asked. "What does that mean?"

Used up. Abel thought he knew what that meant. It was terrible.

"Don't be squeamish," Drey said. "We're changing the world. We didn't break you out of prison to have you sit on the sidelines. We need the best dragons, and you're the best dragon thief. If you won't do it, then you're of no use to us."

Grallup shifted behind Lina. He had a stun gun in his hand, ready to use. She didn't turn, but she flinched a little at the sound of it powering on behind her back.

"I know it seems harsh," Drey told her, resting a large hand on Lina's shoulder gently. "Especially after what happened at the raceway . . . but imagine the power the Sky Knights will have when *we* control a flock of super-dragons. No one will need to pay the Thunder Wings for their armor or weapons because we can engineer dragons that don't *need* armor and extra weapons. We can design custom dragons, genetically modified to be whatever the buyer wants them to be."

Abel thought about the glowing pangolin from the Burning Market. He thought about the invention of dragon peppers. He thought about all the cool things science could do—and how it could all be bent to horrible ends by wicked people. Smarts and talent were just as dangerous in the wrong person as a ten-ton Reaper with the wrong rider.

"Once they can buy our superior dragons, no one will *want* old-fashioned natural breeds," Drey said, warming to his little motivational speech. Lina looked like she was drinking it up. "We'll sell to everyone. We can even donate dragons through our charitable foundations. And after our dragons are in every last corner of Drakopolis . . . we'll unleash our code to take control of them. We'll control everything. We can remake Drakopolis as we want. No more Red Talons or Thunder Wings. No more Dragon's Eye. We'll make a more just, a more *free* Drakopolis."

Lina nodded along with the speech, but she didn't clap or swoon or even smile. Drey looked disappointed in her response.

"I need to know I can still count on you," Drey told her, leaning down to look into Abel's sister's eyes. "No matter how many dragons we have to destroy, no matter how many dragons we have to steal, I need to know you are a true *believer*."

He tapped the infinity dragon symbol on his neck, then the one Lina had on her forearm. Abel had never seen it before. She always concealed it at home. His heart sank. Maybe she was already a true believer.

Lina took a deep breath. The stun gun buzzed in Grallup's hands. She nodded.

"Bring us your brother's dragon," Drey said. "Or Grallup will do it *his* way."

The KISS officer grinned.

Abel felt his heart breaking as his sister met Drey's eye and said, loud and clear, "I'll do it. I'll bring you my brother's dragon."

Abel didn't want to cry, but tears hot as dragon's breath streaked his cheeks. He didn't want to watch whatever they were about to do to Lu's wyvern either. But he couldn't stop them, not alone. He fled into the hallway and ran back toward the platform that had brought him.

"I don't know if you can hear me," he said into his earbuds. "But we need a plan. . . . We have a lot more than one dragon to save!"

A PALL HUNG OVER THE crowd back at the finish line.

Everyone knew that Lu had won the race but lost her dragon, and everyone knew that Abel had lost the race on a technicality but had tried to help Lu anyway. None of them knew what Abel had found.

When he got back, he just told Lu that he lost the thief in traffic. She looked like she was going to protest—to say that their deal was off and she'd won Brazza, so she was going to take her—but Brazza made it clear that was not going to happen. Lu relented. She was too heartbroken to put up much of a fight. Her Red Talon buddies led her away. Arvin gave Abel one quick glance before leaving, and an almost-invisible thumbs-up.

"We still trust him?" Roa asked.

Abel nodded. "We do," he said, and that was good enough for Roa.

He didn't want anyone else to know about Lina, not before he had a plan. He trusted Roa, Topher, and Arvin to keep it to themselves. He didn't need to tell his mother, though. She knew instantly.

"It was Lina, wasn't it?" she asked him on their way home.

After he'd gotten Brazza settled in for the night, his mother paid for them to take a taxi home, rather than taking one of the Nightwing buses.

"I could never keep that girl in her crib," she sighed. "I guess Windlee Prison didn't stand a chance." She didn't ask him anything else; she just let him rest his head on her shoulder, where he fell asleep.

He woke up late Sunday morning in his own bed and heard voices talking low in the living room. He padded across the room and noticed he was in his pajamas. Abel felt a twinge of embarrassment that his mom had changed his clothes while he was asleep, but that quickly turned to a bolt of shock when he saw Silas on the couch.

And sitting next to Silas was Lina.

Neither his brother nor his sister looked happy to be there, and his parents didn't look that happy either. The family hadn't all been together at the same time in months, and this was not the sort of reunion his parents would've chosen.

"Finally!" Silas slapped his hands on his silver uniform pants when he saw Abel. "You get in serious trouble if you oversleep like this at the Academy."

"Good thing we're not at the Academy," Lina snapped at their brother.

"I'd have you thrown in the brig if we were," Silas replied. "You're a fugitive. I should call for backup right now and have them haul you away."

"I dare you to try it!" Lina dared him to try it.

"Both of you, quiet!" their father roared with more ferocity than any of them had heard in a long time. Silas and Lina settled down with their hands in their laps, docile.

Docile. Roa had told him it meant easy to control and eager to obey, like a loyal pet.

It reminded him of the army of docile super-dragons the Sky Knights were trying to create, and of what happened to Carrot Soup Supreme when their experiment went wrong.

"Why are you here?" Abel demanded.

"Ask them." His sister hitched her chin toward their parents. "They're the ones who lured us."

"We did not *lure* you," their father said.

"Well, we kinda did," their mother admitted.

"We *asked* them to come," Dad explained. "We told them it was important."

"And you didn't mention *she'd* be here," Silas grunted.

"Hey, you're the one who tried to arrest me," she grunted, elbowing him in the side.

"I'd do it again too!" Silas shoved his elbow into hers.

"STOP IT!" their mother shouted. "How come Abel is the youngest of you and he's the only one acting like a mature adult here?"

Abel straightened his back and gave a nod of respect to his mom. He didn't admit that the only reason he'd been silent was because he hadn't thought of a good insult for Silas and Lina yet.

"We have a problem as a family." Mom waved Abel into the room. "Silas, we know you made Abel fly that race."

"We do not approve," their father added.

"But we also know you only did it to try to clear Lina's name," their mom said.

Lina flinched. She gawked at her brother in disbelief. He avoided making eye contact with her. She never would have asked for Silas's help herself, and he never would've wanted her to know he was helping. He even blushed a little as he met Abel's eyes.

"I can't believe you told."

Abel had broken the first rule of spies and of siblings: Don't snitch.

But he was tired of lies. Dr. Drago didn't rely on deception and betrayal to save the day, and neither would Abel. A hero wasn't just made by what they did but how they did it. Abel wasn't going to play Silas's games anymore, or let Lina get away with betraying him.

"Abel is the only one of you who is ever honest with us," their mom said. "Even though it took him a while to come clean. However . . ." She cleared her throat. "All that is in the past. We need to think about the future. Your futures."

"My future is just fine," Silas said. "I serve something greater than myself."

"So do I," said Lina. They glared at each other.

"You *will* get caught, Lina," their mother said. "And needless to say, you are not going to steal your brother's dragon."

Lina sat upright so fast it was like she'd been electrocuted. "What? How did you know I—"

"I was there," Abel said. "Under the parking lot on Leviathan Avenue and Burner Street."

Lina's jaw dropped. Her mouth hung open like a dragon trying to shoot fire, but hers only let out coffee breath.

"You don't understand," she said. "Whatever you think, the Sky Knights are trying to *change* things. Everything they do is to make our city better for people."

"What do the dragons that you 'used up' think about that?" Abel said, finding he was much madder at her than at Silas. Sure, Silas had put him in danger, but Lina was putting dragons in danger. "How many dragons have been *used up* because of you?"

"I didn't . . . I'm not the one who . . ." She didn't have a defense. She knew she was in the wrong. It was like the time she'd been caught sneaking out in ninth grade to go to an underground dance party, even though Dad was in the hospital with Scaly Lung.

They had waited up for her till morning. When Lina had finally got home, Mom had simply rose from her chair and said, *I expected better from you.*

Lina had broken down crying. Not because she was in trouble, but because she knew she'd been thoughtless and cruel. Abel had watched the whole scene from the door to his room, and never forgot how Lina didn't get punished for sneaking out. She didn't need to be. She punished herself. Lina believed she was a kind person, but there was no arguing with how unkind she'd been to their family. Abel wasn't sure her relationship with their mom had ever been the same after that night.

People tell themselves stories about themselves, Abel thought, *and it hurts when they realize those stories aren't always true.*

Abel wondered what stories he told about himself, and how he'd react if he found out they weren't true. Would he cry? Lina was tougher than he'd ever be, and she was crying now.

Their dad went to the couch and put his arm around her.

"I didn't mean to hurt any dragons," Lina said between sobs. "But I can't just stop either. The Sky Knights have good ideas, but they're ruthless. They're not going to let me or Abel or anyone else get in their way." She looked up at Abel, eyes puffy. "If I don't take your dragon, someone else will. You know that, right? You're just a kid. There are more thieves in this city than noodles at a noodle bar. One of them will get Brazza eventually."

Abel imagined a noodle trying to steal Brazza, and he laughed a little. He knew it was just his brain reacting to stress, but he couldn't help it. Everyone stared at him.

"Brazza is not so easily gotten," Abel said, dead serious again. "She almost kills me every time I ride her, and she *likes* me. So let's see these thieves try it." He cocked his head at her. "Whoever they are."

"Abel, don't threaten your siblings with a killer dragon," their dad said. "And, Lina, I really wish you'd find another line of work than stealing dragons for a dangerous kin."

"I do *actually* work in the bookstore," she said. "Fitz doesn't just give out that employee discount to anyone."

"Fitz's bookstore is a front for criminal activity," Silas said.

"Then why hasn't the Dragon's Eye shut it down?" Lina stuck her tongue out at him.

"Because it's the best bookstore in the city," Silas said. "We have our priorities."

"Or is it because Fitz bribes the Dragon's Eye?" Lina replied. "Your precious secret police aren't as honest and law-abiding as you think. They're just another kin, only with the law on their side."

"The Dragon's Eye are law *enforcement*!" Silas popped up to his feet. "They are not just another kin! I should arrest you for saying that!"

"And I should toss you out a window for being stupid!" she replied. "Good thing we don't live our lives by 'should.'"

"Yeah," Silas told her through gritted teeth. "Good thing."

"Mom, can I go back to bed?" Abel groaned. He was tired of watching his siblings fight, and even more tired from his late-night dragon flights. "These two are just gonna argue. They won't be any help."

"They will," his mother said, crossing her arms. "Here's what's going to happen. I am going to make breakfast."

"It's almost lunchtime," Silas grunted.

She frowned. "I am going to make *brunch*," she said. "And we are going to eat together as a family, and there will be no arguing, no kicking each other under the table, and *absolutely* no threatening each other with imprisonment, death, or dismemberment."

She glared at her children from one to the other.

"Fine," Silas grunted.

"Fine," Lina grunted.

"I could eat!" Abel said.

"Excellent." Their mother smiled. "And after we eat, we're going to make a plan *together* on how to get each of you out of the messes you're in."

"And free all the dragons from the lab," Abel added.

His whole family looked at him like he'd just dumped a pile of dragon dung on the living room floor. "I won't be part of any plan unless it frees the dragons they're using for their experiments. I'd rather go to jail than leave them in that place."

Lina looked like she wanted to object, but Abel gave her the kind of look a dragon gives a rider before throwing them off its back.

"Fine," his mother agreed. "And free the dragons."

"And arrest the Sky Knights leadership," Silas said, crossing his arms. "*I* won't be part of any plan that lets those criminals go free."

"Silas," their father said. "Your brother and sister are both criminals themselves."

"I know that," he grunted. "They can go free if I get to arrest more important criminals."

Lina frowned, but to Abel's surprise, she didn't complain. Abel sort of wanted to complain, though. He wasn't sure if he objected to being called a criminal or being called an unimportant one.

So he kept his mouth shut. As long as the dragons got free, he was willing to compromise on anything else. He'd even go to

Windlee Prison if he had to. The thing about taking responsibility, he realized, was that it didn't free you from consequences. He was willing to face the consequences if he still got to do what was right.

Judging by the heavy silence around the living room, everyone else in his family was pondering the same kinds of thoughts: what they should do, what they were willing to do, and what price they were willing to pay.

"But first, brunch," his mom reminded them.

And after brunch, all together, they hatched a plan.

"Our kids are idealists!" Their dad beamed. "Crooked, criminal, dangerous, and deceitful . . . but idealists nonetheless!"

He looked weirdly pleased about it.

And as difficult, dangerous, and deceitful as they could be, by the time they were done making their plan, Abel was really glad to be part of this family.

PART FOUR

"HE'S LUCKY I HAVEN'T FED
HIS WHOLE FAMILY
TO ANYTHING YET."

IT WAS ABEL'S TURN TO sneak up on the son of the Red Talon leader. The plan they'd hatched to rescue the dragons required getting Jazinda Balk and the Red Talons' cooperation, and Arvin was their best hope.

Abel had brought Topher and Roa in on the plan, with his parents' permission. They'd agreed to help without any hesitation. He thought his friends were as much a part of his family as his brother and sister were.

"Like you could keep us away," Topher said.

"We'd never let you go into danger alone," Roa said.

Roa wanted to prove they were just as smart as Arvin was, and Topher didn't want to miss out on any hijinks. (He actually used the word "hijinks," which . . . *who did that?*) Abel was glad they were with him, whatever their reasons.

Silas agreed to sneak them onto the campus of the Dragon Rider Academy to find Arvin, but Abel wasn't allowed to bring Brazza. They had to look like actual cadets, so Silas found them all uniforms. Abel's smelled like smoke.

"That's because the cadet who last wore it was burned to a crisp," Silas explained. When Abel balked, Silas shrugged at him. "What about a dragon-riding military academy did you think was safe?"

Safe or not, the campus was way nicer than Abel's municipal school. Silas's government wyvern landed a block away, and they walked the rest on foot. The front gate was set into a high stone wall that had guard platforms evenly spaced along it. Abel saw the silhouettes of White Flame Reapers and Nightshade Infernals on each platform, dragons with ferocious long-range breath weapons. They might as well have hung a sign outside that read: INTRUDERS WILL BE INCINERATED.

Beyond the gate, there was a huge green lawn. It was more grass than Abel had ever seen in one place before. The rooftop parks he knew were tiny, and most were covered in fake grass. Silas swiped his ID card, and a small door beside the gate opened.

The campus itself was as much like a city park as a wyvern was like an iguana. On either side of the lawn were thick stands of trees. Paths cut through trees with neon signs embedded in some of them. Around the lawn, Goatmouth dragons with their wings bound to their bodies gnawed on the grass, while tired-looking gardeners guided them along, paying Silas and the kids no attention.

They walked to the main entrance of the central building, where they faced another imposing wall. This one was decorated with what had to be millions of shining dragon-glass tiles embedded in the steel and concrete, forming a mural of cadets and dragons working together to build a great spiraling city.

Above the scene, there were images of riders on dragonback crushing, burning, and tearing apart all the different kin symbols.

The Thunder Wings' lightning dragon was held in the grip of a ferocious wyvern. The Sky Knights' infinity symbol was shredded by a Ruby Widow Maker's jagged gem breath, while the Red Talons' dragon sun was being ripped in quarters by four Golden Reapers who'd locked their jaws on it. Only the laughing dragon of the

Wind Breakers kin was missing. Abel figured that was because no one thought they mattered enough to put in the mosaic.

Below the ornate scene, a figure peeled itself off from the shadows. It was Silas's partner, Kai, dressed in the school uniform. Clearly he was trying to look like he was a student rather than an officer of the secret police. Kai didn't even glance at Abel and his friends as he approached Silas, whispered in his ear, and then melted away into the shadows again.

"We'll find Arvin in his dorm," Silas announced.

"Kai's not sticking around?" Abel asked.

"Kai has better things to do than assist in our conspiracy," Silas said, though he looked wistfully toward the dark where Kai had disappeared. Abel knew that Lina had a crush on Kai; he wondered if Silas did too. Now that he was himself a teenager, Abel wondered if he'd start getting crushes on everyone all the time too. He hoped not. He was easily distracted enough without going all googly-eyed for every person with a nice smile. Lu had a nice smile, and being drawn in by it had earned him a snapdragon wedgie.

Silas noticed Abel watching him and waved them all forward. "Come on," he grumbled.

They went through the gate under an imposing statue of the eyeball-headed dragon wielding a curved sword. "They say that the sword will come down and behead any traitor who tries to pass through the gate." Silas narrowed his eyes at his brother. "I wonder if you'll make it."

Abel scoffed but kept his eyes locked on the stone as he passed under it, just in case. He noticed his brother's smirk and chose to ignore it. This was Silas's territory now. If they wanted any hope of success, Abel couldn't antagonize his big brother.

He *really* wanted to antagonize his big brother. He was proud of himself for resisting.

They walked around the main building and along a path across a central quad of dorms, toward a big domed building that was shaped like a beehive made out of giant black dragon scales. It was almost invisible in the dark. The other dorms were built the same way, in different colors.

"That's Arvin's dorm," Silas said. "There's a student common room on the first floor just inside. Kai says Arvin's in there."

"You're not coming?" Roa asked.

Silas shook his head. "I'm a cadet major as far as anyone here knows. Officers don't go into student dorms. If I show up, there will be questions."

"But no one knows us," Roa pointed out. "Won't *that* raise questions?"

"This is a military academy, and you are in the uniform of junior cadets," Silas explained. "We make sure our junior cadets don't ask questions they aren't invited to ask. So act like you belong, move like you have discipline, and find Arvin fast."

"What if someone recognizes us?" Topher asked.

Silas rolled his eyes. "We *want* Arvin to recognize you so he'll go with you. No one else knows who you are. If anyone asks, your preferred pronouns are Cadet and only Cadet. Your names are Cadet. Your religion is Cadet. You have no identity but Cadet, get it? Neither does anyone else and you can remind them of that. They'll be embarrassed to have suggested otherwise. It's how they're trained."

"Sounds like a great place," Abel grumbled.

"We learn to protect and serve Drakopolis," Silas told him. "It's bigger than any one of us. When we put on the uniform, our old neighborhoods no longer matter. The kins no longer matter. Our families or lack of them, our money or lack of money, who we loved or how we prayed or what we believed about anything no longer matter. We don't live for ourselves anymore. We live for our city. Get it?"

Abel's big brother looked like he was about to cry. Abel knew he believed what he'd said, but he was also breaking the laws of Drakopolis to help his family, so they *did* still matter to him. He was torn between what he wanted to believe and what he actually felt. A person could only hold so many different versions of themselves before they started to crack. Silas was cracking. Abel, for once, felt no urge to annoy him. He found he actually wanted to hug him.

He didn't, though. Abel certainly wasn't cracking.

Instead, he nodded and promised his brother they'd be out soon with Arvin. Then he and Topher and Roa stiffened their spines, clenched their jaws, and walked into the military dorm like soldiers in training.

They had not expected a killer beat.

• • •

The common room of the dorm was decorated for a dance. All the furniture was shoved to the edges of the room, and the cadets had shed their long jackets to cluster together in the center. They danced in clumps. Bouncing clumps. The air was thick with the smell of cologne and perfume and sweat and deodorant.

And also feet.

In spite of the spinning lights and gleaming holograms they'd used to make it feel like a grown-up nightclub, this was still a dorm where a few hundred teens and preteens lived and worked. There were a lot of sweaty feet.

"How are we going to find Arvin in this chaos?" Roa wondered.

Abel scanned the crowd. All the kids had versions of the same dragon rider haircut. They were all wearing basically the same clothes and dancing basically the same way. The music was so loud it rattled Abel's ribs and threatened to reset his heartbeat. The lights flashed and pulsed and obscured everyone's faces. It would be hard to find Arvin without wading through.

"At least no one will be able to see us clearly either," Topher pointed out.

"Aren't we lucky?" Abel sighed. His head swiveled back and forth around the room, searching for some sign of the Red Talon boy.

Just then, another cadet broke away from their dancing cluster and approached Roa.

"Hey!" they shouted over the music, leaning in close to Roa's ear. "I don't know you!"

Roa hesitated for a moment but regained their composure. "Yes, you do, Cadet!" they shouted back. This time the cadet flinched and studied Roa's face, nodding slightly.

"Oh, right!" they finally said, not wanting to be caught not knowing someone they were supposed to know. Abel was impressed. He'd never been able to lie with so much confidence. "Want to dance?" the cadet asked Roa.

"I— Well—" *Now* Roa was lost.

"They're with me!" Topher grabbed Roa's hand and held it up, making both Roa and the other cadet flinch this time.

"I didn't mean to, like, you know—" The cadet tried to recover, then turned toward the crowd and pointed over their heads toward a makeshift stage made out of dining tables pushed together. "Oh, look, Ruby Scales is about to perform!"

The cadet stepped away fast, just as a smoke machine belched thick fog across the floor and a spotlight lit the center of the stage. Topher hadn't let go of Roa's hand yet, and Abel noticed. Before he could comment, a performer stepped into the spotlight, wearing huge red-sequined platform boots that caught the light and shot it back in a thousand directions.

The music thumped, and the performer spun in a glorious gown of glass scales with silk wings, their face made up like a Jewel dragon's. For a second, Abel thought it was the world-famous Raina Terror, but then he noticed the eyelashes bedazzled with flaming-red rubies, and one red stud glittering in their nose.

"Is that—" Roa gasped.

"Arvin," Abel finished the sentence.

With a flourish and a twirl, Arvin, dressed like a ferocious Jewel dragon, began to sing.

"I'd burn one thousand villages for one glance!" he belted over the heavy bass of the music. His voice carried. "I'd destroy one million knights in armor for just one dance!"

Through the lights and the fog and the scrum of military cadets, Arvin caught Abel's eye. He hesitated for a breath, gave a look to the side of the stage where an emergency exit sign flickered, and then continued his act like nothing was amiss.

"Impressive dancer," Roa noted.

"That kinner can *sing*," Topher observed.

"We need to meet him outside," Abel told them both, then made his way through the distracted crowd.

No one paid Abel and his friends in their bland uniforms even the slightest bit of attention. They slipped through the emergency exit, just at the peak of Ruby Scales's performance. Arvin hit a high note, and a life-sized hologram of a real Jewel dragon dove over the crowd, roaring and raining down holographic rubies.

As his fans went wild, Arvin slipped out unseen.

• • •

"I knew you were coming," Arvin told Abel once they were all standing outside in the cool air. His makeup still sparkled. "I made sure I had a dramatic exit. So . . . what do you want from me?"

Abel was still too mesmerized by the performance to answer. He felt like Brazza when she watched the rainbow sparks fall before the race, dazzled speechless.

Just then, Silas stepped from around the side of the building, and Arvin took a defensive stance. Abel moved between his brother and the boy to keep the peace if he needed to. *Why*, he wondered, *do I feel protective of Arvin, of all people?*

"Take us to your mother," Silas barked, like someone used to giving orders and having them obeyed. Abel was supposed to do the asking, but Silas had gotten impatient.

"We need the Red Talons' help," Abel clarified.

Arvin adjusted his gown, straightened the silk wings on his back, and nodded. "I'm not sure you'll be welcome. My mom has a bounty on all three of you."

"I know," Abel said, shuddering at the memory of the snap-dragon wedgie. "But this is bigger than our grudge. The Sky Knights could wipe out the Red Talons if we don't stop them. At least a hundred dragons are suffering in that underground lab."

"Maybe leave out that second part," Arvin said. "I don't think my mom will care."

"Some of them are her dragons," Abel said. "The stolen ones."

"Stolen by your sister, right?" Arvin asked.

Abel nodded.

"Family is complicated, isn't it?" Arvin winked, and the rubies in his eyebrows shined. Abel found himself at a loss for words again. "Mind if I get changed first?" Arvin added. "The Red Talon kin doesn't know I'm—"

"Amazing," Abel blurted before he could stop himself.

Roa quirked an eyebrow at Abel, but Arvin gave a gracious bow. "That I'm friends with her enemy."

"Oh, we're friends now?" Topher pressed him.

"Yes." Abel cut off any bickering that was about to start. "We are."

Arvin looked pleased. "Let's hope my mom doesn't have you eaten before you can ask for her help."

"Yeah," said Abel, doubting his family's plan for the first time since it was hatched. "Let's try not to get eaten."

Arvin snapped his teeth at Abel so they clicked, then let out a laugh. "No promises," he said. Abel's heart beat louder than a Cloudscraper's wings. "Be right back."

With that, the heir to the most dangerous kin in the city slipped inside to change out of his wings and sequined gown.

"How lovely of you to visit!" Jazinda Balk hugged her son warmly and then turned to Abel, his brother, and his friends. "And you brought snacks for Jo and Kiki!"

She gestured toward two Stoneskin dragons behind her. They were small short-wings, about the size of an eighth grader, and instead of scales, they had hard gray skin with random patches of shimmering diamond that grew from their bones. They had no eyes, but the long tendrils of skin and diamond that hung from their chins like wind chimes let them sense through smells and vibrations, like moles.

Stoneskins were extremely rare and hard to catch because they lived in tunnels underneath the Glass Flats outside the city, tunnels they carved with their oversized claws. Each horrid little dragon cost more than Abel's entire building paid in a year of rent, and each one could eat as much as everyone in Abel's building ate in a year too.

Their tendrils flicked up toward Abel.

"They're not food, Mom!" Arvin groaned. He sounded like any other kid talking to their embarrassing parent in front of new friends. Of course, Arvin's embarrassing parent ruled the largest criminal empire ever created, had fed more people to dragons than Abel would probably meet in his whole life, and was currently sitting on a luxurious red leather couch in front of a floor-to-ceiling window in the fanciest apartment Abel had ever seen. She had views of Drakopolis in every direction, looking down at all the dragons flying about their business, all the lights blinking, and all the armored battle dragons that circled the building to stop unauthorized visitors. Arvin had to show his ID seven times just to get in to see his own mother.

"They're friends," he told her.

This time, neither Roa nor Topher objected.

Arvin's mother sighed and drummed her jeweled fingers on her plush armrest, then pointed at Silas. "This one too? You know he's a Dragon's Eye agent?"

Silas tensed. He'd changed into regular clothes for the meeting, his favorite plaid pants and black leather jacket. Abel could tell by how he looked at himself in the mirror outside the apartment that he'd been proud of his civilian attire. He'd even taken a selfie.

Jazinda Balk deflated him with one withering up-down dart of her eyes. "You can't be friends with the Dragon's Eye. They're like dentists. You pay them to keep things working so you can eat whatever you want. But they'll still hurt you the first chance you give them."

"We are not dentists!" Silas objected.

"Does your commanding officer know you're here?" Jazinda laughed. "Or your partner, Kai?"

She smirked; she was showing Abel's brother that she knew everything about him. She had power over him. "You know half your barracks are on my payroll, don't you? And yet, you never take a bribe."

"And I never will." Silas crossed his arms. The Stoneskin dragons pointed their tendrils his way.

"Disappointing," Jazinda huffed. Abel found himself a little proud of his brother. Sure, Silas was a self-righteous goober, but he had principles, and Abel was starting to respect that.

"Mom," Arvin interrupted them. "We need your help."

"We?" She raised her eyebrows at Arvin. "You're really with these kin rejects?"

Arvin nodded. "We can get our dragons back."

"*Our* dragons?" Now Arvin's mother was interested. She leaned forward in her chair. "The ones we had stolen from us?"

Arvin nodded. "Abel found them."

His mother scowled. "The last time I made an agreement with Abel, he poisoned Grackle, beat Sax in battle, and released my dragon into the wild."

"He won," said Arvin. "Fair's fair."

"That doesn't mean I want to do business with him again," the kinner boss replied. "He's lucky I haven't fed his whole family to anything yet."

"You can't feed us to what you don't have," Abel told her, feeling like he needed to speak up for himself. He had to show Jazinda Balk he wasn't afraid of her. "And if you don't help, the Sky Knights are going to take everything from you."

"Are they now?" She looked curious.

"They're hacking dragon DNA," Roa explained, "to turn regular dragons into super-dragons they can control by remote. If they perfect the process, you and your kin won't stand a chance against them."

"I was fighting off enemy kins before you were even born," Jazinda told them. "I don't need some schoolkids telling me how to defend what's mine."

"They're torturing dragons, Mom!" Arvin objected with tears in his eyes.

His mother shot to her feet instantly, grabbed her son by the shoulders. "NEVER show your gentleness to others! I've warned you about this! Your enemies will destroy you the first chance they get. Even your allies! Drakopolis is not for the gentle!"

Her eyes darted around the huge room. She had two guards with her by the door, big people covered in Red Talons tattoos and scars from Red Talons battles, people who looked like they were about as gentle as meat cleavers.

"You have to be tougher than this, Arvy," she told him. "If you're to rule when I'm gone, you *must* be merciless, pitiless, and unsentimental, even about your beloved dragons."

"But I don't want to rule," Arvin whispered back to her. "I want to protect dragons."

His mother snorted.

Abel tried to stay as still as possible. It was super uncomfortable to be standing there for someone else's family drama. He looked at Roa and Topher, who were also acting like they weren't hanging on every word of Arvin's argument with his mom.

The only child of the Red Talons boss didn't want to *be* a Red Talon. If word got out, it would cause a nasty war for control. Jazinda knew it, and now she knew that Abel, his friends, and his brother did too.

She turned to them. "So, you all want me to help you rescue some dragons from my enemies?"

Abel nodded. "Yes, Boss Jazinda," he said. He was trying to show her some respect so maybe she wouldn't have them tossed out a window.

"You're Dragon's Eye," she said to Silas. "Why not just call in the reinforcements?"

"Well, you see—" Abel started to explain, but Roa cut him off.

"We're not snitches, boss," they said. "We came to you first."

Jazinda smiled. *That* was how you showed respect to a crime boss. Abel was glad to have a friend who was smarter than him. He could tame a dragon, but Roa knew how to tame people.

"So you want me to, what?" Jazinda asked. "Attack their underground base?"

"No," said Abel, "it's way too secure to attack. I have a different idea." He looked at his brother, at his friends, and at Arvin, who was regaining his composure. "I want the Red Talons to challenge me to a race."

"And let me guess," she added. "You want us to lose on purpose?"

Now it was Abel's turn to smile. "No, ma'am. You won't have to lose on purpose. Me and Brazza will win no matter what you do."

"Brazza and I," Roa corrected him, but no one corrected him about winning. He and his dragon were the fastest Drakopolis had ever seen, and they all knew it.

And when they won, Lina was gonna steal her.

26

THE SECOND PHASE OF THE plan began at school the next day. There was no time to waste, so Silas made excuses for Arvin at the Academy. Arvin arrived at Abel's school, disguised as a new student. He had the school tie and fake glasses and a beat-up school computer. Turns out, he was really good at disguises.

"Everyone puts on a costume," Arvin said. "Kinner, officer, student, whatever. Some of us just like to *choose* what costume we show the world. Like when I do my dragon queen act. It's not dress-up; it's controlling what part of me people get to see. It's nice to be someone other than Jazinda Balk's son for a while."

"Except you still look richer than anyone who goes to this school," Abel said.

Arvin shrugged. "A dragon can't change *all* its scales."

"What now?" asked Topher.

"Officer Grallup is our target, right?" said Arvin.

"So we have to get him to trust us?" Abel asked.

"Not quite," Arvin explained. "Like my mother always says: In a good scam, any emotion can reel a sucker in. He doesn't need to trust Abel. He just needs to trust what he *feels* about Abel."

"Dislike," said Roa.

"More like disgust," said Topher. "Hatred," he added. "A desire to grind him beneath his boot and let the sewer serpents feast on his sweet blood. A fervent hope that Abel's hair will get lit on fire by an enraged Infernal and that his eyeballs will be gnawed on by—"

"Okay, enough, we get it!" Abel interrupted. "The guy doesn't like me. How are we gonna use that to get him to do what we want?"

"You brought your jacket?" Arvin asked.

Abel nodded. He pulled it out of the backpack where he'd stuffed it. There were signs and pop-up ads all over the city, with blurry videos of a figure in that jacket flying laser-fast from the police. Other than in the race against Lu, Abel hadn't worn it in public since the police chase.

"What if he just arrests me right away?" Abel asked.

"He won't," said Arvin. "We know he's working with the Sky Knights. We have to tempt him with something he can't resist."

Abel took a deep breath and put on the jacket. If they were wrong about what Officer Grallup would do, Abel would be on his way to Windlee Prison before first-period math class. He hadn't done his homework in days, so that might be a relief.

Grallup saw him coming. A grin split his bushy beard as soon as he recognized the jacket. He actually licked his lips as he made his way through the hall toward Abel. His left hand moved to the plastic cuffs on his belt.

Abel was going to get arrested. Grallup probably figured it'd be easier to steal Brazza after Abel was gone, and he'd get the credit for arresting him too. He could win at his day job and his night job at the same time.

"I think we were wrong," Abel whispered to his friends. That's when Lu and her cronies intercepted him from a crossing hallway, just like they'd planned, on orders from the boss of the Red Talons herself.

Of course, the orders didn't say to slam Abel so hard he fell down. Lu added that touch on her own.

"Watch it, loser!" she snarled, loud enough for Grallup to hear. "You see a Red Talon coming, you make way or you make trouble."

From the corner of his eye, Abel saw that Grallup had stopped to listen. The big officer pressed himself against a row of lockers and, as is the way of mediocre spies everywhere, pulled out his phone to pretend he was looking at something, not eavesdropping on the kids.

"Watch it yourself!" Topher, still on his feet, shoved Lu back. A crowd formed around them. Abel got up again. "You only won because you cheated. You're no real dragon racer."

"A win's a win," Lu said. "And a kin's a kin! My kin is better than yours."

Grallup's eyebrows went up over the top of his sunglasses. He was definitely listening.

"How about a rematch?" Abel snapped at Lu. "Or are you too scared?"

"I'm not scared," Lu said. "But I'll need a new dragon."

Arvin smirked. It was his turn to tempt Grallup with something the corrupt officer couldn't resist.

"You can borrow one from me!" Arvin announced, making sure to unwrap his scarf so that the Red Talons tattoo was revealed in a dramatic way. He was *very* good at drama. "It belongs to my mother, Jazinda Balk!"

They all pretended not to hear Officer Grallup suck in an excited breath. They had him. He was going to do exactly what they wanted: tell Drey and the Sky Knights about a race where they might steal *two* amazing dragons for their experiments.

"Then it's settled," Abel told Lu. "Midnight. Tonight! We race again. I'm not gonna lose to some cheap trick this time."

"No," said Lu. "You're gonna lose the old-fashioned way. I'm gonna get that dragon of yours *and* give you a snapdragon wedgie so hard you'll never wear underwear again."

She winked at him. Grallup had fallen for it. He was already walking away like he hadn't heard them but was probably texting Drey already.

A few minutes later, Abel's phone pinged. It was Lina, messaging a thumbs-up.

The Sky Knights were sending her to prove her loyalty. Everything was falling into place.

"Tonight," Roa said as they watched Grallup skulk away.

"You know you *really do* have to win," Arvin said. "Lu wasn't joking about that wedgie thing. She might be on our side, but she wants revenge."

"I know." Abel nodded. "But, Arvin?"

"Yeah?" said Arvin as the bell for first period rang.

"*You* really do have to come to math class with us."

"But I don't even go here!" Arvin sighed as he trudged after them to the classroom.

Even devious plans to raid secret underground lairs had their boring parts.

ANOTHER MIDNIGHT, ANOTHER DRAGON RACE.

Abel stood in his colorful leather jacket, yawning in the runny light of a buzzing neon sign.

No crowd had gathered this time. There was only Fitz to run the race.

"I don't know what game you're all playing," he told Abel from the back of his serpentine dragon, "and I don't want to know. I just hope you're being careful."

"I'm always careful," Abel said, though they both knew that was the opposite of true.

Lu arrived on the back of a sleek gray Steelwing, whose claws were tipped with rubies and whose teeth were polished with gold. *This* was a real racing dragon.

"You told her not to throw the race," Arvin said. "So she sent her best. When you win, it's yours, you know?"

"When I win, I'm releasing it," Abel replied, to which Arvin nodded.

"My mother will *hate* that." He looked gleeful at the thought.

"Will she forgive you?" Abel asked.

"I'm her only son." He shrugged, which wasn't exactly a yes.

"Well, if my plan works, she'll have some of her dragons back and have helped wipe out the leadership of a rival kin," Abel said. "She can't be mad about that, can she?"

"She doesn't get mad," Arvin said ominously. "She gets even."

Abel shuddered. He really needed this plan to work.

"Just win the race first," Roa said. "Worry about what happens after, after."

Fitz explained the rules one more time, the same as the last race. They'd fly a course that he'd laid out, passing checkpoints on the way. They'd have five seconds added to their time for every checkpoint they missed. Whoever had the fastest time at the end, won.

"And no violence," he reminded them. "This is a race, not a battle."

"Not a battle yet," Topher whispered just loud enough for Abel to hear.

"Riders, mount up!" Fitz shouted.

Roa and Lu climbed onto their dragons, side by side.

"Hey, Brazza." Abel rubbed his dragon's flank. "Sorry to ask you to do this again."

The dragon swung her head around to look at him, nodded once, then set her eyes forward. Her gaze locked on Fitz's, and Abel felt her body tense, preparing to fly. She understood the race, and she seemed to understand the stakes too. Or maybe she'd just embraced her competitive side. Either way, when Fitz's dragon launched a rainbow fireball starting signal, Brazza was off the ground at the same instant as Lu's Steelwing.

Abel saw immediately that the new dragon was not used to losing. The moment Brazza pulled ahead of it, the Steelwing thrust its long neck forward, snapped its wings, and wouldn't let itself fall behind. They flew side by side for the first checkpoint.

Almost immediately after it, the second checkpoint was a steep drop down by the pavement. Both dragons dove in unison, flapping madly along the wide empty street for checkpoint three.

"You really need to go faster, Abel," Roa said into his ear.

"Um, thanks, I hadn't noticed," he said back. "Just focus on telling me what I need to know, please?"

"Okay, dragon rider," Roa said. "You *need* to know that you need to go faster. There's a turn coming up. Checkpoints laid out down the third alley on your right. And Lu's got the inside advantage. Unless you get ahead of her, you'll be stuck behind her when the alley narrows."

"Savvy," Abel replied. The Steelwing was on his right, and so was the upcoming turn. Even if they turned at the same time, Lu would be ahead of him, and he'd have to go under or over her to pass. It was really easy to block a dragon that was behind you if your dragon had a strong enough tail.

The Steelwing's tail was barbed from the tip to the base with thick gray spikes strong enough to pierce another dragon's scales. Any attempt to pass would be risky. Brazza might survive a direct hit from the Steelwing's tail, but Abel sure wouldn't.

He leaned away from the Steelwing, which Brazza answered by edging closer to it, so close their wings were nearly touching, then with a lurch, raised her claws, like she was about to attack.

"Brazza! No violence!" Abel shouted at her.

"Abel, no violence!" Roa shouted in his ear.

"AHH! Violence!" Lu shouted in general over the roar of the wind.

The Steelwing screeched and pulled back, and Brazza cut in front of her, rolling over. Then she straightened out, taking the sharp right turn on the inside. They were in the lead.

Abel had to duck as they passed the blinking checkpoint drone.

He exhaled and pressed his face against Brazza, wrapping his arms around the base of her neck. He felt her body shuddering. For a moment, he thought she might be hurt, but then he realized . . . she was laughing.

"Oh, you clever lizard," he whispered.

"What?" Roa said. The microphone broadcast his whispers loud and clear to his friend's ear.

"I think Brazza understands the rules," Abel said. She was weaving back and forth in the narrow alley, slashing her hooked tail around like a live wire. It blocked every attempt Lu made to pass. The Steelwing roared in frustration. "She didn't actually *do* any violence," Abel explained. "And there's no rule against threatening another dragon, right?"

"But how could she know that? She's a . . . Dragons don't . . ." Topher stammered.

"We have no idea what dragons know and don't know," Abel said. "But this one, right now, knows we have to win."

He leaned back, and Brazza dove where the alley split into two levels, one above, one below. A blinking drone hovered behind some laundry strung across the lower level. Lu didn't see it in time, just saw her chance to pass him, so she took the upper alley.

As Abel ducked to avoid some boxer shorts with heart-eyed cartoon wyverns on them, he caught a glimpse of a drone on the upper level too, lurking right next a purple-and-orange neon sign.

"Fitz set two different routes!" he explained. "Sneaky!"

"He doesn't know it's a fake race," Roa reminded Abel.

"Except it's *not* a fake race," Abel reminded Roa. Brazza accelerated just below the low ceiling of the alley. Overhead lights buzzed past his head. He had to stay almost lying down on Brazza's back to keep from being clotheslined by literal clotheslines.

Brazza flew effortlessly past Fitz's drones. Her eyes were sharper and her reflexes faster than any human's; she didn't miss a single one. She even took a quick diving detour to the bottom row of shops, where a cake seller had laid out his latest three-tiered celebration cake.

Brazza swallowed it in one gulp, then flapped up fast, right through the next checkpoint.

"Sorry!" Abel yelled, hoping his dragon hadn't just stolen *too* expensive a cake. "I didn't even know dragons ate cake," he muttered, but Brazza heard him. She risked a head turn to stick out her long forked tongue.

They burst out of the alley into the night sky, just before Lu's Steelwing burst out from a completely different opening above them.

They were closer to the next drone, but Lu, being so high up, had the advantage as she dove, gravity adding to her speed.

They were neck and neck again, side by side, each dragon pushing itself to fly as fast as its wings would allow. Abel felt his vision narrowing. His ears buzzed, and Topher's g-rig went to work, clearing his head again. On the next turn, he was sure they pulled at least eight g's.

"Doesn't she remember that the winner's dragon gets stolen?" Abel groaned into his mic through gritted teeth. He was pulling back on the reins with all his strength so that Brazza pulled against them with all hers, faster and faster.

The Steelwing matched her wingbeat for wingbeat.

"Some dragons will starve themselves in their lairs if they

think their treasure hoard might get stolen while they're out hunting," Roa said. "And some people will break their backs and wreck their hearts, if they think it will protect their pride."

"Huh?" Abel replied.

"Roa's saying some people are fools," Topher cut in.

"No," Roa snapped back. "Some people just have different hurts than we do. Like, when you twist your ankle, you try to keep the weight off it, right? Well, Lu's pride is her twisted ankle. Maybe she's willing to do a lot to keep from hurting it again, even if it hurts her worse."

"Like I said," said Topher. "Fools."

Abel cleared his throat, reminding his friends that *he* was the one flying at four hundred miles per hour on the back of a dragon between gleaming skyscrapers and shimmering pavement. Maybe they could save the mental health discussions for another time.

"Right, sorry," Roa said. "Left turn coming up in half a mile."

Abel took the turn when it came, then weaved between a staggered row of billboards where Fitz had set the drones up in a zigzag pattern. The Steelwing matched him turn for turn, dive for dive, as they came into the final stretch.

The drones were in stair-step pattern, starting high and dropping down to the finish line, forcing the dragons to dive nearly straight down at times, then level out to hit the next checkpoint, then dive again almost instantly. It was a sickening, lurching descent. The Steelwing stayed at Abel's side the whole time. He couldn't do anything to get Brazza moving any faster, and Lu's dragon was at the limits of its speed too.

But Brazza didn't like to lose.

As they came to the last drop to the last checkpoint, Brazza didn't dive. Instead, she folded her wings in front of her body, turned into a ball, and spun past the checkpoints and over the finish line, accelerating past seven hundred miles per hour.

Even the fancy g-rig couldn't protect him from this.

Abel would've cheered his victory, except he'd blacked out.

• • •

When he woke up, Lu, Roa, Topher, and Arvin stood over him, spraying him with a shook-up can of Diet Firebreather Soda.

"Come on, Abel!" Arvin whispered urgently in his ear. Topher shook his shoulders so hard he might've woken up even if he hadn't survived the landing. "You won! You gotta go!"

His vision cleared just in time to see he was lying on the pavement about fifty feet from his dragon. Arvin had changed into the exact same outfit Abel was wearing . . . except for his one-of-a-kind jacket.

"Gimme," Arvin said bluntly, and though it felt like every organ in Abel's body had switched places, he sat up and shook off his beloved jacket so that Arvin could slide it on. The boy popped on his helmet and lay across the pavement, pretending to be Abel. His friends crowded around, cheering and coaxing his double, while Abel used the distraction to slip away.

He belted himself into the harness that he'd tied to Brazza's belly before the race, just as the dragon thief showed up.

The final phase of the plan to infiltrate the lab and liberate the dragons had begun.

"I hope you know what you're doing," Lina whispered, climbing into Brazza's saddle. "Because if I can't control this dragon, we're both in a world of trouble."

"Don't worry," Abel told her. "Just act like you normally would when you're stealing a dragon."

She shrugged and jostled the reins. Strapped underneath, Abel stroked Brazza's belly. "Play it cool, girl," he said. "She's with me."

Brazza took off, allowing herself to be stolen, and no one on the ground but Abel's friends knew he was still attached to her. He was a little nervous to be stowed away underneath his own dragon without his jacket or helmet, flying to a hostile underground lab, but Brazza was taking the much bigger risk.

If something went wrong, she'd be turned into a science experiment. Abel wouldn't be able to save her, or save the city from what she'd do.

FOR A SECRET LAB, THE Sky Knights' security was pretty relaxed. Lina flew Brazza in right on schedule, without being stopped or inspected. The Sky Knights trusted Lina, in as much as *any* criminals trusted one another.

Too bad for them, Abel thought with some satisfaction.

"You have any trouble?" Captain Drey asked. Lina acted like she was steering Brazza on foot down the wide central corridor. In reality, Abel was underneath, keeping her calm and nudging in the direction they needed to go by pulling the underside of her reins and saddle straps. It'd been hard enough to remember to pull in the opposite direction when he was sitting upright in the saddle. It was even harder hanging upside down.

"Hey!" Drey shouted up at Lina. Brazza had turned left when she was supposed to turn right, nearly trampling him. "You fry your brain on video games like the rest of your generation?"

"Sorry, boss," Lina said. "She's a tricky dragon. Might not be worth experimenting on?"

Drey snorted. "She's the fastest dragon we've ever seen. Why don't you let the scientists do their job, and you stick to yours, dragon snatcher."

"Savvy," Lina grumbled. Abel poked Brazza's belly so that she snapped her jaws in surprise. Drey nearly jumped out of his skin. Abel could feel Brazza's belly ripple with dragon laughter.

When they reached the big door into the laboratory, Lina slid off Brazza's back. She took out her phone to check the time, then made a casual proposal—which Drey needed to accept for their plan to work.

"So I'll go back for the other dragon now?" she suggested. "It was fast too. And we need more dragons, right?"

Drey smiled. "*That's* the spirit! Go get 'em, Lina!"

Abel grinned. So far, so good.

Lina had done her job and been ordered back out into the night. No one would suspect her of treachery if she wasn't here when the treachery occurred.

The plan now was for her to leave a door open for the Red Talons on her way out. *They* were waiting to bust in and seize control of the facility. Arvin would hack the computers from inside the lab and release the dragons one by one. The Red Talons would take theirs back—it was an unfortunate but necessary compromise—and the rest would be quietly led out through the secret entrance and taken to the edge of the city, to be released into the wild.

Once they were out, Silas and the Dragon's Eye would raid the lab in a big show and arrest all the Sky Knights. And because Lina wouldn't be there when the raid happened, Silas could clear her name. She'd no longer be a fugitive. Things could go back to the way they were before.

As long as Lina got out of there right away.

"Not so fast," a voice bellowed before Lina left the room. Abel's knuckles went white gripping the lower saddle strap. He knew that voice. Officer Grallup.

"Where is your brother right now?"

"My guess is he's still at the finish line," Lina said as innocently as possible. "Either recovering from a concussion or crying over his stolen dragon."

She showed him video of the finish, the moment when Brazza rolled across the line. She'd tossed Abel from her back, sprawled across the concrete. Grallup actually licked his lips when Abel's helmet smacked the street. Then Abel's friends gathered around, to cover Abel and Arvin's costume change. The next thing Grallup saw was the helmeted Arvin pretending to be Abel, standing up on shaky legs.

"May I go now, *Officer*?" Lina said, making the word sound like the worst thing you could call a person. Abel's sister almost never used curse words, but she could make totally innocent words sound like them. She'd once been grounded for two weeks for saying the word "pancakes" in a way that made their father cry. "Some of us have actual jobs, not just spying on schoolchildren."

Grallup's hand lurched toward his stun gun, but Drey gave him a look that stopped him from drawing it.

"Lina, just go," Drey told her.

The moment Lina was gone, Grallup told the Sky Knight boss, "I don't trust that girl."

"She's a dragon thief," Drey said. "But she's *my* dragon thief. And she's the best there is."

"The whole family is sneaky."

"We've got the dragon," Drey said. "What can they possibly do now?"

"I guess you're right," Officer Grallup told him. "If you'll excuse me."

He trudged out of the laboratory. Abel took a deep breath and let himself relax for a brief moment. Brazza waited while the scientists prepared their big magnetic cuffs. As the first one approached, Abel stroked her belly to keep her calm. The man bent down with the first of the cuffs—and was startled to see a kid hanging underneath the saddle ringing.

The scientist froze.

"Heya," Abel said cheerfully. "This is the part where you want to run away."

The scientist dropped the cuff on the floor as Abel swung himself out of the straps, scrambling onto Brazza's back. He felt like quite the action hero.

Except his foot got caught. Abel ended up flopping sideways across the saddle, his rear end pointing at the ceiling, his chin bouncing off Brazza's side with an "Ooof!"

She didn't need him in the saddle to do her part, though, and she didn't care so much if Abel felt like an action hero. Dragons don't really care if eighth graders feel cool or not. She reared up on her back legs and snapped her wings open, knocking Drey and all the unlucky scientists over.

If she was the type to make noises, Brazza might've roared. Instead, she let her claws do the talking. She swiped aside the huge injection machine, toppling it, then smashed a table covered in computer tablets. Brazza lowered her head and lunged forward, using her horns to burst through the doors into the rest of the facility.

So far, there was no sign of the Red Talons.

Abel tapped his earbuds to make sure they were working. "Check, check," he said. "Anyone copy?"

He got no answer, which meant they weren't inside yet. *Where are they?* Abel worried. *Surely Lina would have the doors open by now?*

Brazza, in the meantime, was enjoying herself in the way only an ornery dragon could. She ran from the lab and snatched one of the scientists in her jaws by the waistband of his pants. She hoisted him off his feet.

"AHHH!" the unfortunate scientist yelled. Abel felt bad for the wedgie the scientist was getting as Brazza bounced him furiously up and down. He might've been the first person in history to get a wedgie from a dragon. "Stop!" he pleaded, his voice rising an octave higher with every brief-breaking bounce of Brazza's head. "I'M juST a TECHniCIAN! PleASE!"

Abel was finally sitting upright in the saddle, just in time to answer the poor man's begging. "You do experiments on dragons," he snarled.

"It's my job!" the man cried out.

"Well, you should've quit," Abel said. "Now you get to open all the doors for us."

"I can't!" the scientist said. "If I do, they'll—"

"What?" Abel interrupted him. "Feed you to a dragon?" Brazza shook her head, tossing the man side to side. Abel didn't think he needed the reminder that he was currently dangling from a dragon's jaws, but the man's yelps made Abel smile a little.

What does that say about me? Abel wondered. *Am I enjoying this?*

Abel had never taken pleasure in another person's suffering before. The thought that he did now chilled him. He'd known bullies all his life: the kinners who shook down everyone in the neighborhood, the kids at school who tripped other students, and the onlookers who laughed and filmed it instead of helping. The kin bosses. Abel hadn't ever imagined being like any of them. He thought of himself as a hero. But would a hero use his dragon to hurt someone until he got his way?

The only difference between a hero and villain, Abel thought, *is what they're willing to do to get what they want.*

Abel decided not to become a villain.

"Put him down," Abel said with a sigh. Then, remembering his manners, he added: "Please."

Brazza hesitated, then lowered her head until the man's feet were touching the floor. She let him go, and he collapsed, his pants halfway up his back.

"Stop right there!" a Sky Knight yelled. Abel looked around for any sign of the Red Talons, but still, they weren't inside. Brazza turned to face the kinners who'd followed her.

Not only did the Sky Knights have huge stun spears and handheld stun guns, a trio of guard dragons had arrived in the wide corridor. There was an Emerald Widow Maker, a pale blue Fog dragon, and a bright orange Reaper that Abel recognized immediately because he'd been seeing it in his dreams every night since the tragedy at the raceway: Carrot Soup Supreme.

It was a ridiculous name for what had been transformed into a truly terrifying dragon.

THE ORANGE DRAGON HAD NO RIDER.

Instead, Drey stood beside it with his phone.

"Abel," he said. "Nice to see you again. Thank you for bringing such a wonderful dragon for us."

"She's not for you," Abel replied. "None of them are. We're getting out of here!"

Drey laughed. He tapped an app on his phone, and Carrot Soup Supreme formed a ball of fire in its throat. The last time Abel had seen Carrot Soup Supreme, it didn't have a breath weapon at all.

"I don't think you are," said Drey. "You see, our experiments are going well, but I haven't tested the control program in battle conditions yet! I'd love the chance." Drey paused with his finger over his phone screen. "Unless you want to surrender quietly? It'd be a shame to injure your amazing specimen, but I supposc we can extract the DNA from her after you're both destroyed."

I really should have let Brazza keep that scientist hostage, Abel thought. He looked down the corridor, searching for any sign of the Red Talons. *I could use some ruthless, criminal, dragon-battling backup right about now.*

Drey pursed his lips, considering Abel's long silence, then shrugged and tapped his phone. With that simple flick of his human finger, the big orange dragon roared and spat a white-hot ball of fire.

Brazza's tail snapped around the length of her whole body. The gleaming hook on the end of it batted the fireball aside.

Drey tapped a few more commands in his app, and the orange dragon roared again, the Fog dragon shrieked, and the Emerald Widow Maker simply charged.

"Let's see what they can do!" Drey cheered.

Abel pulled on the reins, trying to turn to escape, but Brazza wasn't the sort of dragon to back away from a fight—or to forgive anyone shooting fire at her.

She planted her four legs and braced herself, ready to go claw to claw against all three dragons.

"I admire your guts," Abel told her. "But there is no way we can win this fight!"

Brazza didn't seem to care. She raced like she couldn't lose, and now she was going to fight the same way, even if speed was her gift, not violence. Abel gave up on trying to command her. He thought about jumping off and making a run for it now that all the people who weren't riding dragons had hidden behind the nearest heavy equipment they could find.

But instead, he held on to her back. He shut his eyes, remembering her crouched in her stall at the Burning Market, alone and abandoned, angry at everything. She'd been craving someone just to sit and read her a story. No wonder Brazza was so angry. She thought she was alone in the world. Abel wasn't going to let her think that again.

He held her neck and whispered to her, "Whatever happens, I'm here."

He felt a shift. Her weight moved toward her front legs, and Abel tilted ever so slightly forward. He dared to open one eye, and the other snapped open on its own at the same instant his mouth opened to scream.

All three dragons were closing in on them, mouths wide and breath weapons blasting. Abel lost track of Drey, but he was on his phone somewhere, controlling the three.

Flame, fog, and jagged jewels shot toward Abel, but Brazza's shift had been just enough for her to fall forward into a perfect shoulder roll under the attack. Her wings curled around to protect Abel while she crashed through the legs of all the three dragons, tripping them with their own momentum.

The dragons fell into a tangled heap. Brazza popped up again; then she jumped into the air, spreading her wings while Abel was still catching his breath.

"You have *got* to warn me next time you do that!" Abel pleaded.

Brazza flapped forward and burst over the three dragons' heads, racing straight for the entry platform they'd used to get inside. She was going to try bursting through the doors and escaping.

"Wait, no!" Abel cried out. "We can't leave! We have to stick to the plan! We have to wait! We have to get the rest of the dragons out!"

Brazza ignored him, flying fast for safety. But the huge door was sealed, so she turned with nauseating speed and went back over the scrum in the corridor, speeding up in the hunt for another way out. The three dragons were just getting on their feet again when she blazed over their heads and zipped around the corner. A flurry of jagged gems slammed into the wall behind them, sinking several inches deep into the steel where Abel's body had just been. The Widow Maker screeched.

The corridor was a blur of lights. Sky Knights fired their stun spears at Brazza as she flew over them, but they didn't even come close to hitting her. She was too fast.

"I know it's scary!" Abel cried out to her. "But we can't just leave! We have to find a way to help these dragons! We have to slow down!"

Behind them, the pale blue Fog dragon unleashed a thick mist, which rolled toward them.

The mist from normal Fog dragons makes people feel drowsy and silly—almost pleasant. Until, of course, they fall asleep and get eaten. But Abel heard sizzling on the walls and realized quickly that *this* Fog dragon had been engineered so its mist was acidic. The steel it touched bubbled and blistered and began to run in metallic beads, melting to the floor.

If it caught up with them, it would do worse to Abel's flesh.

"Okay, you can speed up!" Abel said, and pulled the reins again. Brazza accelerated, the mist behind them fading. Carrot Soup Supreme joined the Fog dragon in the chase.

Abel spotted another exit platform just ahead. Although it was closed, it looked like Brazza was going to try to slam through it, like she had in the department store.

"Listen, dragons like gold, right?" Abel tried desperately to reason with her. "Well, humans have this thing, the Golden Rule. It means you treat other beings like you'd want them to treat you. And, well, how would you feel if you were being held captive here? Wouldn't you want someone to rescue you?"

Brazza sped up and lowered her head. She was going to ram the door with her horns. Abel was pretty sure it was reinforced against a dragon, even one flying as fast as she was. This was no department store wall. If she hit this door, their bodies would be shattered and it'd *still* be shut.

Behind them, all three attack dragons were in pursuit but had slowed down, ready to devour whatever was left after they splattered against the steel.

"So I know it's not, like, literal, actual gold," Abel pleaded. "But the Golden Rule gives you something more valuable. Not every treasure can be held in your claws, you know? Sometimes the invisible treasures are the most valuable!"

Abel was no philosopher. He'd actually read that last part in the fortune cookie that came with Brazza's take-out food last week, but Brazza didn't know that.

Just before they hit the door, all three dragons behind them fired. Brazza dove at the same moment, tucking her head under her body like a swimmer turning laps in a pool. She shot straight back below the pursuing dragons.

Their breath weapons hit the door at the same time. An instant later, it exploded open.

"Did you get that from a fortune cookie?" Topher's voice filled Abel's ears. He was receiving a signal again!

Over his shoulder, through the blasted door, a flock of armored dragons poured in, Red Talon riders on their backs. Behind them, Arvin piloted a midnight-blue long-wing Colossus, with Roa and Topher in passenger harnesses.

"A little late!" Abel said. "And yes, I *did* get that from a fortune cookie. Wisdom is like dried gum on the sidewalk. Once you start looking for it, you can find it anywhere."

He'd gotten that from a gum wrapper.

Now the three attack dragons were outnumbered by Red Talons. *Where's Lina?* Abel wondered.

"Surrender!" Jazinda Balk yelled from the back of a sleek red

Heartrender Reaper. Her two Stoneskins flapped at its sides. Her goons spread out around her, riding every manner of dragon Abel could think of, and some he didn't even recognize.

Sax and Grackle, two Red Talons who'd terrorized Abel's neighborhood for years, rode matching wyverns, which they steered down to the floor and stopped directly in front of Drey. Poison gas clouds bubbled in the dragons' mouths. It was nice to see the kinners threatening someone else for a change.

"You really think you can beat us?" Drey called up to Jazinda. He held his phone up to hit the buttons, but Jazinda Balk fired a single pulse from a stun gun at her hip, frying the device in his hands.

"Ouch!" He dropped it.

Jazinda grinned, but Drey's voice came out fierce and furious as he stared at the wreckage of his phone on the floor.

"You fool! If I die today, there will be a hundred more Sky Knights to take my place and carry on the work. We aren't like you! The Sky Knights believe in something."

"The Red Talons believe in something too!" Jazinda Balk laughed. "We believe it's better to be on a dragon's back than in its jaws. Which is where you'll be in five seconds, if you don't put your hands up and lie on the ground."

Drey smiled at her and nodded. "Well played," he said, putting his hands in the air. "One thing, though . . ." he added.

Abel's heart thundered in his chest. When a kin boss smiled and said they had "*one* thing" to add, it was never something good. Just once, couldn't they ominously offer an extra slice of pizza? Or spring the surprise of, like, free movie tickets?

Nope. Definitely not this time.

Drey slammed his palm down onto a computer panel on the wall next to him. "If I don't get out of here alive, neither do any of you!"

An earsplitting siren blared. A line of code projected into the air and then vanished.

"Good luck," said Drey as every door to every dragon stall slid open along the corridor. From inside, the captive dragons smelled their first whiffs of freedom.

This was *not* part of Abel's plan. Some of them roared. Others screeched. They had been released, not one at a time like Abel had planned, but all at once.

And with his phone in pieces on the ground, the mutant dragons were no longer under Drey's control.

They were no longer under *anyone's* control.

There was a moment of terrible, eerie silence, the only sounds the beating of dragons' wings in the dark.

And then came the mayhem.

DRAGONS BURST FROM THEIR STALLS up and down and all along the walls, like bees swarming out of a hive. Many were confused and disoriented in the sudden light of the corridor. Some dove for the floor, some launched toward the ceiling, and some just stopped where they were and blasted fireballs into the air. They bumped into each other, screeching, breathing fire, breathing fog, breathing acid and poison gas and ice.

But there were also dragons who'd had stranger experiments done to them. There was a dragon that spat gumballs, another that belched huge clouds of bubbles, a dragon that spat slivers of bone.

"The monsters," Roa gasped over the earpiece.

"It's not their fault," Abel said. "The scientists did this to them."

"I'm *talking* about the scientists," Roa replied.

Through the chaos of dragons, Abel saw Arvin's Colossus dive into the fray with a roar. It smashed a stack of crates with one swipe of its huge foot and sent three lab technicians scrambling for cover.

One of them was scooped up by a dragon that looked like a cross between a Frost dragon and Sunrise Reaper. It was blue as ice but sparkled like starlight. It tossed the scientist aside just before colliding with a Green Cloudscraper ridden by a Red Talon kinner. The dragons tore at each other in the air, and the rider had to jump for his life.

"We have to do something!" Abel cried.

"He had some kind of doomsday code in his program!" Arvin shouted. He'd given Roa the reins of his dragon as he frantically typed on a laptop strapped to himself. "I can't get into the app. I can't hack into anything here— Watch out!"

Abel saw he'd been warning Roa. A mutant with translucent scales and skin dove at them, three hearts visibly beating in its chest and a ball of blue flame growing in its gullet. Roa rolled the dragon out of the line of fire. They weren't a bad pilot, but Arvin took over and got them to a safer perch. Sax and Grackle chased the strange clear dragon away.

The corridors echoed with dragon roars and human screams.

Abel felt helpless against the melee. In a kin battle, the riders kept their dragons from hurting each other too badly, but this was more like the dragon battles in the ancient stories, fights to the death that had nearly driven all dragons to extinction.

The Red Talons flew through the corridors, defending themselves and chasing down Sky Knights, blasting their supplies. Many of the newly released experimental dragons were flying and fighting, in states of pure panic. This wasn't the quiet breakout Abel had planned. This was a riot.

"I didn't mean for this to happen," Abel muttered. He felt sick to his stomach.

A torrent of flame filled the air just over his head. He had to duck to keep from catching fire. Brazza flapped backward, pulling away from the battle, frightened in a way Abel hadn't seen her frightened before.

Tears streaked down his face. Lina was missing, the dragons were out of control, and he didn't have a way out for any of them.

He'd been such a fool to think he could lead a plan this complex and have nothing go wrong. He was just a kid, one who thought he was cleverer than all Drakopolis. Now everyone was paying the price.

As he struggled to keep Brazza steady, an eyeless dragon with huge hooked foreclaws and nothing but spikes on its face came flying straight for him. Its spikes opened to show a mouth that was rows and rows of more spikes all the way down its throat. It screeched as it attacked. Brazza couldn't fly backward fast enough to get away.

Just before the spiked dragon hit, a wyvern with a mechanical claw smashed into it, knocking it off course. Lu's wyvern, Felix! His claw had somehow been fused into his scales during the Sky Knights' experiments, and the one blind eye had been replaced with a new robotic one, like a cyborg. The cyborg wyvern tossed the spiked dragon to the floor, then dove to grapple with it jaw to jaw and claw to claw.

Near the floor, Abel saw Jazinda stalking Drey on her Heart-render. A Heartrender Reaper shot narrow needles of super-hot fire that could cut right through the seams in any armor worn by man or beast.

Drey wasn't wearing any armor at all, and he wasn't on a dragon. He was trying to find a place to hide. The two Stoneskins were at Jazinda's side, protecting her from attack while she stalked her human prey.

At the other end of the huge corridor, Carrot Soup Supreme had cornered Arvin's long-wing on the ground. Topher leapt off its back, waving a stun stick, trying to scare the orange dragon away.

It was not working.

Abel coaxed Brazza to dive for them, landing heavy at the blue dragon's side. She lashed her tail over her head like a scorpion, pushing Carrot Soup Supreme back.

"Nice to see you again," Arvin called over to him through the earbuds.

"Thanks for taking care of my jacket," Abel told him.

"Looks better on you." Arvin smiled and tossed it to him across the distance between dragons.

Abel wasn't sure how to take a compliment from the heir to the Red Talon kin in the middle of a deadly dragon fracas, but he seemed a little lighter in his saddle at the thought. He smiled as he put it on. He felt more like himself again.

"We need to get out of here," he said.

"What about the rest of these dragons?" Roa asked.

Abel looked all around and blew out his cheeks. "I'm not sure we *should* be letting them out," he admitted. "Look at them. They've gone berserk, every one of them. How can we let them out into the city like this?"

"How can we leave them here?" Roa replied.

It was like a trick question on a test, one with no right answer, but where not answering wasn't an option either. Abel wished someone else could just tell them what to do, but there was no instruction manual for doing the right thing. Would it be wrong to free them? They were dangerous and wild, but that's what free dragons were, right? And maybe, in the wild, away from human technology, they'd regain control of themselves.

Was it guaranteed? No. There were no guarantees in freedom.

Was it safe?

Also no. But freedom wasn't the same as safety, and these dragons had a right to be free.

It might be dangerous, but it was also necessary.

Sometimes you just had to make the best choice that you could in a bad situation, and Abel's best choice had to be on the side of dragons. He still had to get them out.

He was about to explain that to his friends when the situation went from bad to worse.

All the lights in the facility turned red.

A siren blared again.

"This facility is under quarantine!" a mechanical voice announced. "Decontamination to commence in T-minus ten minutes. All personnel evacuate immediately. Have a nice day."

"What does that mean?" Abel asked.

"I think 'have a nice day' is pretty obvious," Topher replied. Four mutants had started circling above them. Arvin's Colossus kept its head up, watching them with narrowed eyes and a blue flame glowing behind its snarling teeth.

"I meant the other part," Abel said.

"That means this whole place is going to be flooded with gaseous acid in ten minutes," Roa said. "Dissolving anything that's still in here."

"The Sky Knights are destroying the evidence of their crimes," Abel said.

"It's not just the evidence they're destroying," Roa said. "It's the witnesses too."

"Us," Topher added.

Huge steel bars slid down over the huge steel doors. Sky Knights were slipping out of access halls and vents, sealing the escape routes behind them.

"Can you hack the building?" Abel asked Arvin.

Arvin shook his head. Even on the back of gigantic fire-breathing long-wing Colossus, he was helpless against a few invisible lines of computer code.

"Decontamination in nine minutes," the mechanical voice announced.

"How come time only ever slows down in school?" Topher wondered. "Never when you actually want it to."

"We have to stop the countdown!" Roa said.

"We have to get out of here!" Topher said.

"We have to get a copy of their program!" Abel said, and he leapt off Brazza's back.

"What are you doing?" Roa shouted.

"We might not be able to deprogram the dragons," Abel called over his shoulder. "But someone is going to be able to." He ducked into the nearest human-sized doorway. "Don't leave without me!" he added.

He ran to the first computer console he could find. Abel pulled out his phone and plugged it in to one of the data ports. A hologram popped up, flashing red and showing a countdown clock.

8:27

8:26

8:25

He swiped it away and saw a screen with a long list of file names and codes and things he didn't understand at all. He didn't *need* to understand them. This was just like copying someone else's math homework; you could never explain what you were looking at if anyone asked you to, but it might be enough just to keep you from failing. Not that Abel would copy someone else's math homework. That'd be cheating. He wasn't a cheater. Except that one time, but they were doing a thing in geometry that he just couldn't get his head around and Roa tried to explain it to him fifteen times and it—

Focus, he told himself. *This is not the time to do that distracted thing.*

He found the Copy button in the File menu and hit Select All and Download.

A little progress bar popped up as the download commenced. Outside the door, there was screaming, roaring, flashes of light, and the sounds of bone scraping metal.

"You all still alive out there?" he asked.

"For now!" Roa replied. "Hurry up, though. Brazza is looking impatient."

"She always looks like that," Abel said.

"Yeah, but this time, I agree with her," Roa replied.

"Decontamination in eight minutes," the mechanical voice announced.

"My mom's made an opening at the other end of the facility," Arvin said. "We have to go, now!"

Abel looked at the progress bar. It was a little over halfway done.

"Go without me," Abel told them.

"What? No!" Roa replied. "We don't leave our friends behind. Come on!"

"I have to finish downloading this data," Abel said. "This is how we prove what they did. This is how we deprogram the dragons and bargain for my sister's freedom."

"Your sister wouldn't want you to die saving her!" Roa argued.

"I'm not gonna die," Abel answered. "I'm gonna get justice."

"It's Drakopolis, Abel," Arvin told him. "There is no justice."

"There will be this time," Abel promised. "There will be justice."

"Then we wait with you," Roa declared.

"My mom is not gonna be happy about me dying for a bunch of kids she hates," Arvin said. "So I guess that's a good enough reason for me to stay."

Abel smiled. He was sad his friends had to risk their lives for him but glad they'd decided to. He felt scared and righteous too. It was hard to hold all those feelings in at the same time. He felt like one of these experimental dragons himself, packed full of too many different things, all the emotions clawing at each other inside. It was hard to feel like you were a hundred different dragons at the same time.

Maybe that's how all people feel, Abel thought. *We're all made up of too many different dragons.*

"Decontamination in six minutes," the mechanical voice announced. Abel had gotten lost in his thoughts again. When he looked at the download progress bar, it was just finishing. Sometimes being distracted by his own brain had an upside: He could tune out the boring parts.

He snatched his phone out of the data port and turned for the door back to the corridor.

"Got it!" he announced. "On my way to y —" He froze. Someone stood between him and the door, someone he really didn't want to see.

Lina.

She was supposed to be long gone. Instead, she was in the grip of Officer Grallup, who held a thick dragon-talon knife to her throat.

"I'll take that phone, kid," he told Abel. "If you want your sister back with her head still attached."

OFFICER GRALLUP PRESSED THE SHARP tip of the knife against Lina's neck. He'd stuffed a gag into her mouth so all she could do was grunt and squirm in his grip. Red lights flashed all around them, and the roars of the dragons in the corridor shook the whole structure. For a moment, Abel felt dizzy. This was like a vision of some terrible underworld, the afterlife you're sent to when every choice you ever made was the wrong one.

"Turn over the phone," Grallup commanded.

"If I give it to you," Abel said, "my sister goes back to jail."

"If you don't give it to me," Grallup replied, "then your sister dies right here. I'm not negotiating with some middle-school punk. I'm here to take the files. After that, maybe you'll get out alive."

"If I make it out, I can still testify against you," Abel said.

"Who would believe you?" Officer Grallup said. "You're a wanted criminal. I'm the decorated Kin Intervention Safety Specialist who first identified you as a dangerous kinner and emerged with priceless data on how to hack a dragon. *If* you get out of here, you'll join Lina in Windlee Prison. I'll be given a parade."

Lina grunted something Abel didn't understand.

"You'd sell out the Sky Knights?" Abel asked.

"I'll sell this data to the highest bidder—the Dragon's Eye, the Sky Knights. Whoever. Grallup is loyal to Grallup. And your time is up."

"You're not offering me much of a choice," Abel said.

"I tried to warn you, kid," Officer Grallup told him, grinning. "Once you get involved with the kins, there are no good choices."

"Decontamination in five minutes," the mechanical voice announced.

"Abel, are you okay?" Roa's voice came through his earbuds.

"Just give me a second," Abel said, both to Roa and Grallup.

"You don't have a second," said Grallup.

"We don't have a second," said Roa at the same time.

Abel sighed. He tossed the phone toward Grallup, who shoved Lina forward. Grallup caught the phone one-handed, grinned, and raced out the door.

Except he walked right into Brazza's waiting mouth.

Officer Grallup didn't even have time to make a sound before Brazza's jaws closed around him.

Roa sat proudly on her back. "Brazza let me ride her!" they announced.

Brazza showed her teeth in a wide draconic grin. There was Grallup, standing terrified on the tip of her tongue, reaching out between her teeth like a prisoner behind bars.

"I'm sorry!" he pleaded. "Take the phone back. Take it! Please don't let her eat me!"

"You deserve to be eaten!" Abel snarled. Grallup yelped.

This is what power feels like, Abel thought. *Life and death at my command. This is how dragons feel all the time.*

Abel's heart raced at the thought, but he exhaled. *Power doesn't create you*, he thought. *It reveals you. This is not who I am.*

He put out his hand to take the phone from the terrified officer and then rested a hand on Brazza's snout.

He didn't say anything, but the dragon understood. She spat Grallup out, covered in hot dragon drool. He curled up, whimpering, on the floor.

"If I were you, I'd start looking for a way out," Abel said.

"And I'd lie low if you do get out of here," Lina added, spitting her gag out. She held up her own phone, which had been recording in her pocket. "You're not going to find many friends in Drakopolis."

She hit Play. *"I'll sell this data to the highest bidder—the Dragon's Eye, the Sky Knights. Whoever. Grallup is loyal to Grallup,"* his own voice played back to him as his eyes widened.

He scuttled to his feet and ran, his boots making wet squishing sounds with every step.

"Think he'll make it?" Abel asked.

"People like him always make it," Lina said. "He'll find some rock to crawl under." She looked at Abel. "You're a good kid for letting him go."

"Thanks," said Abel. "Now it's our turn."

Abel and Lina climbed onto Brazza's back, and Abel took Roa's spot in the saddle again. "You two need to hold on tight," he said. "There's only one safety harness. Getting out of here is going to be tricky."

"It's going to be impossible if we don't get a move on!" Arvin yelled from the back of his Colossus. The dragon shot a fireball into the air just as Carrot Soup Supreme dove for them, sending it swerving in another direction.

"So, we gotta get all these dragons to follow us out," Abel said. He looked over at Arvin and Topher, then over his shoulder at his sister and Roa. Then he patted Brazza's neck. "Ready to pick a fight?"

Brazza didn't give any sign she understood, except to flex her legs and jump. She snapped her wings open and slipped right behind Carrot Soup Supreme.

The orange dragon whirled on her, and she dove below, taunting it to follow. The chase was on.

"You're wild, Abel," Arvin said over the earbuds. "Absolutely wild."

"Hey, let's go annoy some killer mutants!" Topher cheered.

Arvin joined the chase, drawing more mutants' attention, and they raced for the exit Arvin's mother had made.

"Make a left up ahead," Arvin told them. "The Red Talons blew open a door at the end of that corridor— Watch your six!"

The orange dragon was right on Brazza's tail, spitting fireballs, forcing them to weave and dodge. She made the left turn so sharp, Roa and Lina were nearly thrown off her back, but the orange dragon didn't slow. Its DNA had been altered so it was just as fast as she was.

Its next fireball nearly hit them, but Brazza batted it away. One ember caught in Lina's hair.

"Your sister's on fire!" Roa shouted as they patted the flames out.

"Warned you getting out of here would be tricky!" Abel shouted.

"Decontamination in three minutes," the mechanical voice announced.

"What happened to four?" Abel wondered.

"Time flies when you're having fun," Arvin answered in his ear.

Abel dared a glance back and saw Arvin's long-wing weaving and dodging, pursued by dozens of berserker dragons. Arvin was trying evasive flying while Topher stood on the big dragon's back with his stun stick up, swatting the diving snouts and claws as they circled and mobbed.

"I see the exit!" Roa shouted. Abel saw only a dead end of solid steel ahead. "Up there!"

It turned out the Red Talons had not blown open a door but rather blown a hole in the ceiling, making an opening to the street above. Loose wires sparked, and broken pipes dripped and sprayed water and other liquid that Abel wished was water.

"No way out but through," Lina said. Abel leaned forward to turn Brazza straight up, just as Carrot Soup Supreme spat another ball of fire at them.

They erupted from the ground like a burst of lava from a volcano. The fireball burned up into the night.

Stars and neon lights blazed over them but were suddenly blotted out by a dozen spotlights.

A new voice blared over a loudspeaker, but it wasn't a mechanical computer voice this time. It was Silas.

"This a police action!" he announced. "Land your dragon and surrender immediately. We have you surrounded!"

One quick glance down at the street around the hole showed that the Red Talon kinners had all been arrested the moment they emerged, outnumbered by a massive Dragon's Eye force of long-wings and Reapers and wyverns and drakes and every other military dragon that Drakopolis could muster. Lu was lying on the pavement beside her Steelwing. Grackle and Sax were on the pavement next to their wyverns. Some Sky Knight scientists had been arrested and were already being loaded onto a prisoner carrier on the back of a heavily guarded blue long-wing. Even Arvin's mom was lying on the pavement, all three of her dragons locked in magnetic control cuffs.

The night sky above, and the surrounding streets, were completely filled with Dragon Safety Officers and Dragon's Eye agents. There was no escape. The Red Talons were supposed to lead the mutant dragons out through the garage quietly. Getting arrested along with the Sky Knights was not a part of the plan—and they did not look happy about it. The chaos below the streets had changed Silas's plans. He was now making the biggest kin arrest in the history of Drakopolis.

Silas had three problems, though.

The first was that Brazza's drool had shorted out Abel's phone. He needed the data on it to trade for their freedom.

The second was that the underground laboratory was about to be destroyed by poison gas, which led directly to the third and most immediate problem for everyone, from the kinners to the police surrounding them.

Every last enraged mutant dragon had followed Abel's escape route, and at that very moment, they burst into the night and straight into the police blockade.

Silas might've been asking himself at the very moment, *How do you stop a hundred mutants whose brains have been hacked?*

Abel already knew the answer, though: You couldn't.

"LAND IMMEDIATELY!" SILAS WARNED. THE
spotlights blinded Abel. Brazza thrashed in their white glare.

"AH!" Roa yelled, tossed from Brazza's back.

Lina's hand shot out, catching Roa before they fell.

"Got you!" she yelled, holding Abel's best friend by one wrist.
Below their dangling feet, the broken hole in the concrete flashed
red. The distant mechanical voice announced one minute to
decontamination.

"Abel!" Silas called his name over the loudspeaker, for all the
kinners, cops, and TV cameras to hear. "You have to surrender!"

There was panic in his brother's voice. He was supposed to arrest
the Sky Knights inside the facility, not have them burst out into the
street. He'd been taken by surprise, and Abel had known since
stealing Silas's towel one time at Serpent's Paradise Water Park, his
brother was most dangerous when he was surprised.

Back then, the worst he could do was pummel Abel until their
parents stopped him. Now he had an entire battalion of wyvern
riders at his command.

Brazza thrashed and bucked, trying to escape the bright lights.

"Don't make this harder!" Silas pleaded over the loudspeaker. He
sounded desperate, which was even worse than surprised. "Don't
make us—"

He didn't get to finish his sentence. At that very moment, the eyeless spike-headed dragon shot out from the lab, burst past Brazza, and slammed directly into Silas's wyvern with a blood-boiling screech.

An all-white dragon with gleaming red eyes blasted huge blobs of sticky tar from its mouth; they smacked into the spotlights and blotted them out. The rest of the hacked dragons swarmed after them, and a new battle over the streets of Drakopolis began: military dragons against berserker mutants.

"They're supposed to be going free," Abel cried out. "Not attacking each other!"

Silas's wyvern was tangled claw to claw with the spiked dragon, turning and tumbling in the air, while Kai tried to blast the attacking dragon's soft underbelly with a flamethrower. It had no effect. The spiked dragon didn't *have* a soft underbelly. It was engineered to have no vulnerable spots, not even eye sockets. Silas's wyvern was holding her own in the fight, but she couldn't last forever.

The other military Reapers, wyverns, and long-wings engaged with the attackers, crashing into them, firing their breath weapons—and being met with breath weapons in return. The military dragons had armor and enhancements like lasers, blades, and super-heated flame. They were a living deck of DrakoTek cards.

But the mutants had been designed not to need that stuff. They were their own living weapon systems, and they were out of control.

A brown-scaled dragon the size of a bus opened its huge mouth in front of three military Reapers, but instead of hitting them with a breath weapon, it shot rainbows. The Reapers roared in confusion, crashing into one another to scramble away, unsure if it was some kind of poison rainbow.

It was.

Their armor sizzled, melting away.

On the ground, the kinners saw the chaos as their chance to escape. Drey hopped onto the back of a Sky Knight's Diamond Drake, and the two blew past Brazza. Drey glared at Lina as they passed. She'd chosen a side, and it wasn't his.

He made a claw with his hand, then mimed tearing out his own throat.

"Rude," Lina grunted, masking the hurt in her voice.

She'd given her all to the Sky Knights, and she wasn't just kicked out now: She was dead to them. If they caught her, they'd give her a lot worse than a snapdragon wedgie.

"I'm sorry, Lina," Abel told her. And he meant it.

Before Drey flew into the night, he pointed at Abel and made the same gesture.

"I don't think Drakopolis is going to be safe for any of us," Abel said as Lina finally hoisted Roa back onto Brazza.

"It never really was," Lina sighed.

Brazza beat the air, hovering in place. She dodged the occasional rainbow or bolt of lightning. The final alarm sounded below the street, and a sickly green gas filled the underground lab. A little mist of it seeped onto the street, sizzling on the concrete.

"Anything left in there is destroyed," Roa said.

"Anything left up here is gonna be destroyed too!" Topher's voice shouted in their ears. Abel saw Arvin doing his best to fly through the chaos of the police line and the escaped dragons, but the sky was too thick with breath weapons. He couldn't find a path out. Other kinners were having the same problem. Some of their dragons were injured and forced to land, where Dragon's Eye agents had been forced down too. Some were taking cover, others chasing down kinners on foot.

Jazinda Balk had been surrounded by a dozen more officers. They weren't about to let two kin bosses escape their blockade. She was being led to her own private armored prisoner transport, though she didn't look worried about it. She kept looking to the sky to see if her son had gotten away.

Sax and Grackle were currently cornered by a group of agents. Abel thought they'd be caught again, but Lu's Steelwing swept over them with its claws extended and scooped the two goons away. Rescued from the law by Abel's bully.

Her uncle's wyvern, now a cyborg, was past rescuing. It was currently grappling with a Dragon's Eye Infernal, high above the Mbalia Bank and Trust building.

Meanwhile, Silas had escaped the spike-headed dragon and made a high turn to chase down Drey and the Sky Knights. He'd almost caught up when Carrot Soup Supreme crashed into him.

Silas's wyvern fought the orange dragon with everything it had. The sounds of their fight made Abel's skin crawl. Silas was a good rider, though. He fought hard and smart and kept his dragon safe, never exposing a weak spot to the orange dragon's talons. He even got a few good blasts from his own weapons in.

More of the hacked mutants escaped into the city to wreak havoc on civilians. Already, the rainbow-shooting dragon was firing its deadly colors into late-night traffic, melting stoplight drones and causing buses and taxis to crash into each other in roaring tangles.

"They're all so angry," Abel despaired. How could he tame over a hundred angry dragons that humanity had so thoroughly broken with their technology? If the experts could even access the data on his broken phone, it might take weeks to unscramble and deactivate the dragons. By then, they might have wrecked half the city or all been hunted down and killed in the process.

Abel didn't know what to do. Not even Dr. Drago had ever faced a situation like this. These dragons weren't anything like the ones in comics. Each was unique in all the world, and each was angry in its own unique way.

Just like Brazza.

That was it! He thought he was supposed to be the hero of his plan, saving the dragons as only a noble human could. But what if dragons had to save dragons? What if being a hero was knowing when you couldn't be *the* hero?

"Hey, B," Abel said to her, leaning forward. She could always hear him, even if he wasn't shouting, and he knew by now that she understood most of what the people around her said. Maybe that's why *she'd* fallen silent. People had talked *around* her and *about* her and *at* her for her whole life. Maybe she just needed someone to talk *with* her.

"So, like, I don't know what to do here," he said. "But you've felt just like these dragons do. And, well, I really need them to stop attacking the city. Do . . . um . . . you have any ideas how to get through to them? Because I could use your help."

For a while, Brazza just beat her wings against the sky like she hadn't heard. Then he felt a ripple in her muscles below the saddle. Abel wondered if she was about to bolt away again, leave this whole sorry scene behind, and drag Abel, Roa, and Lina along with her.

Instead, she rose, flapping her wings in long strokes like she was pulling the skyscrapers down around her. Soon, they were at the top of a gleaming office tower, and she perched on its spire.

"What's she doing?" Roa asked.

"I think she's helping," Abel replied.

Brazza settled her back feet on the ledge. She looked up at the moon and the stars. She bathed in the neon lights of the city below, and she opened her mouth to roar.

But she didn't roar.

She sang.

The first note was a high, screeching sound that warbled and dropped to a deep bass. Then it rose again in short, staccato bursts. Soon, it turned from one note into two, each sung simultaneously. Somehow, Brazza was able to use the vibrations in her throat and movements of her jaw to harmonize with herself! Two notes became four, four became six, a whole chorus from one mouth.

"BURRRREEEERRRREEE!" Abel's earbuds screeched feedback. He popped them out quickly with a hiss of pain. Looking around, he saw everyone else on dragonback was doing the same. Dragon's Eye agents took off their helmets, and kinners popped out their headphones. The holographic ads around the city flickered and changed into strange pulses of light and color.

"Is she doing *that*?" Roa marveled.

"*What* is she doing?" Lina cried.

Abel couldn't find the words to answer, didn't dare add his own voice to the glorious and terrifying music she was making.

Every dragon stopped fighting. The ones on the ground and the ones in the air all turned their heads toward Brazza.

She kept singing.

The kinner dragons and the police attack dragons and even the civilian dragons snarling in traffic calmed themselves. No matter what their riders commanded, they fluttered to the ground. They listened to the music.

Arvin's Blue Colossus had settled on a high landing platform of a nearby building, and Abel saw Arvin and Topher scurry off its back. The earbuds didn't work, so Abel waved down at them, trying to tell his friends it was okay, everything would be okay.

He couldn't explain how he knew it, but with the music pulsing through his bones, he simply felt it. Feeling was a kind of knowing, wasn't it? It was hard to measure, difficult to describe, and impossible to argue, but none of that made it matter less. Maybe that was how dragons spoke, in a language that was absolutely true and absolutely impossible to translate. You just had to feel it.

And the mutant dragons felt it. They understood Brazza's song.

They flew toward Brazza, a hundred of them sweeping up to her eye level and hovering in place. At first they arrived one at a time, then by the dozens. None of them made a sound. Only Brazza's song filled the air between them.

As she changed pitch, the entire wild scrum of winged beasts spread out into a formation, creating the shape of a single giant dragon in the night sky. A hundred different dragons with a hundred different minds formed one giant dragon, and then the giant dragon answered Brazza's song in one perfect, ear-rattling harmony.

There wasn't a human below who didn't shed a tear at the mournful beauty of the sound. Abel felt Brazza's weight shift. She leaned to the side and lowered one wing to the rooftop.

A ramp.

She stopped singing and looked down her neck at Abel. It felt like the entire city, in its tens of millions, simply vanished. There was only Abel and the dragon perched between the city and the star-soaked sky.

"You want me to get down?" Abel asked. He was vaguely aware as Roa and Lina climbed off, but he stayed in the saddle, not ready to dismount his thrilling, frustrating, ferocious, and surprisingly loyal friend.

The dragon nodded. Abel tightened his hands on the reins.

"You're going to lead them away," he said.

Again, Brazza nodded her head one time.

"But we're not finished reading our book yet," Abel pleaded, his voice cracking. "You don't know the end!"

He knew it wasn't a convincing argument, but held some hope that a good story might keep the dragon with him a little longer. His goal all along had been to set the dragons free, Brazza included, but now that the time had come, he didn't want her to go. He wasn't ready. She was exciting and generous in her own dangerous way. And funny too, if an eight-ton dragon could be said to have a sense of humor. She was his friend.

He remembered Karak right then, the Sunrise Reaper who'd let him become a dragon rider, and how he'd let him go too. Abel didn't want to then either. It wasn't fair! Why did he always have to let go? Why did doing the right thing have to hurt so much?

Normally, in school and at home and just living his life, Abel's mind flickered and threw out sparks like a malfunctioning neon sign. He had trouble paying attention and was forgetful, and sometimes he fixated on a minor setback and turned it into a major catastrophe. But with Brazza he felt calm, focused, and even, for flickering moments, heroic. He didn't want to give that up. He liked how the dragon made him feel.

"That's not fair to you, though, is it?" he said aloud, like she could read his thoughts. "You don't exist to make me feel good. Your life is your own."

She just stared at him more; her eyes were gentle, but unwavering.

"I have to let you go," he said, surprised that he wasn't crying. He felt a calm kind of sadness wash over him, like listening to a sad but beautiful song.

Brazza blinked. She was patient, but she would not be changing her mind. Abel let go of her reins. He dismounted slowly and slid down her wing to the rooftop. He rested a hand against her scaled side and felt the warmth through his fingers.

She turned to face the formation of dragons, but then she hesitated. She looked back at Abel, and his heart thundered. Then her head snapped forward, jaws open and long teeth gleaming.

Abel flinched as her mouth snapped shut on a hovering drone just above his head. It sparked and whirred where she crushed its motor with her fangs. Then she set the broken thing at Abel's feet. The lights on the drone still blinked in vibrant colors.

"Is that for me?" he asked, laughing.

The dragon snorted. She wasn't a talker and wasn't about to waste her song answering a question Abel already knew the answer to. Dragons don't give away their treasure to just anyone. Whatever became of Brazza out in the wilds beyond the city, her gift had told Abel, much clearer than words could, that they were friends.

Abel smiled. "Goodbye, my friend."

Brazza opened her wings and leapt. She flew right through the center of the formation of mutant dragons, and with a single note from her booming voice, the entire flock followed her. They flew together, fast from the city and into the endless Glass Flats, beyond the reach of humans.

Abel let out a long breath. Roa and Lina approached from behind, each putting a hand on one of Abel's shoulders. They let him take all the time he needed to watch Brazza become a distant speck in the neon sky.

"Sorry, fam." Silas's voice rose behind them. Abel snapped around to see his brother mounted on his armored battle wyvern, now perched on the rooftop opposite them. The spotlights snapped back on as dozens of police dragons regained their blockade.

"But you're still all under arrest."

ABEL SAT ALONE IN A holding cell for a long time. He didn't know what had become of his friends or his enemies in the kin. He didn't know who'd been arrested or who'd slipped away. He didn't know where Lina had been taken, or why Silas hadn't come to see him. He didn't have his phone because the Dragon's Eye had seized it to see what data they could recover. He didn't even know what time it was. Morning, he guessed.

His plan had gone awry, but at least the dragons were free. Even if Abel wasn't. The Dragon's Eye would probably accuse him and his friends of violent kin activity, disturbing the peace, unauthorized dragon use, destruction of property. Lina was an escaped fugitive and a known Sky Knights thief, so she'd be in a lot more trouble. Silas might be able to help, but they already had the phone. He had nothing to bargain with. As for Abel, they had him on camera racing illegally on Brazza's back, coaxing her to control the hacked dragons, all while wearing the same jacket he'd worn in the police chase. Silas couldn't make that just go away. Abel would be going to prison, probably for the rest of his life.

Which wouldn't be long.

His stomach flipped at the thought. Windlee Prison was terrifying by design. It was filled with kinners. Red Talons, Sky Knights, and Thunder Wings were all doing time behind Windlee's walls, and none of them liked Abel. The Red Talons weren't going to forgive him for screwing up the plan, even though it wasn't his fault. And the Sky Knights weren't going to forgive him for screwing up *their* plans, which was totally his fault.

He wondered if there were Wind Breakers there who could protect him. He'd caused more chaos in Drakopolis than criminals three times his age. That had to count for something, right? Maybe he'd be a prison celebrity?

He tried to reassure himself, but it wasn't doing much good.

Abel shifted his weight on the hard bench. He tried not to think about wedgies or Windlee or what would become of him. He cleared his head like he did when he was on Brazza's back. With his eyes closed, he imagined the wind in his hair and the city racing by.

He hoped she and her flock had made it from the city by now. Maybe she'd found Karak in the wild. Maybe they talked about Abel together, in whatever way dragons do. He pictured them around a little table with tiny cups and flowery hats, like at a toddler's tea party. The thought made him laugh.

Clearing your head was hard. Abel was not good at meditation.

His cell door slid open.

"Napping?" Silas asked, closing the cell door behind him. They were alone.

"Thinking," Abel said. "Or trying not to think."

"We study mindfulness at the Academy," Silas said, his voice gentler than usual. "I can teach you some breathing exercises if you want."

"No thank you," Abel grunted.

"So listen." Silas squatted down so he was at Abel's eye level. "We've got a problem."

Abel looked around his tiny dark cell. It didn't even have a window. "I noticed."

"Jazinda Balk and her son have already been released," Silas said. "Officially, they were just in the wrong place at the wrong time. Between us, I think she paid a very large bribe."

"I'm glad Arvin's out at least," Abel said.

"He asked about you," Silas told him. "Wanted to make sure you were okay."

"Am I?" Abel asked.

"You could be," Silas said. "If you do what I say."

"Seems like doing what you say got me into this mess," Abel said.

"So let me get you out of it," Silas told him. "No one we arrested is confessing to anything. And we haven't gotten your phone working yet—dragon drool is awful for electronics—so any confession or accusations would just be from you, Lina, Roa, and Topher. Not the most reliable witnesses. I don't think *any* of you should make any kind of official statement."

"Are you telling me to *lie*? *To the law?*" Abel sat up a little straighter. It wasn't like Silas to choose his family over his duty to the Dragon's Eye.

Silas didn't say yes, but he didn't say no either. "Your friends will be okay if they keep their mouths shut. In fact, you and Lina and Mom and Dad will too."

"How?" Abel said. "I've been on the news twice now!"

"The City Council doesn't want to admit that over a hundred experimental dragons were created, hacked, then escaped out from under them," Silas said. "They don't even want to admit the technology to hack dragon DNA exists. They're afraid it'll make it look like they're not in control."

"But they're not," Abel said.

Silas shook his head. "Officially, they are. They aren't letting any of the images from last night be broadcast, and they're arresting anyone who posts videos of 'the incident' online. They're calling it all a military training exercise. Nothing to worry about."

"So they're lying to everyone in the city?" Abel said. "And they expect people to believe them?"

"They don't care if people believe them," Silas said. "They only care that people obey them. And most people just want to live their lives and go shopping and eat at restaurants and watch the latest episode of *Celebrity Dragon Lookalikes*. They're not gonna go against the government over some video that has nothing to do with them, even if it's an obvious lie."

Abel thought about the Burning Market, how people pretended it just wasn't there, that reality was just what everyone decided to believe.

But Abel knew what was real. He knew what had happened was as real as dragon song.

"So the government just covers up the truth and no one stops them?" Abel was incredulous.

Silas shrugged. "That's politics."

"Well, what if I won't let them?" Abel said. "What if I speak out?"

"Forget about it, Abel," Silas told him. "This is Drakopolis. They'll vanish you into Windlee Prison before you can convince a single person you're telling the truth. Mom, Dad, and Lina too. They'll tell the kins you snitched so that they take you out while you're in jail. In fact, that was their plan until a few minutes ago."

Abel's stomach dropped like Brazza in a high-g dive.

"I spent all night convincing them there was another way," Silas continued.

"What way?" Abel didn't like that Silas was the one deciding the fate of his family and friends, but it seemed like it always happened that way. Being the youngest meant Abel never had any say, and being the oldest meant Silas always did. It wasn't fair. But, like Silas said, this was Drakopolis. Nothing was fair.

"Exile." Silas dropped the word in front of him like a sack of dirty laundry. "The whole family goes to one of the mining towns out on the Glass Flats."

"The *whole* family?" Abel asked, with his best attempt at an eyebrow raise.

"Don't make that face," Silas snapped. "You look like you're pooping. And yes, the *whole* family."

"Even you?" Abel asked.

"Even me," Silas said. "In spite of what you think of me, I *am* a part of our family. In fact, I'll be responsible for all of you. If no one says a word about what happened here, and no one causes any trouble in our new town, everyone stays out of prison. And I get to be a sheriff's deputy. No more secret police."

"You? A sheriff?"

"A deputy," Silas said. "It's a promotion. Sort of."

"And what about my friends?"

"They can't come. In fact, you're not allowed any contact with Roa or Topher. For their own safety and yours."

"And Arvin?" Abel asked.

Silas shook his head, then did something very un-Silas-like. He put his arm around his little brother. "I know it sounds bad, but this is what it's gonna take to protect the family. Sometimes being a hero doesn't mean flying around on a dragon blasting your enemies with fire. Sometimes it means doing something boring, like moving to a new town without your friends and putting on a brave face about it. It's still your choice, but I really hope you'll make the right one."

"Did Lina already agree?"

"Without hesitation," said Silas. "The moment I told her it would protect you." With that, he stood to leave Abel alone in the cell again.

But then Silas stopped. He pulled out a brand-new phone from his pocket and tossed it to Abel. "I'll be back in ten minutes for your answer. In the meantime, call your friends. Say whatever you think you need to."

When Abel was alone, he stared down at the phone. He thought about everything he'd seen and everything he'd done. He was willing to go to jail for it, now that the dragons were free, but he didn't think it was fair for the others to go too.

He hated to admit it, but Silas was right. Being a hero wasn't always exciting, and you weren't always celebrated for it. Sometimes being a hero hurt worse than dragon fire on bare skin.

But a hero does what's right anyway, even without the glory. Even when it hurts.

He made his decision.

Abel started dialing his best friends, thinking about how to say goodbye.

ABOUT THE AUTHOR

Alex London is the author of over twenty-five books for children, teens, and adults, with over two million copies sold. He's the author of the middle grade Dog Tags, Tides of War, Wild Ones, and Accidental Adventures series, as well as two titles in The 39 Clues. For young adults, he's the author of the acclaimed cyberpunk duology Proxy and the epic fantasy trilogy the Skybound Saga. A former journalist covering refugee camps and conflict zones, he can now be found somewhere in Philadelphia, where he lives with his husband and daughter, or online at calexanderlondon.com.